ANGELS

RACHEL CHURCHER

ANGELS

First published by Taller Books, 2023
Text copyright © Rachel Churcher 2023

The moral right of the author has been asserted.

This is a work of fiction. Names, characters, places, and incidents are the product of the author's imagination, or are used fictitiously. Any resemblance to actual persons, living or dead; events; or locales is entirely coincidental.

ISBN 978-1-9163868-6-0

Cover design by Rachel Churcher
Typeset in Baskervville
www.tallerbooks.com

"Hope" is the thing with feathers –
That perches in the soul –
And sings the tune without the words –
And never stops – at all …

Emily Dickinson

Part 1

Loving Kane

Chapter 1

June 2008, Age 5

The billboard was the largest I had ever seen. It touched the roof of the building, towering above me in the crowd. I felt my father's fingers tighten around mine as we pushed our way along the pavement, and I squeezed back, terrified of losing him in the maze of legs and bags and trampling feet. I must have been five years old. My mother stopped, cradling my baby brother in his sling as she stared up at the man in the photo. My father tugged on my arm, pulling me into the safety of our family group. We stood on our patch of pavement, jostled by the endless river of people blocking the road, all of us staring at the image that hung over Oxford Circus like a miracle.

A man with golden wings.

Real wings. Beautiful feathers spilling from his shoulders, arching upwards in graceful curves, lifted outwards as if he was about to fly away from this unexpected attention. His face was turned to the side, his eyes cast down, watching us as we watched him.

His back was bare under the feathers, his muscles tight and contoured under his tanned skin. On one arm he wore a beaded bracelet, and on the other a silver watch strap gleamed. More than that, I couldn't see.

The crowd hemmed me in, surrounding me and my parents and brother like a moving forest.

All around us, people were pointing, talking, taking photos of the photo. Posing in front of the extraordinary billboard. The sound was a murmur, flowing around us like a tide, soft footfalls joining the voices as the crowds drifted past. Somewhere I could hear shouting, but the people around us spoke with quiet voices, all their attention on the angel.

My father tugged my hand.

"Can you see?"

I shrugged. "Only the top."

He made a sad face.

"That won't do, Pumpkin," he said. "Want a boost?"

He held his arms out, dropping my hand, and for a breathless moment I was alone in the crowd. Unconnected, I reached up into his grasp and he lifted me, ducking his head and planting me firmly on his shoulders. He flicked his ponytail out from under my knees, and took my hands again.

"Better?" he asked.

I glanced around at the sea of people milling past us, and I felt a hundred feet tall. No danger of being dragged away up here – I was safe, and I could see everything. People filling the road in front of me. Cameras, held up to capture the image we had all come to see. A group in the distance with placards, chanting – too far away for me to hear their words.

"Better!" I said, smiling.

And then I looked up.

I could see the whole of the billboard. The man's bare back. His muscular arms. Bracelet, watch, and wings. And the black jeans, slouched at his hips, a red label stitched onto the back pocket. I followed the lines of his legs with my gaze, to where the jeans tucked inside black leather boots, their tops loose and open, echoing the shape of his wings.

His impossible wings.

I stared, one of thousands drinking in the shocking image. A real angel, modelling jeans on a London street.

The other shops boasted similar photos – girls with long blonde hair and crop tops, moody boys with leather jackets and sunglasses – but none of them covered a building from pavement to roof, and none of them could fly.

A man stumbled against the curb next to us, apologising as he recovered his balance. He turned to look at the image, pushing a hand-rolled cigarette and a lighter like my father's into the pocket of his jacket.

"Woah," he said, shaking his head. He held his hands in front of him, framing the angel between his yellowed fingers. "Wings. *Wings*."

He grinned up at me, and I gave him a smile.

"So they can fly, right?" He looked at my father, who shrugged, his shoulders flexing under my legs. The man stared up at the angel.

"Hard to keep tabs on, someone like that. Someone who can stretch their wings and fly away." He fluttered his hands, like a butterfly. He wasn't talking to us. He was talking to the crowd. He stared some more, tracing the shapes of the feathers and muscles with his fingers, then took a breath. I felt my father's shoulders tense.

"I wonder what he'd be like to f–"

"Hey!" My mother stepped in front of him. "There are children here. Keep your fantasies to yourself."

"Sorry, Lady," he said, and shot me a goofy grin. "Sorry, princess."

I shrugged, and smiled. I had no idea what he was going to say. But I understood his fascination with the angel.

He was beautiful. Shameless. Showing his wings as if there was nothing strange about them. I loved his confidence, and I loved the crowds for supporting him.

The man stumbled away, and my mother smiled up at me.

"Are you glad you came, Melodie?" It's what she always asked when we did something special together. I nodded, looking up again at the golden wings.

"Remember this, Pumpkin." My father gripped my fingers. "This is the first step towards a better world."

Chapter 2

They had been here forever, my grandfather said. We'd always had angels, living among us. He'd known one, back in his army days, but when the commanders found out, the angel was told to leave. My grandfather tried to talk to him as he packed his bags, but the base had posted guards on the barracks, and no one was allowed in until the *abomination* had been marched to the gate and bustled into a waiting car.

I didn't understand *abomination*, but I understood the story.

"How he got through his medical, I'll never know." My grandfather shook his head. "How he hid it from all of us."

"Where did he go?" I asked, confused and frightened by the idea that someone could be removed from your life so quickly, and so finally.

"Somewhere he could show his wings." He shrugged. "Or somewhere he learned to hide them. All I know is that he never came back."

I thought about the man in the photo. About all the people staring up at him.

"So why is it OK for us to see *his* wings?" I waved my hand to suggest the tall billboard, and my grandfather must have understood. The photos had been all over the papers and the news.

"You saw him? In London?" I nodded, and my grandfather laughed. "Times are a-changing, Mel," he said. "Times are a-changing."

"It's a random mutation," my mother explained as she folded the clean clothes from the washing line. When she found one of my brother's onesies or socks, she'd toss them to me across the table. I was in charge of the baby clothes, and I was gathering a pile of folded organic babygrows and a colourful selection of odd footwear.

"What's a random mutation?" I asked, concentrating as I paired two yellow socks, turning one inside-out over the other and placing it carefully in a new pile.

My mother put down the T-shirt she was folding.

"Well," she said, her paint-stained hands still bunched in the fabric. "You know that some people have light hair?" She smiled. "Blonde, like yours, and mine."

I nodded.

"And some people have dark hair, like Sam?"

I nodded again. Sam was my friend. His skin was dark brown, and his hair was black and curly. My mother bought me a special dark brown crayon, so I could draw Sam in my pictures.

"A very long time ago, when the first people existed, they probably had dark hair. But today people have brown hair and blonde hair and red hair ..."

" … and black hair!" I said, thinking of Sam.

"And black hair."

"So what's a mutation?"

"A mutation is what happened when the first person had brown hair instead of black. Or red hair instead of brown."

I nodded, thinking about the angel on the billboard.

"So it's like a new way to be a person?"

My mother smiled, and reached out to take my hand. "Yes, Melodie! Exactly. It's a new way to be a person."

I smiled back, happy to have understood.

"Could I grow wings?" I was almost hopeful, thinking about the man in the photo. About the beautiful feathers curving from his shoulders.

"Sorry, Melodie." She shook her head. "It doesn't work that way. A mutation happens before you're born. While you're still growing in here." She patted her tummy.

"So it's a surprise? When you have a baby, it's a surprise if it has a mutation? Like purple eyes or green hair?"

"It is," she said, laughing. "It's a big surprise."

"But Grandad says we've always had angels."

She nodded. "That's probably true, give or take. But it's like blonde hair. The first one grew wings because of a mutation. Something that made them different from other people."

"And now? How do angels happen now?"

"Well," she said, slowly. "Angels mostly have babies with other angels, so they pass on the mutation."

"They keep making the new kind of person?"

"Exactly." She smiled again. "And sometimes someone else will have the mutation. Someone whose parents aren't angels. That's what 'random' means. Sometimes we don't know why it happens."

"OK," I said, nodding.

She pulled her hand away, and picked up the T-shirt, but stopped when she saw the look on my face.

"What's your question, Melodie?" she asked, dropping the T-shirt again.

"So ..." I was still thinking about the angel on the billboard. About all the people in the street, and all the newspapers and the TV news. The fuss they were making because the man in the photo was showing off his beautiful feathers.

Something didn't make sense.

I took a deep breath, and my mother raised her eyebrows, waiting.

"Why is it OK to have blonde hair, but it's not OK to have wings?"

She sighed, and gave me a thin smile.

"That," she said, "is an excellent question."

Saying goodnight to my father was best on a summer night, when he'd be sitting in the garden with my grandfather smoking cigarettes they rolled themselves. The smell was comforting, like herbs and pine trees and cut grass, and the smoke coiled up through the strings of fairy lights hanging between the trees outside my mother's painting studio.

"Pumpkin!" my father called as I walked along the gravel path between his neatly tended vegetable beds. "Come to take your leave of the day?"

He always asked silly questions when I came out to say goodnight. If I asked him what he meant, he'd only use longer words to explain, and my grandfather would laugh at us both – me making faces as I tried to understand, and my father waving his hands and trying to make sense.

I had more important things on my mind.

My father lifted me onto his lap and wrapped an arm around me.

"You know, when you wake up in the morning, you'll be a whole day older."

"And taller," said my grandfather, holding his hand out to judge my height, and raising it by a tiny bit.

"And taller! How much taller are you going to get, Pumpkin?" My father ducked his head and grinned. "You're nearly as tall as me already! Look!"

I stretched my hand up, as high as I could reach. "Taller than a building!" I said, looking up at the fairy lights.

My grandfather smiled. "Still thinking about your angel, Mel?"

I nodded.

"He made quite the impression, didn't he?"

My father leaned back in his chair, and I lay against his chest, breathing in the grassy smell of his glowing cigarette. It was quiet in the garden, and I watched the strings of lights, white against the slowly darkening sky. I thought I understood – about random mutations, and giant billboards – but there were still pieces of the angel's story that didn't make sense. Things I wanted to ask.

"Can they really fly?" I thought about the man next to us in the crowd, talking about flying away.

My grandfather shook his head. "Not like a bird, or a plane."

My father laughed, sweeping a hand through the air. "Not like Superman, either!"

"So …" I said, thinking. "What can they do?"

"Glide," said my grandfather. "Catch themselves if they fall."

"So it looks like flying?"

My grandfather nodded. "Sometimes." He waved his cigarette in the air, and the end glowed brighter. "But not everyone learns to do it. It's hard. Like swimming really fast, or running a marathon."

"Does it hurt?"

"I don't know, Mel." He sighed. "I guess you'd have to ask an angel."

I stared up at the lights.

"Why don't we know any angels?" I whispered, just loud enough to be heard.

My father looked sad for a moment.

"Oh, we do, Pumpkin. We do."

My grandfather smiled. "Just because you haven't seen someone's wings, that doesn't mean they're not an angel. It just means they don't trust you with that information yet."

"What's trust?" I asked, sitting up.

My grandfather took a puff on his cigarette, and thought for a moment.

"It means that someone can tell you something – something secret – and they know you won't tell anyone else. They know you're a good person, and you won't go talking about their secrets to people who might not like what they hear."

I thought about what he said.

"So there are still people who don't like angels?" It sounded stupid, but I had to ask.

My father nodded. "Yes, there are."

"But why?" I couldn't believe that anyone would not like the man on the billboard, with his beautiful golden wings.

I felt my father shrug. "Jealousy. Some people wish they had wings. Some people don't like the idea that other people are better than they are – or think they're better. Some people think it would be better if there weren't any angels – just people. Some people would like everyone to be the same."

My grandfather laughed softly. "And what a boring world that would be!"

"But—"

"It's complicated, Pumpkin. And it's time for bed."

My father swept me up in a tight hug and planted a kiss on the top of my head.

"Sleep well," he said, glancing at my grandfather. "Remember – you'll be taller in the morning!"

But when I tried to fall asleep, I couldn't stop thinking about the angel. About his amazing wings, and all those people in the road, watching his photo.

The people who loved him, and the people who wished he didn't exist.

Chapter 3

July 2019, Age 16

"Spying, Mel?"

Sam taps my shoulder as I catch my breath. I didn't hear him walking up the path. I'm too busy watching my mother and her model in the studio.

"No!" I whisper, shrugging his hand away. He points at me, at the studio, and back at me, a look of exaggerated puzzlement on his face.

"OK, yes. Fine. I'm spying." And I turn back to the open doorway.

Sam leans round me, letting out a gasp as I push him back.

"That's …" He breathes, his eyes wide. "That's Kane." I nod. "As in 'all over your bedroom wall' Kane. *That* Kane."

"I'm aware," I murmur, keeping my attention on the angel.

"I don't blame you for the spying," he says, under his breath. "I don't blame you at all. That's one fine angelic specimen, right there."

I nudge him with my elbow. "Don't let Faisal hear you say that!"

He grins.

"Faisal has … a thing for wings. He'd forget all about me with a view like that."

I make a sad face. "That's too bad. A good-looking guy like you deserves someone's full attention."

He runs a hand over his close-cut hair and shrugs. "Good-looking I may be, but we both know I can't complete with an angel."

I nod, but I'm already looking back through the door. I have to stop myself from yelping when Sam pokes my back.

"See? You've forgotten me already."

He's right. My friend can't compete with the man whose face and torso are slowly appearing on my mother's canvas.

I can't drag my eyes away. The bare-chested angel, wings spread wide in the small room, feathers shimmering with every breath – impossible as it sounds, this is the same man I gazed up at from my father's shoulders, on a giant billboard in London. Everyone knows his face, and his wings. Kane is the most famous angel in the world, modelling for all the biggest names in fashion, but that's not who I see from my hiding place outside the door.

This is my first angel – my first glimpse of wings – posing as my mother picks out his image in paint.

This is personal.

"I know you're there, Melodie," she calls over her shoulder, her eyes never leaving her painting. "Do you need me, or are you just gawping at our guest?"

Behind me, Sam bites back a laugh. My mother turns from the painting, one hand on her hip.

"I didn't realise we had an audience. Are you selling tickets now?" She looks past me. "Sam," she says, nodding.

"Sorry, Mrs Abbott. I was—"

"It doesn't matter, because you're leaving now." She waves a paintbrush at us. "Both of you. I'm sure Kane would prefer our portrait session to go unobserved."

I glance at the angel, and my breath freezes. His lips twitch into a smile, and his eyes meet mine.

Blue. Blue like the sky. Blue like sapphires. Blue like ice.

He holds my gaze, still smiling, and tilts his head to one side. His wings flutter, fragments of golden light dancing across the studio's white walls.

I feel as if I'm staring at the sun. As if I'm glowing.

As if the ground has disappeared.

I lose my balance, falling. Stumbling backwards into Sam's strong arms. When I look back, Kane's eyes are fixed on my mother, his smile extinguished. Sam pushes me onto my feet and takes my elbow, dragging me away from the door and across the garden. I'm still breathless, looking back over my shoulder, searching for a flicker of gold, a shard of reflected light – but my mother has closed the blinds.

At the back door Sam drops my arm, and we both sink back against the weathered sun-warmed bricks.

Sam laughs. "Did that just happen? Kane – *the* Kane – in your mum's studio?" He waves his hand at the garden. "Here?"

I nod. "Every day for a week, now."

"So you've been spying for a week?" He punches my shoulder. "Why didn't you tell me?"

I shrug. "I'm not supposed to know. No-one is supposed to know."

"But—"

"And I haven't been spying. That's the first time."

Sam narrows his eyes and gives me a sarcastic nod. "Sure," he says. "First time."

But it's the truth. I figured out who the mysterious model was on Monday, but I've been too scared to go near the studio.

"It's taken me this long to dare myself to do it. And then I went and ... oh god." I hide my blushing cheeks in my hands. "I fell over. He looked at me, and I fell over." I can feel the floor vanishing under my feet. I can see his smile. His eyes. Heat builds on my skin – I think my whole body is blushing.

Sam laughs. "Angel eyes, right? One glance is enough to knock you out cold." He shakes his head. "That was a proper swoon, Mel. Like, movie-level, full-body, you-rocked-my-world *drama*. You need to work on that – I won't always be there to catch you. Can't have you swooning like that every time you see an angel."

"Wait ..." Sam says, over his glass of fresh lemonade. "This isn't for that exhibition, is it?"

I try to look innocent, twirling the lemon peel in my glass. I'm not supposed to tell anyone. "What exhibition?"

"It is! It's for the Queen's exhibition." He waves a hand in the air. "The angel celebration thingy."

I stare at my drink, trying not to react, but I can feel the blush returning.

"Oh my god, it is!" Sam bounces in his chair, pointing at the studio through the kitchen window. "Your mum's painting an angel for the Queen!"

'Queen' comes out as a squeal, and I can't help laughing.

He bites his knuckle, a grin growing on his face.

"Ohmygod ohmygod ohmygod, Mel! Your mum is painting *Kane* for the *Queen*!"

I force the smile from my face and watch his reaction.

"I mean, I knew she was famous ... but this? This is ..." He shakes his head. "This is *huge*!"

I want to grin with him. I want to squeal and tell him he's right, but I can't. No-one can know.

"Yes, Sam. My mother is a famous painter, and sometimes she has famous people in her studio. They pay her lots of money to recreate them with paint and canvas, and then they leave and we never see them again." I point at the studio. "Who knows why Kane is here?" I shrug. "Maybe he wants a portrait for his new mansion. Or maybe it's a present for his mum."

"Or his lover?" Sam places a hand on his chest and gives me a wistful look before shaking his head. "No. Nope. This one's for the Queen. I know it."

"Well, then," I say, sighing. "You'll just have to promise not to tell another living soul."

He grins again, and I find myself smiling back.

"Our secret, Mel," he says, crossing his heart. "And as a bonus I won't tell anyone that he swept you off your feet with a single glance."

I aim a kick at his knee, under the table.

The evening sun paints my bedroom in gold. Kane left hours ago, smuggled out by a member of his staff through the back gate to a waiting car. My mother is still working on her top-secret royal commission, so my father cooked home-grown vegetables for dinner. Sam left to meet Faisal somewhere, and the men of the house are smoking in the garden, my brother paying close attention as they roll their organic leaves into neat paper tubes.

I close the door, shutting myself inside my shrine.

It takes a moment for me to lift my eyes to the images papering the walls. From a hundred photos, a thousand magazine cuttings, and my own rough sketches, Kane's eyes gaze back at me. Modelling jeans, shirts, sunglasses, watches. Selling boats, cars, planes, jewellery and aftershave. Posing on red carpets from London to LA, Beijing to Bollywood. Arms around beautiful, muscled men and gorgeous, flawless women. Dressed in everything from shadows (artfully photographed) to dinner jackets, modified with tasteful slashes to show off his wings.

I touch my fingers to his face on a photo – black and white, very classy – and let my hands drag across the wall. Photos and cuttings pass under my fingertips. An extreme close-up, his eyes an impossible blue. The interview where he explained that his name means 'gold', and revealed his favourite albums – all of which became instant bestsellers. The Limited Edition Kane-branded gold eyeshadow and nail varnish advert on the same page – both sold out within a day. His iconic first billboard, towering above a London street. The crowds gathered to see his wings.

Everyone he's with – male or female, human or angel – is perfect. Chiselled muscles. Stunning makeup. Designer gowns and impossible heels.

And everyone is smiling. Enjoying their moment with the world's most famous angel.

Kane belongs to no-one, and we must all compete for our moment in his orbit. My stomach sinks as I realise my moment was this afternoon, in the studio. His eyes met mine, and I …

… I fell. I stumbled, and fell, and it was over.

Hopeless. Wasted.

I'm such an idiot. My cheeks catch fire again, just thinking about how I must have looked. How I lost control of my legs, right in front of a man who has *actual wings*. How my knees gave out, just because he looked at me. How I needed Sam to rescue me.

A sixteen-year-old schoolgirl forgetting how to walk. Forgetting how to *stand*.

Idiot.

But I still remember the feeling as his eyes met mine. The ground dissolving as my balance shifted towards him. As he became, just briefly, the centre of my world.

I'm not stupid. I know there's no chance for someone like me, with someone like Kane.

With an angel.

But I can't help finding beauty in his golden wings and sculpted face. In the image where I first saw him, as tall as a building and as golden as his name.

In his eyes as he looked into mine.

And there's no harm in dreaming.

Chapter 1

September 2019, Age 16

"Is that the *actual* Queen?"

Sam's whisper distracts me from the glossy programme in my hand. I glance up, catching sight of a sunflower-yellow hat over the heads of the guests queueing in front of the National Gallery. She disappears into a car, and the motorcade idling in the street alongside Trafalgar Square pulls away towards The Mall.

Faisal rolls his eyes. "Of course it's the actual Queen! Didn't you get the memo? *Royal* preview?"

Sam nudges his boyfriend with his shoulder. "Yeah, but … she was right there, Fai!"

The boys exchange a grin, and Faisal shakes his head. "You are going to lose your shit when you see Kane."

My fingers tighten on the programme, creasing the expensive paper.

Kane will be here. Kane is coming to see his portrait.

And I am my mother's guest of honour.

The gallery gave her three extra tickets. One for me, one for my father, and one for my grandfather. My brother is too young to be trusted around priceless art, my communist father refuses to attend a royal event on principle, and my grandfather offered to take them both to the cinema instead. So here I am, pretending to be grown up enough to represent my mother's family at the most important exhibition of her career.

The Queen has completed her viewing of the paintings she commissioned. In a moment it will be our turn.

Around us, the families and plus-ones of the other artists straighten their jackets and ties, and sneak final glimpses of their makeup in pocket mirrors and phone cameras. I tug on the snug short sleeves of my mother's second-favourite dress and arrange the dark blue pashmina around my shoulders. Faisal straightens Sam's tie, putting out his hand to stop Sam from pulling it loose again. I check my gold nail varnish and tap nervously at my hair, piled on top of my head in a posh messy bun, and set in place with enough bobby pins and hair spray to stop a bullet.

"Looking good, Mel." Faisal gives me a wink. I nod, nerves beginning to flutter in my stomach. Both boys look so much older than their sixteen years, and I feel like a fraud next to them. Faisal's olive skin glows golden under the spotlights in front of the gallery, and Sam's white shirt shows off his dark complexion. They look amazing, like models in a magazine. They look as if they belong here.

I'm starting to sweat into the vintage saree-fabric floor-length gown, and I can only hope that the midnight blue silk will be enough to disguise the damp patches under my arms. I fan my face with the programme, trying to ignore the heat on my skin.

Kane is inside. Kane is with my mother, and her portrait. There's no way our paths won't cross this evening.

I try to remember to breathe.

The exhibition space is underground, in the Sainsbury Wing. Museum staff check our invitations at the door, and we drift down the stairs with the other guests towards the murmur of voices and the notes of a string quartet. I have to stop Sam from taking the champagne on offer at the door, and ask for three sparkling elderflower cordials instead. *No alcohol*, my mother had said as she pinned my hair in place. *And no messing around. Tonight, you're grown-ups.* It's not as if anyone can tell – the drinks look the same in the glasses.

We follow the other guests into the gallery, and immediately my breath catches. Spaced across the whitewashed walls, the paintings of the Royal Angel Exhibition glow under their spotlights. Each picture is different, catching each subject in a unique pose, but all with their wings outstretched. All with their glimmering feathers dominating the canvas, like icons in a cathedral.

All breathtaking.

There are oils, watercolours, photographic projects, detailed collage, and minimalist charcoal sketches. More than one artist has chosen to show the angel in shades of grey, but recreated their wings in bright, eye-catching colours. Every picture tells a story, offering a personal insight into the subject's life. Among the sports stars, media personalities, and famous musicians, some of the artists have captured doctors, teachers, craftspeople – angels without a public profile who have been brave enough to bare their wings and show who they really are.

And at the far end of the room, dominating the space, is my mother's portrait of Kane.

I've seen the completed painting in her studio, but here, in this spotlit, church-like space it has become something magical.

In the image, Kane stands as I saw him from the doorway. Wings spread, his naked chest centred on the giant canvas, his eyes burning out of the frame and gazing straight at his audience. In a nod to his history-making billboard, he wears low-slung jeans and combat boots, untied at the top. A beaded bracelet circles one wrist, and on the other he wears a watch that glints in the light.

My mother has captured him in shades of bronze acrylic paint and picked out his wings in gold, her bold brushstrokes suggesting the constant shimmer of his feathers.

His eyes are blue, like sapphires.

I can't look away.

"Steady," Sam whispers from behind me. "Keep your feet on the floor."

I stifle a laugh as we make our way past the other paintings to where my mother stands, answering questions from journalists and posing for photos with her creation. Her green silk dress catches the light as she moves, and I feel utterly out of my depth here, surrounded by famous artists and their glamorous guests. I might be rocking the poshest outfit I've ever worn, with hair and makeup that wouldn't look out of place on the cover of a magazine, but I feel like a fraud. Knowing my friend is behind me gives confidence to my steps.

"Catch me?" I whisper back, over my shoulder. I can feel my knees shaking already, and I'm mentally awarding myself adulting points for choosing shoes with flat heels. Sam wraps his hand round my arm.

"I've got you," he says.

I feel the rush of air from Kane's wings before I realise he's right beside us, striding towards his painting with a glass of bubbly in each hand. Sam's fingers tighten and for a moment he's the only thing holding me up. Gravity swims, and the air feels like a hurricane. I'm close enough to reach out and touch the angel's feathers, and he doesn't even know I'm here.

Sam slips an arm around my waist. I didn't realise I'd stopped walking. I'm standing, eyes tight shut in the middle of the gallery, swaying as I try to feel the floor under my feet.

"Hey," Sam says in my ear. "Queen of the dramatic swoon." I nod, eyes still closed. "Are you done now?"

I make myself breathe, centring my weight over both feet.

He's just a model. He's beautiful, and fit, but he's just a model. He doesn't save lives, or paint pictures, or write heartbreaking songs. I've been head-over-heels in love with him since I was five years old, but he's an angel, and I'm ... me. I'm ordinary.

But I've spent those eleven years dreaming of Kane, and now ...

Sam's arm shifts at my waist, and I take a calming breath.

"Can I let go?" He whispers, "Or is this a full falling-over routine? If so I'm going to have to confiscate your drink."

His concern is enough to break Kane's spell, and I open my eyes, lifting my glass out of his reach.

"You're good?" His voice is soft, and I'm so pleased he's here. I give him a quick smile, my face warming under my makeup.

He smiles. "Then let's go meet your angel."

My mother spots us, waving over the shoulder of the journalist she's talking to, and we're trapped. I can't walk away from her. I can't turn my back on Kane and his painting. I feel Sam's hand on the small of my back

– a gentle push to make sure I'm moving – and I make myself put one foot in front of the other.

The journalist sees he's outnumbered, and excuses himself, leaving us facing my mother, and Kane. The angel whose face stares out from a hundred photos on my bedroom wall, whose wings took my breath away when I first saw him on the iconic billboard, is standing in front of me, and smiling.

My mother is introducing me, but I can't hear anything past the rushing of my blood and my shallow breathing.

He's wearing white trousers with black combat boots, and there's a sheen of gold body glitter across his arms and chest. No top, no jacket, and I can see his wings flexing, scattering shards of gold under the gallery spotlights as he turns to me.

His eyes catch mine, and it doesn't matter how many photos I've pinned to my wall, or how many times I've watched his red-carpet appearances on YouTube. This isn't a photo. This isn't a carefully crafted video moment. This is raw and real, and I'm losing myself in sapphire blue, framed with mascara and golden eyeshadow.

He's even more beautiful in real life.

And his eyeshadow matches my own. I almost laugh at the realisation, and that's enough to keep me on my feet.

"Melodie," he says, glancing back at my mother. "From the studio! I remember." His smile is enough to light up the entire gallery. "Lovely to meet you properly."

I can feel every pin in my elaborate hairstyle, pressing against my scalp. Every place where my dress touches my skin feels like sandpaper. My shoes pinch against my toes. The glass in my hand is icy cold.

Time isn't working.

"And you," I hear myself say. I think I'm smiling, but my face feels numb.

"What do you do, Melodie?" He asks. "Are you an artist like your mother, or do you have other miraculous skills?"

His full attention is on me, and I feel like one of the paintings. Something to be gazed at and admired, caught in his personal spotlight. I feel unreal, like a ghost of myself. As if I shouldn't be breathing.

And suddenly I need him to think I'm older. I can't imagine telling Kane I'm a sixth-former and watching his interest fall away as he realises he's talking to a schoolgirl. The drink in my glass looks like champagne, and I'm wearing my mother's dress. With my hair up and the make-up to match I know I can get away with stretching the truth.

I messed up our first meeting, and he's giving me another chance.

"I'm studying art," I say, surprising myself. It's true, and I'm definitely going to take art at university, but my lungs feel too small as the half-truth escapes. My skin is burning, and I hope he doesn't ask me anything else.

I wish I could disappear, before I screw up this perfect conversation. Before I do something stupid in front of Kane.

I grip my glass with both hands, trying to stop them from shaking. My dress feels damp under my armpits, and I hope no one can see how much I'm sweating.

"Ah," he nods at my mother. "Like Alice!" He smiles. "Good for you." He looks around the room, at all the gorgeous artworks. "What's your medium, Melodie?" He asks. "Does a talent for painting run in the family?"

My mouth is dry, and I have to concentrate to take a breath.

"I paint. Oils and acrylics, mostly." I glance at my mother and she gives me an encouraging nod. "But I'm learning a bit of everything at the moment. Pen and ink, sculpture, collage, photography. I might get to make a video piece next year."

"And are you studying here in London?"

I nod. Another half-truth.

"Then I hope you'll invite me to your next exhibition." He lifts a hand and points to the paintings around us. "It's intoxicating, this place. So many talented people. So much beauty in one room."

All I can do is nod as he reaches for my hand. I can't take a breath, and I can't feel the floor under my feet.

Sam is beside me, but all I can think about is Kane, watching me as he talks about beauty and art.

I peel my fingers away from the glass and hold my hand out for him to shake, but he has other ideas. His blue eyes stay fixed on mine as he raises my hand to his lips, and places a gentle kiss against my knuckles.

My cheeks flare with heat. My skin prickles. I swear I'm floating in the middle of the room.

Kane is kissing my hand.

He glances at my gold-painted fingernails and his eyebrows rise.

"Very nice," he says. "Is that a deliberate reference?"

"To your interview? Yes. Of course." The words rush out of me before I can stop. "I have the magazine cutting on my bedroom wall."

He lifts my hand and admires the colour before letting my fingers fall.

"A true fan," he says, smiling, and I have nothing left to say.

"These are family friends, Sam and Faisal." My mother waves a hand at the boys as she introduces them, and I take a step back. I make myself breathe, grateful that Kane's attention is shifting away from me. I can't believe I told him about the interview. After trying to sound sophisticated and mature, I had to give myself away as nothing more than an adoring fangirl.

My hands are shaking. I think my makeup is melting off my face, and I don't want to think about what I'm doing to this dress. The air feels hot and thick as I concentrate on breathing. I really am an idiot.

The angel gives the boys a warm smile.

"Sam," he says, reaching out to shake my friend's hand. "Thank you for coming, and supporting the woman who captured my soul on her canvas."

My mother beams, and Sam shakes his hand. My effortlessly handsome friend has to clear his throat before he can reply, and I'm relieved to find that I'm not the only one struggling to form simple words.

"It's a pleasure," he says, as Kane turns to Faisal.

"It's an honour to meet you, sir." Faisal is talking before Kane can speak, and I realise he's is going to start babbling. He's having no problem finding words, and I wonder whether we'll have to stop him. I watch, holding my breath as he dips his head in a bow. "Can I say, you're looking ..." he shakes his head as he looks Kane up and down, then presses his fingers together in the shape of a heart. Somehow he manages to make *his* fangirl reaction look cool, and Kane smiles.

"Thank you," he says, nodding at Faisal's sharp suit and artfully tousled hair. "You're looking pretty hot yourself."

Faisal clutches his jacket against his heart, and Sam reaches out to put a hand on his arm.

"Boyfriend," he says, loud enough for Kane to hear. "No swooning."

Kane laughs. "You're a lucky man," he says, winking at Faisal. Sam grins, and I swear Faisal is glowing.

Now that the attention is no longer on me, I know how he feels.

Chapter 5

We take our drinks and wander the gallery. My mother has more journalists to speak to, and there's a growing crowd of people who want to meet Kane, and shake the hand of the angel who changed everything.

We must all compete for our moment in his orbit.

I'm still breathless from our conversation. Casually chatting to Kane about art – it feels impossible. Dreamlike.

I don't want to wake up.

"Stannis!"

Faisal pulls me out of my daydream, catching my arm and dragging me to a life-size photo of a man with ebony skin, neat dreadlocks, and silver wings. The image is printed in shades of grey and blue, and overlaid with sketches of red football shirts, players in motion, and the bright green grass of a stadium. Over his heart he holds an eye-catching full-colour photo of a young girl in a neon-pink dress, long cornrows trailing over her shoulders, her own wings flared behind her outstretched arms.

"Legend," Sam breathes as he gazes at the image. The first angel to play openly in the Premier League smiles back at him from the photo.

Faisal glances round the room. "Do you think he's …"

I check my programme. *Nolan Stannis is unable to attend the Royal Preview.*

"Sorry, Fai," I say, showing him the page, and his shoulders slump. Sam drapes an arm round his shoulder.

"I think I'm OK with that," he says, waving a hand at the artwork. "I'm not sure you'd ever look at me again if you met Stannis in person."

Faisal shrugs and grins, moving on to the next painting.

Something on the programme page catches my eye, and I stop. Alongside the artist's notes is another photo of the little girl. Stannis's five-year-old daughter is dressed in a red football shirt, her wings tucked behind her as she watches the artist setting up the lights for the portrait session. She rests her chin on one hand and her elbow on an equipment crate, her attention held by the assistants connecting cables and positioning softboxes.

Five years old, and showing her wings to the world. The same age I was when I first saw Kane's billboard.

I wonder what it would be like to be born an angel. To grow up with wings. To learn to balance with feathers pulling against your shoulder blades.

Another piece of your body to protect and take care of and keep clean. Another part of yourself that you might be forced to hide if you live in the wrong place, or the wrong time. Another amazing part of your identity, to be assessed and judged by the people around you.

I stare at the photo, trying to imagine her life. Not just an angel, but the daughter of a famous angel. So much part of his identity that he gave her a place in his artwork.

She looks happy. She looks completely at ease.

My dress tugs at my shoulders as I turn to follow Sam, and for a moment I feel the lack of feathers. The absence in my own body.

I am surrounded by angels, and I am jealous of their extraordinary wings.

When I catch up with my friends, they are staring at a simple sketch. Sweeping pastel lines make up the face of an older woman, the shapes of her wings picked out in bright colours behind her. In one hand she holds a burning candle, and in the other a sky-blue flag with a pair of golden wings in the centre.

Mila Cornell, the sign next to the picture reads. *Angel Activist.*

I thumb through the programme until I find Mila's image.

"One of the first angels to show their wings in public", I read aloud, and Sam nods. "Just after Kane's billboard!"

I had no idea there had been other angels revealing themselves in public at the same time as Kane's first appearance. My surprise makes my voice too loud, and I glance at the people around us. Mila is here, standing with the artist and a group of journalists. I don't think anyone heard my outburst, but I'm blushing as I turn back to the sketch. So many ways to embarrass myself tonight, even if I don't fall over in front of Kane.

And then I realise that Mila's wings are damaged. The bottom half of one is missing completely, and the other hangs at a sharp angle from her shoulder. The artist has made sure the injuries are visible without detracting from the drama of the image, and when I turn to the group behind me I see that she wears her wings boldly, showing off the unmatched shapes with a plunging asymmetric neckline.

I scan the page in front of me, and learn what happened.

The damage is from an assault, around the time Kane's photo hit the headlines. She unfurled her wings at a demonstration for minority rights. There were people in the crowd looking for trouble, and she found herself under attack. When the thugs were dragged off, the people around her tried to get her to a hospital, but they were turned away. No one knew how to treat wings. No one knew what the risk of infection might be from damaged feathers and shards of wing-bone.

It took hours, and three emergency departments, before anyone stepped up to help, but by then the damage was too severe. She made headlines for a day, but no one wanted to read about angels. No one wanted to be reminded that people with wings lived around them in secret. No one wanted to feel that her blood, and her injuries, were on their hands.

My hands are shaking. I had no idea. I've been so wrapped up in Kane's life, and Kane's image, that I missed this woman's astonishing bravery. It took a commission from the Queen to bring this beautiful artwork to my attention, along with the story behind it.

For the second time tonight, I'm breathless.

We keep walking, checking out the exhibition and looking for our favourite pictures. Sam picks out a mixed-media collage of a doctor in hospital scrubs, framed by his wings. One is depicted as a scientific anatomical sketch, and the other is a ghostly X-ray image. Smaller anatomical diagrams and scans fill the space around him, and the effect is hypnotic.

"He's just an ordinary doctor," Sam says, shaking his head. "He treats everyone, wings or not."

Faisal's favourite, after the footballer, is an oil painting of a librarian. She stands in front of a line of bookshelves and holds a pile of books in her arms. The image is half old-fashioned formal portrait, and half joyous laughter. Her clothes are smart but drab and her wings are the dull brown of a female blackbird, but the books erupt in raucous colour all around her as she laughs. One of the books in her pile is Faisal's favourite – some old cyberpunk adventure – and he decides immediately that this is his guardian angel.

Mine, not counting Kane, is a Winter Olympic medallist. She took the silver in a ski event in Vancouver in 2010, and surprised everyone at the welcome-home party in London when she took off her jacket and showed off her wings. Her coaching team, some of whom had been hiding their own wings, had sworn to keep her secret, and some of them joined her at the party to show their support. The top of her medal is just visible, glinting at the neckline of her plain white shirt. It could have been the focus of the huge watercolour panel, but instead she asked to be painted with her family, sitting together on a bench in the garden of their home.

She's an ordinary angel, and somehow that inspires me more than all the high-profile names and famous faces. She won her place in the world, and then found her own way to be happy. She proved that wings and medals don't have to define who you are, or dictate anything about your life. She is the face of freedom in a gallery full of people trying to meet expectations about who they are, and what they must do to fit in.

The exhibition curator clinks a wineglass to attract our attention, and the murmur of conversation dies.

"Welcome," she says, looking round at us all. "Angels, artists, reporters and guests. It's wonderful to have you here tonight at the launch of this very special exhibition."

She checks a crumpled sheet of paper in her hand before looking up at us again.

"When Her Majesty the Queen expressed her desire to celebrate the angels of the United Kingdom, the

National Gallery was only too happy to co-ordinate the event. We were thrilled when forty-three angels, and forty-three artists, answered the call, and we are very excited to welcome most of you here this evening."

"This exhibition has been several years in the making. Recruiting angels and artists was only part of the challenge. Matching each angel with an artist, creating the teams that produced these amazing tributes, took months. Angel and artist had to spend time together, planning the tone of each image – the colours, the settings, the story each person wanted to tell."

I find myself looking for my mother in the crowd. I had no idea she'd been meeting Kane before bringing him to the studio. Getting to know him, and planning the painting together.

Another angel story I'd missed while my attention was on the cuttings on my wall.

"We are here today to celebrate art, and artists. But we are also here to celebrate the angels among us. Famous faces, and ordinary angels. People we may never have heard of, who have been brave enough show us who they are."

The curator nods at Kane, and raises her empty glass towards his painting. "Among those famous faces is Kane, whose unmissable image draped along Oxford Street first brought public attention to the forgotten angels in our midst. It is hard to fully express the shock, and the media buzz, that surrounded the unveiling of that image, just as it is hard to express the bravery of the man who bared his wings and challenged a generation to accept his existence. Following his example, Mila Cornell showed us beauty, strength and resilience in the face of a fierce public backlash. Between them, these pioneers started a revolution, and it is because of them that we stand here today, able to celebrate their unique achievements in one of the most prestigious venues in London, in an exhibition commissioned by the Queen herself."

Several of the angels start to clap, and soon we're all joining in the applause for Kane, Mila, and the curator.

The curator continues her speech, and people are clapping again, but I'm not listening. I'm still trying to understand the stories I've seen tonight. Mila, with her broken wings and utterly undaunted spirit. Kane, whose appearance was greeted so differently, and inspired so many angels to come forward and fight for rights and recognition. The doctor, the footballer, the librarian – and the Olympic Medallist who chose to show her family, not her triumph.

When I walked into the gallery, I had one story in my mind. One angel experience. A world-famous, charismatic, charming fashion model with a jet-setting lifestyle and the power to make and break trends, brands, and careers. A life lived in the flashbulbs of a thousand photographers, and printed in surgical detail on the pages of every lifestyle magazine on the planet. Knowable and untouchable in the same moment.

I had given no thought to the ordinary angels, and the activists who faced violence and discrimination on the road to acceptance.

I close my eyes, remembering the moment I sat on my father's shoulders and looked up at Kane. The moment I saw his wings.

And I remember shouting, and placards. I hadn't understood it at the time, but those were protesters. People shouting about indecency and deformity. People like the ones who attacked Mila.

"OK?" Sam takes my elbow and whispers in my ear. I open my eyes. "You look ... swoony."

I nod, then shake my head, trying to catch the rest of the speech. He keeps his hand on my arm.

"... and please join me in thanking everyone who worked behind the scenes on this event." The curator raises her glass to the staff on the check-in desk, to the string quartet sitting quietly behind us, and to the floors above us in the gallery. "And in remembering all those angels still keeping their wings hidden. May we, in our small way, open the doors to them – to acceptance, to visibility, and living their authentic lives."

The final applause is much louder, as the angels and artists express their gratitude and excitement at being here, and the rest of us congratulate them on their images, their stories, and their bravery.

Remember this, Pumpkin, my father said as we looked up at Kane's billboard together. *This is the first step towards a better world.*

Here, tonight – this feels like another step. Another important moment, and I was here to watch it happen.

I glance across the room, to where Kane is standing with my mother ...

... and my breath catches as he glances across at me.

I meet his perfect blue eyes, and in a room full of people and noise I feel as if we are alone. I feel as if, in spite of everyone here, I'm the only person he sees. I feel as if I'm floating – as if there's a helium balloon inside my ribcage – and I'm grateful for Sam's hand on my arm.

Kane has my full attention, and in this moment, I have his.

I'm a schoolgirl, and he's a superstar with wings, but there's no harm in dreaming.

Chapter 6

The angels and their artists leave first, heading up the gallery stairs to meet the press outside in the square. The rest of us follow, gathering in the wide stairwell as the photographers outside shout and jostle each other for the best shots.

"Swooning again?" Sam leans close to my ear, and I realise I've been swaying to the fading music of the string quartet, eyes closed, my fingers gripping the handrail for balance.

I shake my head, and Sam puts a hand on my shoulder.

I'm not swooning – I just don't want this evening to end. I want to stay in the beautiful underground gallery, spotlit and peaceful as a cathedral, surrounded by the astonishing images of angels. I want to feel close to the art, and the artists. I want to be part of the celebration. I want to feel as if I belong.

For the last few hours, we've been part of something special. We shared the room with the most talked-about artists of the year. We admired their beautiful, joyous portraits. We walked with angels.

Kane kissed my hand.

I don't want to go home.

When we reach the square the sky is dark, but we are met with a barricade of light. Dazzling floodlights wash the walls behind us in a golden glow, and a thousand cameras flash and glitter from the crowd in front of us. The air is cool, but the lights feel hot on my skin.

Across the space in front of me, Kane talks into a TV camera, praising the artists and thanking the Queen for commissioning the exhibition. His wings are behind him, glowing in the golden light and spread across his shoulders like a cloak. He looks like a Renaissance painting or a graveyard carving.

He's the only angel left outside the gallery, and he looks beautiful. He looks like his painting. And next to him stands my mother, calmly answering questions about her portrait.

The woman interviewing them is blushing, and her hands are unsteady on the microphone. I find myself smiling – I'm not the only one swooning tonight.

Sam nudges me, pointing over the heads of the crowd, and I hear shouting. The photographers are turning, aiming their cameras away from the gallery. The police officers keeping the press in line are starting to take an interest.

Something is happening in the square.

A protester with a placard pushes through the crowd, two officers running to catch him before he can reach Kane. He's shouting, calling angels *unnatural* and *disgusting*. As he stumbles, pinned at the elbows by police in high-viz jackets, his placard falls.

Abomination, it reads in blood-red paint, above a crudely drawn pair of wings.

I can't breathe. Someone is attacking angels. After this evening's celebration, after seeing all those inspiring portraits, this feels like darkness attacking the light. It feels cruel and impossible and evil. It feels like a bad dream.

Kane turns. I can't see his face, but he only glances at the man before turning back to the camera.

The reporter nudges my mother away. One stupid angry man with a placard, and she's not the story any more. No one cares about her gorgeous painting – suddenly this is all about hate and conflict, a million miles from the evening we've spent in the gallery.

The interviewer gives a brief explanation for her viewers, then points the microphone back at Kane. Behind her the officers drag the protester towards a waiting police van.

"The situation seems to be under control. What's your reaction to this protest?"

Kane faces the camera, light playing on his gold body paint. Slowly, he lifts his wings, stretching them to each side and holding them still as the feathers glimmer and shine. He shrugs.

"I've got something they haven't," he says, giving the reporter his best megawatt smile. "I'm happy with who I am."

The woman smiles back, and Kane drapes one wing round her shoulders while she signs off from her report. The reporter thanks him, ducking out of shot as all the cameras start flashing. Photographers are running to find the best spots as he turns towards them, floodlit, wings out, arms slightly raised, posing for all tomorrow's front pages.

I'm shaking. I still can't believe that someone got that close to the most famous angel in the world.

"Are you OK?" Sam is in front of me, his hands on my shoulders. "Mel?"

I nod, brushing tears from my eyelashes.

"That was …" I shake my head.

"Yeah," he says. "It was."

"Melodie!" My mother takes my hand and brushes my cheek with her fingers. "We're OK. Nothing happened. The police were there …"

I nod, and she pulls me into a hug.

"You're OK," I say, still shaking.

I close my eyes. I want to block out the lights, the crowd, the noise. I want to be back in the gallery. I want to rewind the last hour and start over.

My mother's arms tighten around me, and I can almost believe there's nothing wrong.

I can hear the cameras snapping, the photographers calling to Kane, their footsteps as they push round each other to steal the best shot.

I can hear shouting in the square. Police and protesters, angry voices confronting each other.

Unnatural.

Disgusting.

Abomination.

And there's something else. Something that shouldn't be there.

I push away from my mother, spinning to look beyond Kane, beyond the photographers. I don't have time to explain. I don't have time to shout.

I'm running, sprinting towards the angel. And coming towards me, heading straight for us both, is the sound of a revving engine.

Time slows. The photographers begin to scatter. The police are running, too. The world is a progression of flash bulbs, jolting from one image to the next as the cameras clatter and a large black vehicle swerves into the space in front of the gallery. The sound of the engine builds.

Kane turns. At the last moment, he raises his arms and wraps his wings close to his body, and then he's flying.

There's a horrible, splintering crash, and he's flying backwards.

In those final seconds, he doesn't look like an angel. He looks like a broken bird, his feathers splayed and messy as he falls through the flash bulb instants.

He can't fly. He can't lift his wings and save himself. He is thrown by the impact and as his head cracks into the pavement and his feathers scatter around us – I am with him.

I am on my knees, shouting. My hands are on his chest, begging him to take a breath. I'm cradling his head against my dress, but there's a deep cut across his nose and mouth and he's bleeding. One arm is twisted behind him and there's another cut on his shoulder and he's not breathing.

He's not breathing.

I don't know what happens next. I hear cameras and shouting, the roar of the engine and the squeal of skidding tyres. I'm crying out, pleading with the angel to *just breathe*. There's a hand on my elbow and someone is pulling me away but I won't leave. I'm screaming and fighting and I won't leave Kane.

Somewhere there's a crash, and the sound of twisting metal.

More hands, and I am dragged gently back while people in uniforms cluster around him and try to start his heart.

I can hear the whine of a defibrillator. Shouting. The TV reporter is talking again, and the light is so bright and my hands are covered in blood.

The world dissolves into colours and noise. Time is unravelling. I can't feel the ground under my feet. I don't think I can stand up.

Someone is holding me. Shielding my eyes from the lights.

Faisal. Faisal has me in his arms.

"It's OK," he says gently into my ear. "It's OK, Mel. Sam's got her."

I don't understand. I don't understand anything. I think Kane might be dead, and we were all just so happy, and all I can hear is the sound of those bloody cameras – and then I realise what he said.

"Who?" I ask, my face pressed into his shoulder.

He holds me a little tighter.

"Your Mum," he says, one hand stroking my back. "She was hit, but she's alive. Sam's got her."

Chapter 7

I am disconnected from time. I exist only in those flash-bulb moments, as the bone-crushing force met the gold-painted angel.

As he fell through the light towards me.

As I cradled his head and felt his blood on my hands.

If I close my eyes, it all happens again. Slow, moment by moment, time sliced by a hundred flashing cameras.

The hospital is bustling around us, the emergency department treating all the injuries from the gallery. My mother is in surgery. Sam and Faisal sit next to me on the plastic waiting-room chairs.

And Kane is dead.

"Woah." Sam is hunched over his phone. "Mel …" he begins, nudging me.

I lift my head from my hands. He's staring at his screen, tapping on photo after photo on his newsfeed.

"Mel." He turns the screen towards me, his hand shaking. "You're famous."

I was wrong about tomorrow's front pages. It won't be Kane staring out from every newspaper, smiling and showing off his wings.

It won't be the angel celebration making the news.

It's me.

Sam scrolls through news sites, TV channels, social media – and my photo is everywhere. Cradling Kane's head, blood painting my hands, I'm screaming for him to breathe.

Some of the images capture me bending over the angel, my hands on his chest. In others my face is streaked with make-up and tears and I'm ugly crying, looking up into the floodlights and shouting for help.

As we scroll, one image appears more and more. The photographer must have been kneeling at Kane's feet, his lens trained on my face. I'm looking up, tears catching the light. Kane's head rests against my knees, and I'm holding my bloodied hands out, as if in desperate prayer.

It's a stunning photo. I look like a saint or a goddess, begging for healing or calling down retribution for the death in front of me. In the floodlights my skin glows, and the silk of my dress shimmers. Kane's wings spread, broken, around us both.

I find myself thinking about the colours I would use if I was painting the scene. Standing in front of an easel, brush in hand. This really is someone's once-in-a-lifetime photo, and it captures everything – drama, devastation, and pain.

It's beautiful.

But it's not an abstract image. It's not a model in a studio, or a stranger on TV. It's me, frozen in the worst moment of my life.

Like Kane, framed forever by his first, shocking billboard, I realise this is how the world will define me. Whatever I do, whatever I become, however I want to be seen, I won't have a choice. I will always be the screaming girl in the floodlights, ruined make-up on my face and blood on my hands. I will never be able to move beyond the moment when an angel died in my arms.

Sam pushes the phone into his pocket and wraps his arms around me. I'm sobbing, but I don't know when the tears started. In the square, under the lights, everything felt unreal. Disjointed, slow motion, fractured and out of time. But here, now, scrolling through photo after photo of my face, my dress, my hands – now reality crashes down.

I can't relive this. I can't rewind and start the evening again and hope for a different ending.

I'm famous for all the wrong reasons. Kane is dead. My mother is with the doctors, keeping her breathing and saving her life.

And there's nothing at all I can do about it.

We're doomscrolling again, all three of us working our way through news reports and social media updates. More photos are being posted and shared – different angles on me and Kane, some shots of the protesters, and several showing the vehicle that drove through the crowd. The black SUV is crushed against one of the flagpoles outside the gallery. In one image, the police are dragging someone from the driver's seat.

I cry out when I see Sam, kneeling with my mother where she landed. She's gripping his arm with both hands, her dress torn and bloodied, and her leg is a mess. I didn't see the SUV veer away from me and towards her. I had no idea she'd been hit – I was too wrapped up in what was happening to Kane. So distracted by the angel that I missed the disaster in my own family.

Thank goodness Sam was with her.

There's a noise outside the waiting room, through the doors to the ambulance bay. I can make out bright lights, a TV camera, and the reporter from the gallery. Someone is shouting.

A security guard rushes past us from the reception desk and out through the doors, pushing the TV crew back. There's more shouting, and camera flashes up against the glass. The triage nurse picks up the desk phone and calmly requests police assistance. There are more security guards outside, pulling photographers away from the windows and doors.

My heart is racing. I thought we were safe here. I thought they'd leave us alone while we waited for our families and friends – while the doctors treated the wounded. I close my eyes and I can hear the cameras in the square, snapping and clattering and stealing photos of all of us as the driver steered through the crowd and Kane lay bleeding under my hands.

I thought this was over.

"Miss Abbott?"

Sam looks close to tears, and Faisal puts an arm round my shoulder as I glance up at the security guard standing over us. I nod.

"Come with me, please." He tips his head towards the door, and the altercation outside. "Let's get you and your friends away from all this."

I nod again, and stand, and follow him out of the waiting room. Sam follows, hand in hand with Faisal.

I feel numb. I feel empty. The guard opens the door to a private waiting room, and I'm crying before I make it to one of the beige sofas. I don't know where the tears are coming from. I don't feel sad. I don't feel anything at all. I'm so tired all I want to do is lie down here and sleep for a year.

Sam brings me a cup of water from the cooler in the corner. There's box of tissues on the table, and Faisal places it gently on the seat next to me. No one speaks. I curl up in the corner of the sofa and rest my head on my arm, closing my eyes and wishing everything would disappear.

I must have fallen asleep, because when I open my eyes my father is sitting in the chair next to mine, his head in his hands. My grandfather sits on the sofa opposite, my brother curled up next to him on the cushions. Sam and Faisal have gone.

"Mel?" I lift my head and nod at my grandfather. "How are you doing?"

My mouth is dry and my throat aches. I cough before I can speak.

"I'm ..." I shrug. I don't have the words.

"In one piece?" He asks.

I look down at my hands, remembering blood. Someone in a uniform asking me whether I was hurt. Explaining that it wasn't mine. It wasn't me who needed help.

Washing my hands in the hospital bathroom, the water rushing red and brown from my fingertips. Scrubbing with soap until my skin felt raw.

My hands are clean. I'm not hurt. I'm not bleeding.

"I guess," I say without looking up. I'm staring at the gold nail varnish, perfect and untouched by everything that happened tonight.

"Kane ..." I say, and it comes out as a sob. I can't explain how I'm feeling. I can't give words to the gap between Kane kissing my hand in the gorgeous gallery, and Kane broken and dying in my arms. It feels like stepping off a cliff. It feels like falling forever.

"I know." My grandfather's voice is gentle, and I think he understands.

"And Mum. How's Mum?"

My father stirs, sitting up and reaching out to me. I take his hand over the arm of the sofa and he squeezes my fingers.

"They think she's going to be alright."

Something heavy shifts in my chest and I take a breath.

"They can fix her leg?"

He nods. "It's broken in a couple of places, but they're putting her back together."

My grandfather smiles. "She'll be setting off the airport alarms with all the metal pins they're putting in, but they're fixing her." He glances at the clock on the wall. "They wanted us to go home, but we asked to wait. We should have some news soon."

"Sam? Did he …?"

"The boys went home. Faisal's dad picked them up. We convinced them there was nothing they could do here." He grins. "I think Sam wanted to wait with you, but Faisal was … very persuasive."

That makes me smile. Sam is a great friend, but one glance from Faisal's deeply pretty brown eyes and he'll forget about everyone else.

"I bet."

My grandfather must notice my smile fading as I think about my mother, the surgeons putting her back together with metal and stitches.

"So," he says, sitting forward on the sofa. "Tell me about this evening. Tell me about my daughter's royal commission. Tell me everything! Make sure you remember the good stuff, Mel."

So I do, and he listens, his eyes glistening with tears as I tell him about the gallery, and the beautiful paintings, and the angels.

We take a taxi home. We usually catch the bus, but my grandfather insisted on hailing a black cab. I sit with my head resting against the window, watching the streetlights fade in and out as we drive through the night-time city. The road is painted yellow and gold under the lights, and the bright white headlights of passing cars sting my eyes.

My stomach is knotted with tiredness and exhaustion. I feel as if we're moving underwater.

My mother is out of surgery, and they're confident that with physiotherapy and rest she'll make a decent recovery. My father held her hand in the recovery room while the rest of us waited outside.

There was nothing more we could do at the hospital.

I made the mistake of checking my phone while we waited for my father, and I've seen tomorrow's front pages. It's my photo staring out from every newspaper, blood on my hands and tears on my face, screaming.

I'm the face of a hate crime. I'm the story of Kane's murder, condensed into a single image. I'm the girl who caught the most famous angel in the world, falling on a London street.

Everyone will see, and they'll think they understand – but they won't know my story. My story is more than that image.

My story is a billboard on Oxford Street. A bedroom wall filled with photos. A moment, stumbling in the doorway of my mother's studio. A breath caught as the angel kissed my hand in a gallery lit like a church. A lifetime of adoration for the man who died tonight.

There are tears on my face as I think about all those people buying their papers in the morning. Scrolling through their news feeds. One glance at me, a quick scan of the text, and they'll think they know everything.

But they won't hear the engine, revving through the crowd. The constant snapping of the cameras. The crash and the shouting and the screeching tyres.

They won't see his broken wings, falling.

They won't know about the day when I was five, and my father lifted me onto his shoulders to see a beautiful angel on a billboard.

They won't understand.

My throat feels tight and my shoulders shake with sobs I can't control.

Chapter 8

It's been days, and I still can't believe he's gone. His eyes stare out at me from every photo on my wall, every image I've sketched.

It can't be real. That can't be the end of Kane's story. It's too brutal, too ugly for such a gorgeous man.

The news coverage rolls on, my picture a constant presence on social media and news platforms. I make the mistake of reading some of the comments.

There are plenty from fans like me, united in grief and confusion. *Is this really happening? Who would do this? Why did they kill him?* I leave a trail of heart-shaped likes as I scroll through the hashtags – #Kane, #WeLoveKane, #KaneFans, #RIPKane. I stop when I notice people wishing they could trade places with me. Wishing they were the girl in the photos, with Kane's blood on her hands.

I feel sick. I can't imagine why anyone would say that.

And some of the comments are nasty. There are people gloating over Kane's murder.

Finally my girlfriend will shut up about him.

That knocked the smile off his smug face.

The abomination got what he deserved.

Keep looking over your shoulders, angels – we're coming for the rest of you.

There are people with anonymous accounts calling me an angel-whore, and worse. Laughing at my photo. Making fun of my pain.

I report the worst of the comments, and force myself to put my phone down.

This isn't my story, and I refuse to play the role mapped out for me by journalists and haters. They've decided who I am, and there's no way to change the image they've painted of me.

When a reporter gets hold of my number, I switch off my phone and lock it in a drawer. I have nothing to say. The true fans already understand, and everyone else will ignore my words. I want them to remember Kane on his billboard, on his fashion shoots, in my mother's portrait. I don't want to be part of this obsession with the moment someone killed him for being proudly, confidently himself.

He deserves more than that.

"Mel!"

Sam's voice drags me back to my room. I don't know how long I've been staring at Kane's photos, trying to remember how it felt when his eyes met mine. When he kissed my hand.

"You're OK," my friend says from the doorway, and I nod, making space for him on the bed next to me. He closes the door and sinks down onto the hand-printed throw. Blue and white vines map the space between us as he kicks off his shoes and sits cross-legged against my pillow.

"So," he says. "What's new?"

I shake my head, my attention still on the wall of photos in front of me.

"You didn't answer your phone." He tugs at the bedspread. "I wanted to check on you."

I shrug. "Still here," I say, turning to look at him.

He nods, and watches me for a moment. He looks as if he hasn't slept.

"Your Mum's home."

I nod. "Yesterday. Dad went on the bus and brought her home in a taxi."

Sam clasps his hands in his lap and stares at them.

"I'm sorry I didn't stay. At the hospital."

"It's OK."

He twists his fingers, still not looking at me. "I wanted to."

"I know. And I know you can't say no to Faisal. You definitely can't say no to Faisal and his Dad."

Sam grins, and shrugs. "Yeah. They did gang up on me."

"You swooned, Sam." I'm smiling as he looks up. "I wasn't even awake, and I know you swooned. I know Fai's superpower, and I know you swoon just as well as I do."

"Fair." He nods. "But in my defence I knew you'd be OK. You had the full Dad-Grandad-brother army with you. And you were out of it." He snaps his fingers with each word. "Out. Of. It."

"I know …"

"Like, unconscious. You were drooling, Mel! Your Dad wouldn't let me wake you, so I had no choice. We had to disappear, right when you needed us."

I make a disgusted face. "Too much information!"

Sam smiles, pressing his hands flat against the throw. "I'm sorry. For leaving you like that."

"I know. Thank you." I shake my head. "There's nothing you could have done."

We sit quietly for a moment. I reach out to rest one hand on his.

"So how are you really doing, Mel?" He laces his fingers through mine. "That was messed up, what happened. And all the photos, and the stuff online …"

I pull my hand away. "Have you read the comments?"

He nods again, glancing at the Kane Wall. "Yeah. That's why your phone's off, I'm guessing?"

"And locked in the drawer." I point at the desk at the end of my bed. "Just in case I'm tempted."

"Have the journalists found you yet?" I nod. "Yeah. Us too."

"You haven't talked to anyone, have you?"

He shakes his head. "No way. I don't want anything to do with that circus."

"Thank you," I say, quietly.

"You've seen what they're saying. I don't want to get involved." He makes a face. "And some of those commenters are scary. It's not just angels they're gunning for. There are photos of me and Fai all over our social media. I don't want—"

"I know." I reach out and he takes my hand. "I don't want anything happening to you two. Keep your heads down, OK?"

He takes a breath. "It's so unfair. If you're a straight man with your arm round a gorgeous woman, no one cares. You can be loud and proud and rude and obnoxious, and people will cheer you on. But if you're a guy with a gorgeous boyfriend, or a guy who knows she's really a girl, or an angel showing off to the rest of us – that's a crime to these people. That makes it OK for them to ..." He gestures at the wall of photos. "It makes you a target. It means they'll cheer if someone hurts you."

I squeeze his fingers. "Pretty sure that goes for angel-whores, too."

He looks up at me. "You read those?"

"Yeah."

"I'm sorry, Mel. You don't deserve any of this."

"Neither do you." I wave a hand at the photos. "And I might not like the words they use, but they do have a point. I might have a tiny angel obsession."

It's a relief to hear Sam laugh, and I can't help joining in.

"A tiny angel obsession," he says. "Right. An absolute devotion to a single angel for almost as long as I've known you, but it's nothing, really."

And for a moment I can forget that Kane is gone. That I'm the face of his murder.

That everyone knows who I am.

For a moment it feels good to laugh with my friend, before the grief presses itself around me again and I find I'm brushing away tears.

"Sam! I believe I have you to thank for taking care of me outside the gallery."

My mother sits with her feet up on the sofa, propped up with a mountain of cushions, her legs draped in blankets. In spite of the bruises on her hands, she's been trying to draw. Her sketch pad and pencil box sit on a stool by her side, along with a box of hospital-grade painkillers and her hand-painted bamboo water bottle.

"You're welcome, Mrs Abbott."

"None of that 'you're welcome' nonsense. You helped save my life." She gestures to her legs. "When I'm up and about again, you can expect a crushing hug from me."

Sam grins. "I'll be waiting."

"And thank you for taking care of my daughter. You and Faisal were brilliant at the hospital, I'm told. I'm very grateful."

My friend takes a breath, but whatever he's about to say is cut off by my brother.

"You should show him!" He shouts as he runs into the room. "Hi, Sam," he says, breathless, as he reaches my mother's side.

My mother smiles. "Oh, I don't know. He won't want to see."

"He will. It's awesome!"

"Brace yourself," I whisper to Sam. "He's not going to let you go until you've seen the gory details."

My mother is untucking the covers from her legs, and my brother is jumping up and down with excitement. He's learnt not to touch her legs, but he still wants to show everyone what's under the blankets. It's their double-act, whenever someone new comes to visit.

"Ready?" She asks, and my brother squeals. She flips back the blankets.

Sam gasps.

"Impressive, isn't it?" She flashes us a proud smile.

My brother grins. "It's an External Fixation," he announces, pronouncing the words carefully. "It's there to hold all the bits of bone together while they heal. The doctors will take it out in ..." He looks at my mother, who whispers in his ear. "Six weeks," he says, crossing his arms over his chest and looking smug.

I give him a thumbs-up, and he returns the gesture, glancing at Sam.

Sam stares, and takes a deep breath.

"Looking good, Mrs Abbott," he says, eventually, and she laughs.

"Better than the last time you saw me, I think."

I still can't get used to the metal structure embedded in my mother's leg. The bone was smashed by the front bumper of the SUV, and she's lucky that it knocked her out of its path. Sam was with her when she fell, and he saw the damage – he's the one who called for help, and kept her talking while the paramedics arrived – but this is different. This is supposed to be helping, but the metal posts dimpling her skin, threaded through to the knitting bones underneath – they look violent. They look like an injury happening again and again. Under the scaffolding that holds her leg together, her skin is crisscrossed with scars and stitches. Whatever she says, however cheerful she sounds, she will never fully heal from this.

She painted an angel, and it made her a target.

The protesters came for Kane, and we're all living with the aftermath.

Sam's right. This isn't fair.

Chapter 9

I dream of Kane.

We are outside the gallery. Kane stands, posing for the photographers, and I can feel my panic rising. I try to shout. I try to run, but I'm frozen, hearing the engine in the crowd, watching everything happen again.

I don't want to look. I don't want to see him broken and falling. I don't want to watch him die.

I take a breath and try to scream his name, but something has stolen my voice.

The engine roars. The crowd parts. Everything is moving in slow motion.

And then Kane turns to me.

He smiles, and holds out his hand. Before the driver can reach him, the angel takes my outstretched hand in a confident grip. I look into his sapphire-blue eyes, and I see the gaze he gives every partner on every red carpet. The intense, focused, 'I'm so glad you're with me' look. The 'I'm happy you could be here' smile.

The expression repeated again and again in the photos on my bedroom wall. The glance every fangirl dreams of.

The shrieking tyres and the thousand cameras feel far away, and when I look down I realise we're flying. The SUV speeds into the square, the photographers scatter, and the police run to contain the threat – but we are not there.

We are rising through the air, my hand in his, that stunning smile still on his face. He reaches out and wraps his arm round my waist and we climb together into a darkening sunset, his golden wings a gentle shelter around us.

London is laid out beneath our feet like a blanket woven with light.

"You see?" He says, looking into my eyes. "It's beautiful. It's all beautiful."

For a moment there is no sound. No cameras, no shouting, no panic.

"Thank you," he whispers, looking down at my bloodstained hands.

And then we're falling, back towards the light.

When I wake my face is wet with tears. In my chest is a bubble of something like joy.

Part 2

Meeting Jez

Chapter 10

Autumn 2023, Age 20

"The depiction of angels with wings is seen first around the third century of the Common Era. In art from this time period it is still more common to see angelic figures portrayed in non-winged, human forms."

I glance round the lecture theatre. Most of the students are paying attention, scribbling or typing notes while glancing at the slides on the screen behind the lecturer. The sketchbook page in front of me is covered with quick sketches of the paintings he shows us, along with isolated words in block capitals. I'm hoping I'll remember all this later.

"Artists in the Early Christian Era took their cues from religious texts and stories, which describe angels as spirits, or heavenly visitors who appear in the form of men."

I shouldn't be here. This is a History of Art lecture, and I'm surrounded by students who want to write essays and develop an understanding of the work of dead artists. I can't imagine spending three years this close to centuries of creative expression, and never once picking up a pencil or a paintbrush to channel the same inspiration. My tutor noticed a course on religious art, and suggested I try some of the lectures. I'm only grateful I'm not formally enrolled in this department, so I don't have to submit an essay – anything I produce from this experience will be sketched or painted or sculpted, not reduced to dead black words on a harsh white screen.

The lecturer clicks through to a new slide as I turn the page, and I hurry to capture the two simple figures on the screen at the front of the room.

"In this image, from the Catacomb of Priscilla in Rome, we see Gabriel represented in human form."

I know better than to raise my hand. I'm a guest in this room, and this isn't my subject, but I'd love to know what made anyone think that this faded brown silhouette is supposed to represent an archangel. I manage to scrawl *Why Gabriel?* next to my sketch before the screen changes again.

"Some historians have suggested that this move to the depiction of winged figures coincided with the first mutations, and the first appearance of the angels we are familiar with today. But ..."

A new slide appears on the screen, showing a simple terracotta winged figure on a black background.

"... the existence of earlier artworks depicting gods with wings – here we see Eros, in a representation from Ancient Greece, around 5oo years before the Common Era – makes this theory unlikely. Angels have existed among us for far longer than two millennia."

The lecture moves on. I sketch images of figures with bird-like wings, mapping the development of angels in art across the centuries. Some I recognise – Bruegel's rebel angels transformed into terrifying creatures, Bouguereau's musical angels with their white robes and matching wings, the cheeky cherubs in Raphael's *Sistine Madonna* – but others are new to me.

In a painting by Van Eyck, the angel shows off jewelled robes and dazzling rainbow wings. The image reminds me of the paintings in the royal exhibition, where several artists highlighted their subjects' wings in bright, eye-catching colours. Perhaps this was their inspiration.

My hand cramps around my pencil as the lecturer clicks to another image, and another, and I struggle to keep up. I shift my attention between my sketchbook and the screen until I'm dizzy, fighting to note down every example as we head for the end of the lecture. And suddenly I'm looking at Kane.

Sapphire eyes and golden wings, captured in my mother's studio.

I stifle a gasp as the students around me click at their keyboards and scratch pens across paper. It's just another image, to them.

To me, it's a memory. I can feel the ground outside my mother's studio, tilting under my feet as my eyes met his. Sam behind me, ready to catch me as I fell. Kane – in person, alive – his golden wings shimmering as he turned his gaze back to the artist.

"In Alice Abbott's work, *Angel,* commissioned for the Royal Angel Exhibition in 2019, we can see echoes of the work of Carolsfeld in his *Die Bibel in Bildern* of 1860, James Powell's *Four Archangels* of 1888, and even

Sir Jacob Epstein's 1958 sculpture *St Michael's Victory over the Devil*, among other influences. Gilded religious icons inform her use of colour – gold, bronze, and Marian Blue combine to create a striking image of one of our most famous angels."

He looks around the darkened room.

"Can anyone define 'Marian Blue' for me?"

Someone calls out an explanation about the traditional colour for representations of the Virgin Mary, but I can't take my eyes from the screen.

I should be writing this down. I should be noting the connections between my mother's work, and the representations of angels throughout history. *Carolsfeld, Powell, Epstein* – I should be adding their names to my sketches, but I can't.

I can't breathe.

Kane gazes out of the screen, and I'm thrown back into the flashbulb moments of his death. His eyes are alive – not *Marian Blue* as the lecturer confidently asserts, but the genuine, shocking colour that stares out from every photo on my bedroom wall, and every red-carpet video.

I want to raise my hand. I want to tell him he's wrong. I want him to know that Kane was real, and beautiful, and that my mother's choice of colour perfectly captures everything about him.

I want to walk away – out of this lecture hall and into the daylight. I want to pull my paintbox from my backpack and start spreading colours into my sketchbook.

I want to create an angel.

I fight for breath. I feel as if I'm falling.

"For comparison," the lecturer continues, moving to a slide with two images side by side. "Note the parallels between Alice Abbott's depiction of Kane, and his famous first billboard. The clothing, the nude torso, and the details." He points at the painting and the photo as he speaks. "A beaded bracelet, light reflected from his watch, and his unlaced boots all bring to mind the history-making billboard. Which," he says, raising his voice and looking around his audience, "is a reminder that twenty-first century works should be understood in the context of contemporary media, and not solely with reference to earlier art."

I drop my pencil and close my sketchbook, glancing around the lecture theatre. Everyone is concentrating, taking notes, comparing the images on the screen, and paying close attention to the lecture. No one else is drawing. No one else is responding to an hour of beautiful works of art with anything more than notes and essay plans.

No one here is moved by the paintings, or inspired to express themselves with light and colour. They don't feel the brush in their hands, the soft glide of paint onto canvas, or the texture of worked clay against their skin. They can't imagine the intense focus of an artist on a model, the translation of a flesh-and-blood person into the images they've skipped through over the last hour. They've been gifted with the riches of centuries and continents of art, and it's just another area of knowledge to master.

When the lecturer switches off the screen and the lights come up, I'm the only one who floats out on invisible wings.

Chapter 11

"Daydreaming again?" Georgie nudges my elbow, and I wonder how long my flatmate has been walking next to me. "It's not a great habit on a London street, Mel," she says, laughing. "Wouldn't want you wandering into traffic. That would be …"

She stops, noticing as the colour drains from my face and my mind replays Kane's final moments.

"Shit," she says. "Sorry. Not funny."

I take a breath and make myself shrug. "It's true. I should pay more attention."

"And lose that artistic thousand-yard stare?" She throws an arm round my shoulders. "You wouldn't be you if at least half your mind wasn't somewhere else. Away with the fairies." She waves a hand at the sky.

I manage a smile. "Away with the angels, surely?"

She raises an eyebrow, biting back whatever she was about to say.

"It's OK." I nod. "I know who I am. And I'm definitely away with the angels."

She grins, her long red curls bouncing over her shoulders as she walks.

"That reminds me!" She pulls her arm back and rummages through a pocket of her camera bag. "I found something. Thought you might want to come."

She pulls a crumpled flyer from the bag and unfolds it, handing it to me.

It's black, with a heading in neon pink lettering, and an image of two angels in outrageous sequined dresses.

Angel Drag Night, it says, and there's a date, a venue, a time, and a price.

I try to hand it back, but Georgie pushes it away. "Keep it. I have more."

I look back at the photo, and I realise the wings aren't real. They're sequined, to match the dresses. One silver, and one in rainbow colours. I smile when I realise they look like the wings in the Van Eyck painting – stunning and unmissable. Beautiful.

And fake.

"What is this?" I wave the flyer at Georgie as her fingers clamp over my elbow and she drags me away from the lamppost in my path.

"Mel!" She squeals. "Watch where you're going!".

But my attention is on the paper in my hand.

She follows my gaze. "It's a bit of fun, Mel. Performers pretending to be angels. Boys showing off their female alter egos. Probably some girls being boys for the night." She tugs my arm. "Sequins, high heels, songs and booze. It'll be fun!"

"Is this a new thing? Angel impersonators?"

"No idea." She shrugs. "I've never seen them before, but who knows how long they've been running drag nights, right under our noses?"

I study the photo. Two women posing for the camera on a stage, one with a sexy pout, the other laughing. Their make-up is extreme, and I look again.

"Are they women, or men in dresses?"

Georgie laughs and rolls her eyes. "Really, Mel? Who cares? If they're funny and gorgeous and entertaining, who honestly cares?"

"And they're not angels."

She nods. "You're catching on, friend. No one is what they seem to be!" She waves her hands as if she's performing a magic trick.

I'm laughing, but my mind is back in the lecture hall. All those stunning paintings of angels with their feathered wings. Quiet. Beautiful. Respectful.

Everything this isn't.

"Isn't it a bit ..." I screw up my face. "Tacky?"

"I think that's the point, Mel," she says, trying not to laugh. "Fun, flamboyant, sassy ..."

I still can't hold the two angelic depictions in my head.

"If you were an angel, wouldn't you be offended?"

She shakes her head. "Are you kidding? This is the highest form of flattery! These are talented performers who want to have wings! They're showing their love and support for all the angels out there."

I look again at the laughing angel. There's joy here, and pride.

"Maybe—"

Georgie interrupts. "Say you'll come! Please! Please?" She nudges me. "Sam's coming, and Faisal. And a load of people from the journalism course."

"Photojournalists? Or the real kind?" I can't resist the dig at her choice of subject. It's traditional. When we met a year ago in Freshers' Week, it was the question everyone asked. I think she's studying the right thing – I think a good photo is more powerful than words on a page – but everyone else seems to think it's only the writers who matter.

We're fighting them together, one photo and one painting at a time.

She laughs and waves a hand. "Everyone. Words and Pictures. And anyone else they can drag along."

"Well," I say. "If Sam and Fai will be there, they'll never forgive me if I stay home."

"Yes!" She punches the air with both hands.

"But I reserve the right to—"

She interrupts before I can finish.

"Hate it?" I nod. "Sure. If you come along, and you don't like it – if it's disrespectful to your revered angels – then don't come next time."

I can't argue with her. And I don't want to turn down an evening with Sam and Faisal.

And she's right. It might be fun.

"Ha!" She grabs my elbow again. "We should find costumes! Raid the charity shops and kit ourselves out with wings and sparkles!"

"Sure," I say, pushing the flyer into my pocket. "Wings and sparkles. Why not?"

"Looking good, Mel!"

Faisal calls from my doorway as Georgie shields my eyes from a final coat of hairspray. We've spent hours with heated curlers, setting luxurious waves into my long, straight hair. I've been dying it blue-black since I started at uni, and when I check my reflection in the mirror propped up on my desk I can't believe I'm looking at myself.

"Gorgeous, right?" Georgie grins, and plumps the curls round my face. Heavy eyeliner and hot red lipstick make me look like a movie star. Gold eyeshadow and a touch of glitter add some angel chic, and my slinky red dress, knee-high black boots, and cute golden mini wings complete the outfit. Georgie looks just as stunning in a skin-tight silver catsuit, terrifying heels, and almost floor-length dove-grey wings. Where mine are cartoonish and cute, hers are breathtaking. Fully feathered, they rise above her shoulders and drop below her knees, and there's a complicated back-brace system built into the catsuit to keep them in place. The outfit must be left over from some theatrical production, and whoever wore it on stage was exactly Georgie's size. When she tried on the costume in the charity shop, there was squealing.

Our charity shop treasures included both outfits, plus a silver sequined clutch bag for Georgie, and a tiny black shoulder bag on a gold chain for me. We've added angel-wing keyrings to both bags, and we're ready to compete with the drag performers.

"My turn!" She jiggles the chair until I stand up and give her space to sit down. Her make-up is dramatic – dark eyeliner and lips contrast with her porcelain skin, and she's painted silver glitter across her cheekbones and eyelids. Tiny diamond studs sparkle in her ears as she pushes her untamed red curls over her shoulders. She picks up the tiara and bobby pins and passes them to me over her head.

"I give myself to the artist!" She bows to me in the mirror. "Make me fabulous."

By the time her hair is anchored in place by the dazzling silver tiara and a bag full of clips, the others are shouting from the kitchen. A quick spritz of hairspray, and we're both ready to go.

The boys are waiting in the kitchen as we strut down the corridor of our tiny two-person student flat. They've been ready long enough to walk here from their hall of residence and hang around while we finished getting dressed. Fai gives us a wolf whistle, and Sam glances up from his phone.

"Looking good, ladies!" Faisal holds up his hands and squints through the picture frame of his fingers, grinning.

Sam shakes his head. "Wow."

Georgie and I strike a pose, and Fai swipes Sam's phone for a photo.

And then I realise what he's wearing.

It's a tailored jacket in midnight blue, slashed down both sides at the back and lined in scarlet. Feathered wings are pinned against his shoulders, arching out through the openings and showing off the colourful satin inside.

I reach out, stroking the fabric at his elbow. "Where did you ...?"

He smiles. "Perfect, isn't it?"

It can't be Kane's. His clothes are in museums or changing hands for millions online. And Kane's jacket would hang off Faisal's slim shoulders.

But it's a convincing copy.

Sam gives me a proud smile. "The theatre faculty is a goldmine. I might have persuaded the costume department to let me borrow a few things – just for the evening." He tilts his head towards Faisal. "And he does look good in it."

"Well," I say, nodding at Sam. "Normally I'd be expecting you two love-birds to walk together, but today that's not going to work." I glance at Sam's outfit – black jeans, T-shirt, combat boots, and a black leather jacket. No visible wings. "Turn around," I say, twirling a finger at him.

He turns. The back of his jacket has been painted with white feathers, far closer to my costume than Faisal's.

"You're walking with me, Sam." I hold out my arm to link through his. "Fai and Georgie are clearly the angelic couple tonight." I catch Georgie's grin as Faisal solemnly offers her his arm. "We're just the fangirls."

Chapter 12

When we find the club, it's at the end of a narrow alley somewhere in Brixton, but there's no doubt that we're in the right place. A line of people in angel wings and sparkling costumes stretches from the door to the street. A hot pink neon sign lights the grey brick walls, welcoming us to the Angel Club.

"How are we only just hearing about this place?" Sam looks around as we join the back of the line. He pokes a finger into my shoulder. "How are *you* only just hearing about it?"

I roll my eyes. "So now I'm the expert on everything angel-related?"

He gives me a confused look and tries not to smile. "Of course you are, fangirl Mel."

"Well, this must have passed me by," I say, shrugging. "And anyway, Georgie's the genius who found out about it. Ask her!"

"Maybe it's just for angels." Faisal leans in, his voice a whisper.

I point down the line to a tall man, four couples in front of us. His wings are sequined, like the ones on the flyer, and I can see the straps holding them on. "If it is, we won't be the only people who don't fit in."

Georgie's phone buzzes, and she pulls it out of her clutch bag. "The others are inside. They've just opened the doors. Hold on ..." She speed-types on the screen with both thumbs. "I'll ask them to grab us a table."

I don't see what happens next, until it's too late. Someone walking along the street grabs Georgie by the elbow and pulls her out of the queue. Her phone clatters to the pavement, and she's shouting.

Two men in jeans and grubby trainers are tugging at her arms and wings.

"Real, are they?" One of them shouts, and aims a kick at her leg. "One of those abominations?"

"Hey!" Sam pushes one of the men away, and Faisal steps in front of Georgie, his hands held out to protect her. I step up and grab her arm as she trips in her heels. She stays standing, but the other man pulls on her wing. For a moment she's caught between his hands and my attempt to save her, and then she steps towards him.

His eyes widen and he howls in pain as her stilettoed boot heel stamps through the top of his shoe. She wrenches it free, stumbling backwards into me as Faisal stares down the shouting man, and Sam throws out his arm to catch us before we fall.

It's over in seconds. The man backs down from Faisal's glare and helps his friend up from the ground. I'm holding my breath as I wait for him to throw a punch or worse, but he looks up and down the line of people behind us and shakes his head.

"Disgusting!" He shouts as he turns to leave. "All of you. Bloody disgusting."

Sam's hand is still on my back, steadying me as I reach out to Georgie.

"OK?" I ask, taking her hands, and she nods. I pull her into a hug, reaching to avoid her wings, and she clings to me, resting her head on my shoulder. "Do you want to go home?"

She pulls back. "Oh, hell no. We came out to have a good time, and I'm bloody well going to have a good time. Screw those idiots."

"Did they hurt you?"

She shrugs. "I guess. This costume is bomb-proof, apparently. He could have dragged me half way across London by my wings before they broke!"

I turn her gently and check her back. She's right. The costume looks untouched, but pulling on the wings and the hidden harness must have hurt.

"Interesting bruises, then?"

She laughs, nodding. "Interesting bruises."

There's a hand on my arm, and I realise the people from the queue are crowding round us, checking we're OK. Someone hands Georgie her phone, and someone else brings her bag. They're all talking and there are gentle hands on my shoulders and I can't pick out anything they're saying.

Someone offers to call an ambulance and someone else says they're calling the police, but Georgie holds up her hands.

"Thank you, but no. No ambulance, no police. I'm fine." She turns to look at the small crowd gathered round us. "Really. I appreciate the concern, but I just want to have a fun night out with my friends."

There's murmuring and nodding. Sam takes my arm and steers me out of the road.

"Thank you," I whisper. I'm struggling to find any more words. "That was really brave. Thank you."

"Let's get inside." He casts a nervous glance over his shoulder. "We don't want to be here when they come back."

The crowd surrounds us as we head towards the club. I take Georgie's hand in mine, and she grips my fingers. It feels safe, cocooned here among sequined dresses and angel wings. It feels like walking with a team of divine bodyguards, and as we move through the sparkling costumes we find ourselves pushed to the front of the queue.

By the time we reach our table, the story of the last few minutes has made it to everyone in the club.

"Georgie! What happened?" A cute guy with slicked-back blonde hair and an angel T-shirt stands up as we arrive and takes her hands.

"What happened, Patrick, is that a pair of idiots decided I was a real angel." She swings her shoulders to show off her wings. "I've decided to take it as a compliment, and enjoy the rest of the night." She flashes him a grin, and his eyes widen.

"Georgie – that's a story! It's breaking news!" He pats himself down, muttering about a notebook. "Can I get an interview?"

He finds a pen in the pocket of his jeans, and reaches for a paper napkin.

"No," she says, leaning close to him. "From now on, nothing happened, and we're all here to have fun."

He nods, sitting down on the red velvet bench seat, but he leaves the pen and the napkin on the table.

A young man in a crumpled grey jacket sits slouched next to Patrick in the corner of the bench. He glances at me and rolls his eyes, and I can't help smiling.

"Journalists," he says, and returns my smile.

"Hey!" Patrick gives him a glare. "I don't see your notebook."

The man stretches his arms and sits up. "I don't need one. I'm taking notes up here." He taps his forehead and turns back to me. "And the most important question right now is 'who are you, and what are you drinking?'"

If he hadn't been looking right at me, I would have assumed his question was directed at Georgie or Faisal. They're the ones with the stunning costumes, and the target for all the looks thrown our way when we walked in.

But his gaze is intense, and he doesn't look away.

I have to remind myself that my costume is better than most I've seen so far. It might not make me look like a real angel, but it's certainly eye-catching.

And I seem to have caught someone's eye.

He's waiting for me to reply. I don't know whether this is real, or a reaction to the drama outside, but I feel the floor dropping away. He's waiting for me to say something, and I'm falling into his gaze. Grey eyes, the colour of the sea after a storm. The colour of first light under clouds. He watches me calmly as I melt under his spell. There's a bubble in my ribcage, lifting me up, making me smile.

I grip the back of a chair and make myself blink. When I look back he's still smiling. He raises an eyebrow.

Dark hair, elfin features, skin like a marble statue – and he wants to buy the drinks.

"Mel," I say, as confidently as I can when I'm trying not to float away. "I'm Mel. And I'm drinking whatever you're buying."

I can't believe I said that. That's not the first impression I wanted to give, but his smile widens and he waves to a waiter behind me. I don't hear what he orders. I'm too busy wondering whether my face is actually on fire, and whether the blush goes all the way to my toes.

"I'm Jez," he says, and holds out his hand. I take it, and he gives my hand a polite shake. "We should find you a seat."

He turns to Patrick, and the look he gives is enough to make Georgie's friend shuffle away along the bench. I take his place, and before I realise what's happened I'm sitting next to the man with the stormy eyes, waiting for angels.

Across the table, Sam mimes a swoon, and smiles when I glare at him. If Jez notices, he doesn't comment.

"So you're …" I wave a hand at the people round the table. "One of them?"

He folds his hands across his chest and slumps back into his corner.

"Am I a journalism student? Yes." He glances at his friends. "Am I one of them? Not really."

He looks impossibly smug. I find myself wanting to defend a table of people I've never met.

"That seems rude. What makes you so different?"

He waves a hand. "Everything. Nothing." I hold out my hands in a shrug, willing him to say more.

"Ambition," he says, eventually. "The scaling of great journalistic heights."

"Oh," I say, nodding slowly. "You're better than they are." I hope he can hear the sarcasm. He's sitting here, slumped in a corner as if this is the last place in the world he wants to be. He's made no effort at a costume, and he's dismissing everyone else on his course. He might have lovely eyes, but his attitude stinks.

He shrugs, a smile teasing the corners of his mouth. "Do you see me scrambling to write up a street attack on a fake angel in Brixton?" I shake my head. "Ambition," he says, as if he's just won a debate.

I give him my best sarcastic nod, and for a second there's a wounded look on his face.

He sits up, abandoning his nonchalant slouch. "Haven't you ever wanted more than the people around you? Haven't you ever seen more, noticed more – *felt* more than your peers?" He presses his hand to his heart. "Don't you know, in here, that you're destined for something big?"

If I'd heard this speech from anyone else, I'd be laughing. But Jez is serious. He's looking into my eyes, and he's asking me – he's *telling* me – that I'm special. I think about the History of Art lecture. All the students around me scribbling notes and feeling nothing. My need to get away, to paint, to create. The isolation of being the only artist in the room.

I think about the wall in my bedroom at home. Photo after photo of Kane – a lineup of perfection and obsession. More devotion than anyone else I've ever met.

What he says is obnoxious, and I want to tell him he's wrong. I want to pretend I don't know what he's talking about – that I've never been so dismissive of other people and their ambitions. But he sees something in my reaction, and he knows he's found a connection.

"Ambition," he whispers as the waiter brings our cocktails.

Before I can respond, the lights in the club dim. Music pounds from the speakers, and a spotlight illuminates the stage in front of us. The crowd claps and cheers and bangs their fists on the tables.

Sam grins at me in the light from the stage. Georgie whoops, and lifts her drink.

I'm done trying to understand the man next to me.

It's time for the angels.

Chapter 13

The lights dim, the spotlight picks out red velvet curtains, and the applause picks up the beat of the music. When I glance around the club, everyone's clapping along – even the staff behind the bar. It's impossible to resist the rhythm, and I find myself joining in. When I turn to look at Jez, he's slouched into the corner, hands crossed on his chest, and there's a smirk on his lips. I roll my eyes at him and turn back to the stage.

The music builds, the applause shatters into white noise, and the curtains open. Highlighted by a sparkling backdrop, a figure with feathered wings, a short silver dress, and knee-high boots like Georgie's stretches one hand to the ceiling and nods to the beat, looking down at the stage as the cheering grows louder.

I can't tell whether the singer is male or female, angel or human, but they are gorgeous.

There's a microphone in their other hand, and as they slowly raise their gaze to the audience, their smile and the sparkle in their eyes is enough to capture the attention of everyone in the room. Two lines into their rendition of Dua Lipa's 'Levitating' we're clapping along, trying to keep up with the breathless pace of the lyrics.

It's a fantastic performance. By the time the dance moves kick in, I'm sure the wings are fake, but I have no idea about anything else. Dazzling glitter and impossible eyelashes outline the singer's eyes, and their nails flash gold in the light. The dress swings at their hips as they move, and their smile as they completely slay the song is one of pure joy. As the music fades out, half the audience is standing, dancing and clapping at their tables, and we're all singing along.

All except Jez, who shrugs when I glance at him. I'm beginning to regret sitting with him – he's spoiling the mood. It's like sitting next to a black hole.

"Let's hear your cheers!" An older drag queen takes the stage, and I recognise her from her photo on the flyer. Dressed in a floor-length black sequined dress, matching silver wings, a giant blonde wig and outrageous make-up, she holds a hand out to the singer as they take a bow. "Kandy Kane, everyone!"

I almost choke on my cocktail. Sam sends me a concerned look across the table.

"Kandy Kane? Like – *Kane*, Kane?"

"Hardly the real thing, is she?" I only realise I've said anything out loud when Jez answers my question.

"No ... I don't ..." I shake my head, trying to clear my thoughts. "Is this supposed to be a compliment?" I wave a hand at the stage.

Jez shrugs. "Apparently."

I look back at the performers. Kandy Kane turns their back to the audience, places a kiss on the tips of their fingers, and raises their hand. As they walk off stage they let their fingers brush the gold frame of a photo hanging to one side of the backdrop, outside the spotlight's circle.

Kane. Even in the shadows I recognise the image – it's one from my bedroom wall. He's wearing a jacket like Faisal's. His wings are draped around his shoulders, and he's laughing.

I think about the lecturer, discussing my mother's painting. Comparing her choice of colours to religious icons.

And here is Kane, his photo being used as an icon in a club. Fake angels, dedicating their performances to him. Worshipping their murdered hero with their acts and their outfits.

I don't know what to say. Part of me feels offended – this is cheapening his life and his death. Taking advantage of everything he did to show his pride and confidence. I want to be outraged. I want to protect his memory ... but part of me understands.

Maybe this is a compliment. Maybe they are, truly, honouring Kane with their joy, their talent, and their pride.

I take a breath, and sit forward in my seat.

The compère is introducing the next act, and the cheers explode as she walks on stage.

Performer after performer takes the stage. At least two are angels, their real, flesh-and-blood wings arching over them as they make the music and lyrics their own. The costumes are dazzling, and it's not long before I notice a theme for the songs. Everyone sings about flying – like a bird, like an eagle – and the audience loves every word. Every performer gives the same salute to the photo of Kane as they leave the stage. The more I see it, the more I think it is a genuine act of affection.

Sam catches my eye and grins when a tall drag queen with immaculate make-up steps up to a microphone stand and gives a note-perfect performance of 'Rise Like a Phoenix' – Conchita Wurst's winning Eurovision song from 2014. She even waits until the final chorus to reveal the golden wings hidden in her costume. Sam presses a hand to his heart, singing along. When I join in, Faisal lifts his hands in a heart sign, and I return the gesture. Watching Eurovision together has been a Sam-and-Mel tradition for almost as long as I can remember, and Fai loves it as much as we do.

Jez watches everything – the singers, the audience, the bar – from his corner of the bench. I can't tell whether he's enjoying himself or not, but while I'm paying attention to the stage, he's making sure our drinks are replaced. He even orders bottles of water to even out whatever's in the shockingly sweet pink cocktails.

The atmosphere in the club is electric. Everyone sings along to the songs they know, and several people move their tables and chairs to give them space to dance, so I'm completely unprepared when a young woman walks onto the stage with a guitar, and changes everything.

Perched on a tall stool, one foot resting on the crossbar, she begins to play. The noise in the club drops to nothing, and her quiet, husky voice and gentle guitar chords keep everyone's eyes on her as I recognise the song. Her cover of Tom Petty's 'Learning to Fly' is slow, deliberate, and heartbreaking. Echoing the lyrics, she doesn't wear wings, and as she sings I can feel the sadness in her words. After all the songs about flying, and all the joyful angel anthems, a song about not having wings should feel out of place. Instead, the audience is silent, all their attention on the stage, and I realise I'm crying.

I'm crying for her as she crafts the song into something special. I'm crying for Kane, and Mila, and all the angels who still don't dare to show their wings.

And I'm crying for me.

Kane had everything. He had fame and beauty and charisma and wings. I craved my moment with him. I wanted to follow him to fashion shoots and red carpet events and glamorous parties. I wanted him to see me, the way I saw him.

I wanted to be like him. I wanted wings of my own. I feel as if she's singing this for me.

With the final chord the room erupts with applause. I dab at my face with a napkin, hoping my make-up is more resilient than I am. Georgie notices my reaction and stretches out a hand across the table. I take it, and she tugs on my fingers, a look of sympathy on her face. I give her a smile, and she lets go.

The singer steps down from her stool, and the compère gathers her into a hug. I join in the whooping and cheering as she gives us a wave and leaves the stage, touching Kane's picture as she goes.

Jez sits up and leans to whisper in my ear.

"Wing envy?" There's a smirk on his face as he waits for me to answer.

My anger is white hot. I can't believe he's mocking me. I don't stop to think as I pick up the remains of my cocktail from the table and throw the pink liquid onto his shirt.

His eyes widen in shock. The drink is cold, and unexpected, and he gasps as it hits his skin.

We both look down at the spreading patch on his chest.

I freeze. I can't believe I've thrown a drink at someone I've only just met. I'm terrified to meet his eyes. I don't want to look up and deal with his reaction. I have no idea what to do next.

And then I realise he's laughing.

"I guess I deserved that," he says, holding out a hand while I pass him a pile of napkins. "I wasn't expecting so much emotion," he says, glancing at me as the bunched paper darkens under his fingers.

I look around the room, at the people cheering and shouting.

"Maybe you're in the wrong place," I say, pointing over my shoulder at the crowd.

He smiles, and nods. "Maybe." He dabs his shirt and drops the sodden napkins in a pile on the floor. "Or maybe I shouldn't make assumptions."

I wish I could agree. I wish I could shame him for making fun of me, but I know I've made the same mistake. I didn't expect to enjoy this evening. I thought it would be tacky and disrespectful, and I was wrong. I've let the music lift me, and I've let it flood my face with tears.

I know I'm in trouble when the next act's music fades in. When I turn back to the stage, the compère is holding the microphone, and I grab another napkin from the table. With a voice like cigarettes and honey, she begins to sing, and I'm sobbing before the end of the first line. 'Wind Beneath My Wings' is my mother's favourite song, and when the drag queen turns and addresses her words to the photo of Kane, I can't stop the tears.

It's a surprise when Jez reaches out and puts a hand on my shoulder.

"I'm sorry," he whispers when the song is over. "I didn't know … It's Georgie who has the perfect wings. Yours seem … less serious." He takes a breath. "I was wrong about you. I didn't know this would be a big deal."

All I can do is nod, and reach for another napkin.

For the final song, all the performers crowd onto the stage. The compère thanks us for our support and demands that we all stand and join in as the first notes of 'Angels' by Robbie Williams fill the club. There's a roar of approval, and by the end of the first line we're all on our feet and singing at the tops of our voices. Georgie grabs my hand and puts an arm round my waist, and we're swaying together, belting out the words as the singers on the stage pass the lines and the microphone between them.

The atmosphere is fantastic. We're all – everyone in the club – shaping this song together. We're all loving the angels on the stage, and the costumes around us. Fake wings or real feathers, we're all singing the same words, and it feels amazing.

I'm starting to realise that this is a place for people like me. That the performers on the stage saluting their photo of Kane know who he was, and what he stood for. They saw his bravery, and it inspired them. They are dressing up and filling the room with joy, and it's all because of Kane, and Mila, and Stannis, and all the angels in the royal exhibition.

This is genuine. This is admiration and love, for Kane, and for all the brave angels who showed their wings in spite of the danger. And it's for the angels who choose to stay hidden, who choose not to let the world know who they are. Unlike the street outside, this is a safe space. Like the paintings in the gallery, these acts are demonstrations of defiance, acceptance, and celebration. Like the gallery, this is a cathedral of confidence and pride.

At the end of the song I collapse back into my seat. The realisation is making my skin warm and my face burn. I've misjudged the Angel Club.

And as I notice the way he's smiling at me, I realise I've misjudged Jez.

Chapter 14

"So why did you come?" I wave a hand at the stage as Jez finishes his cocktail. "You didn't dance, you didn't sing ..."

He smirks, and places his empty glass on the table.

"That's the only way to experience fun, is it?" He settles back into the corner of the bench and watches me. I feel as if I'm under a microscope.

"No, but ..." I gesture to the tables around us. "It seems appropriate."

I'm drunk. I've had too many cocktails, and the lights in the club are too bright. It's hard to make my thoughts line up.

And Jez is still smirking.

"You really want an answer?"

I shrug. I'm not sure I care. Every time I think I've made a connection – made him smile, or apologise – I feel myself relaxing. Warming to him. Falling into his stormy eyes. And then he smirks, and makes me feel small, and all I want to do is walk away.

Or make him smile again.

I feel like screaming.

My boots are pinching my feet. My dress keeps riding up, and I've started tugging the hem down every few seconds like a nervous tic. When I move, the cute golden wings tap against my shoulder blades. I'm uncomfortable, and I want to go home.

"Sure," I say, just to get rid of the smirk.

He sits up, leaning closer to me.

"I'm here to observe." His voice is hushed, and he glances over my shoulder before he speaks again. "I'm here to watch the human animal in its unguarded moments. Making notes on the human condition." He taps his forehead and nods.

I stare at him. I can't decide whether he's telling the truth, or measuring my reaction. Am I his confidant, or a specimen to be tested and observed? Is he messing with me, or does he believe what he's saying?

"This?" He says, pointing at the people behind me. "This is where you get to see people being real. Moving to the music, moved by the lyrics." He looks into my eyes. "This is where you find out who people are. What makes them tick. How they think and how they feel." He touches a finger to his shirt, still damp and stained with my cocktail, and smiles again. "What makes them angry. What makes them cry."

I want to look away. I want to laugh at him, and tell him he's so full of himself there's no way he's observing anyone else.

But there's something about the look in his eyes. Something bewitching about his focus on me, and I can't move.

He's conceited. He's rude. He's judgemental.

And he's fascinating.

"Mel!"

I don't know how long I've been sitting here. How long Jez has been watching me, watching him. Georgie's voice cuts through the spell, and we both jump at the sound of her voice.

"Am I interrupting something?" She's trying not to laugh, eyeing the front of Jez's shirt, and I can feel my face warming under my tear-streaked make-up.

Jez sits back, and I shake my head, trying to give my friend an innocent look.

"OK, whatever." She waves a hand at the two of us. "More important things. You and me …" She points at my chest. "We're going backstage."

It takes a moment for my thoughts to catch up.

"We're what?"

She grins. "Backstage invitation! I can get you in, and Sam and Fai."

Jez clears his throat beside me, and she shrugs. "Were you attacked on your way in? Did you face down two angel-hating idiots with nothing but your best mates and a pair of killer heels? No? Thought not." She turns to me. "Now, Mel!"

Jez shakes his head, laughing, as Georgie grabs my hand and drags me from the bench.

"I'm sorry," I say, over my shoulder. "I have to …" I point at the silver angel pulling me through the crowd.

Jez spreads his hands in an exaggerated shrug. "Too bad," he says, smiling.

"What's the deal?"

Georgie frowns at me. "How many of those cocktails did you drink, Mel?" She glances over my shoulder. "Or has Mr *I'm So Mysterious* over there scrambled your brain?" She doesn't wait for an answer, and I'm relieved I don't have to explain myself. "Angelica heard about what happened in the queue, and we're getting a backstage tour."

"Angelica is ...?"

She rolls her eyes. "What have you been doing all night?" She frowns. "Actually, don't tell me. If you've been snogging Jez Priestly, I don't want to know."

I feel as if someone's lit a fire under my skin. I'm trying to find the words to tell her that's not what happened, but she doesn't wait for me to explain.

"Angelica," she says, her hands on my shoulders, "is the Queen of Queens." I shrug, and she rolls her eyes again. "In charge of the acts? Black sequins? 'Wind Beneath My Wings'?"

Colour and meaning break through the alcoholic haze. "The drag queen?"

Georgie nods. "The top drag queen. And we're her backstage guests." She looks me up and down. "Are you too drunk to handle this, Mel? I can ask Patrick or—"

"No." I tug the hem of my dress down and make myself stand up straight. "I'm fine. I'm coming."

Georgie considers me for a moment, then takes my elbow and pulls me towards the curtains at the edge of the stage where Sam and Faisal are waiting.

"Darrrrling."

Angelica stands as the security guard shows us into her dressing room. She's taken off her wig, but the wig cap holds her hair in place. She's still wearing her sequins and make-up, and she's very much still in her drag queen persona. She takes Georgie's hand and glances at the grey wings on her back.

"I'm so sorry," she says in her honey-and-ash voice. "No one should walk in fear." She reaches out to touch the feathers. "May I?"

Georgie nods, and Angelica smooths the edge of one wing with the back of her hand.

"They're beautiful. Did you have them made?"

My friend laughs. "Charity shop," she says, and I think I see tears in her eyes for the first time since the attack.

"Wow." Angelica draws the word out, one hand on her hip. "That's one lucky shopping trip. They are spectacular." She taps Georgie's shoulder. "Let me see."

Georgie turns, and Angelica nods. "I can see why they thought you were the real thing." She looks down. "And those boots! Heavenly, even if they are murder on the feet."

Georgie strikes a pose before turning back to the drag queen.

Angelica looks around at the rest of us. "And how did you fight them off?"

We glance at each other.

"Together," Georgie says. "These guys were really brave. They stepped up and put themselves between me and the ..." She chokes on her final word.

"Idiots." Sam cuts in. "They were idiots. And let's not forget you and your killer heels."

Angelica tilts her head at Georgie, who mimes stamping down with her boot.

The drag queen raises an eyebrow. "And where on the unfortunate idiot's body did this heel connect?"

"Top of his foot." Georgie sounds proud, but there are tears on her cheeks.

"Shame." Angelica scowls. "Aim higher next time, Angel."

Faisal digs a packet of tissues from the pocket of his jacket as Georgie brushes her fingers over her face, and Angelica turns to me.

"Oh," she says, taking a half step back. She shivers and wraps her arms across her chest as if she's just seen a biblical angel. "Oh. You're her. You're Alice Abbott's daughter."

It takes me a moment to understand what she's said. I don't recognise myself in this outfit, and I can't imagine anyone else seeing through the dyed hair and make-up. All I can do is nod as she takes a step towards me.

"You're the girl in the photo."

I feel as if the world has stopped. As if the air has rushed from the room. I want to take a breath, but my throat is tight and I feel as if I'm drowning.

I'm back in the spotlights, camera flashes marking time as I try to save the angel. As I try to stop Kane from falling.

"You're the one who was with him when they killed him."

I nod, and feel the tears spilling onto my face.

"Hey." Angelica's thumb brushes my chin, and I realise I'm hanging my head. "Hey," she says. "Look at me."

I force myself to meet her eyes, and her gaze is like steel.

"Thank you," she says. "Thank you for being there." I shake my head. I didn't choose to have his blood on my hands. I didn't chose to hold him as he died. I don't understand what she's thanking me for.

"You've seen what we do here. Kane is our muse. He was beautiful and talented and iconic. He's the reason we stand up on stage. He's the reason we sing, and perform, and—" She shrugs. "He's the reason we wear our wings with pride."

I'm gasping for breath as the tears come. I touch a hand to my face, and it comes away streaked with mascara.

Angelica glances at my shoulders. "You're not ...? You don't ...?"

Her face asks the question, and I shake my head. "I don't have wings."

She cups my face in her hands, and gives me a sad smile.

"Oh, darling," she says. "Of course you have wings. We all have wings. We all have something to be proud of." She leans close enough for me to smell her perfume, and whispers next to my ear. "Sometimes it just takes someone special to see them."

We walk home together – Georgie, Faisal, Sam, and me. Not two by two, but boldly, taking up space on the midnight streets. Angelica's words echo in my head.

No one should walk in fear.

Kane is our muse.

We all have wings – sometimes it just takes someone special to see them.

I saw Kane's wings. I saw who he was, and I saw his bravery.

I saw the wings on all the angels at the exhibition.

And I saw sequined wings on stage tonight, celebrating the angels among us.

Maybe she's right. My wings may not be feather and bone, but I can still fly. I can still be fearless and bold and show the world who I am.

I saw Kane's wings. I saw Mila and Stannis and the others.

Maybe one day someone will see mine.

Chapter 15

"I need to move, Mel."

Sam grimaces as I hold up a finger.

"One moment ..."

"Mel! I've got cramp in my foot and my nose is itching!"

My paintbrush flicks across the paper, capturing the dark velvet of my friend's eyes.

All the art students have a studio space in the university buildings. I figured out that I can get Sam into the studio after hours if I sign him in as my model, so he's been sitting for me while we talk. This term's assignment is to paint the same person in three different styles, and in this painting I'm using a rainbow of acrylics to show off the intensity of his dark skin and hair.

"Mel?"

I step back from the easel, taking in my progress on the portrait.

"OK. You can move."

My model lets out a muffled yell as he pushes himself up from the battered leather armchair, limping and rubbing his nose with his thumb.

"Are you OK?"

He stretches his arms over his head, and nods.

"Now that I'm not a human statue – much better, thank you."

I lean into the painting, correcting the light on the side of Sam's face, and he laughs.

"You can stop now, Mel. The chair is empty!"

"And my hands are full," I say, holding up the paintbrush and palette.

He shakes his head. "I'll come back tomorrow. You can paint again then."

"Or now ..."

There's a shadow under his ear that needs to be darker. A bright spot on his forehead that I want to tone down.

"Mel!"

I look up, confused. I'm still thinking about the painting.

"It's time to go," he says, glancing at his watch. He stretches again. "I don't know about you, but I need dinner."

I give him a smile. "Meeting Fai somewhere?" I'm surprised when he shakes his head.

"Fai has rehearsals for his dance recital. I've been abandoned in favour of boy-tights and leg warmers."

"Ooof," I say, still smiling. "Completely abandoned. You've only been the centre of attention in my studio space for ..." I step into the corridor to check the clock. "Two hours. It's heartbreaking, honestly."

He laughs. "OK. Fair. But he's skipping out on dinner as well."

"Unacceptable." I'm nodding as I drop my palette and brushes into the studio sink. "Fancy eating with me instead?"

"Only if you're quick with the clean-up", he says, grasping his stomach. "I'm beyond hungry."

I turn on the tap, and the wall-mounted pipes shudder with the force of the water.

"Tell me what's for dinner, and I'll clean up accordingly."

Sam ponders his response as I wash the smeared paint from the plastic palette, watching rainbows swirl into the drain.

"Burger?" I lift up the palette and show him that I'm cleaning in slow motion. "OK, OK!" He says. "Not a burger. Fish and chips?"

I yawn, and slow down.

"Food trucks!" He shouts. "It's Thursday. There are food trucks in the park."

He laughs when he sees me scrubbing faster.

"Bao buns! Barbecue ribs! That weird spicy salad thing you like!"

"Sold!" I give him a smile as I stack the palette and brushes into the drying rack. By the time I've shrugged out of my overalls and dried my hands, he's half way down the corridor, shouting about street food.

"You're such an artist, Mel." Sam rolls his eyes and points at my fingers. I'm holding a giant bao bun with both hands, and there's still a cascade of pickled carrot and sticky sauce tumbling onto the picnic bench. I tip my bun, and laugh.

My fingers are covered with streaks of paint, and I think there's a different colour under each fingernail.

"My model didn't exactly give me time to scrub my hands."

Sam shrugs, and holds up his foil-wrapped burrito. "It was a food emergency!"

"Drama Queen." I grin, and he grins back, taking a mocking bow over the table.

"We are what we are," he says, putting on a posh accent. "You mess around with paints, while I aspire to the West End stage."

I almost choke on my bun.

I remember the Angel Club. Jez, leaning forward in his seat. All his talk about being special. About being better than everyone else.

Ambition.

The scaling of great journalistic heights.

I shake my head, and bring my attention back to the park.

"Mess around with paints?" I do my best to sound indignant, but Sam is watching me. "What?" I say round a mouthful of steamed dough.

"You look ..." He shrugs. "I don't know. Something I said ..."

I can feel the colour rising on my face. I don't want to compare my friend with Jez. I know Sam was joking.

He stares at my burning cheeks.

"OK," I say, putting the bun down in its tray. "You sounded like Jez. Just for a second."

Sam raises an eyebrow. "Tell me more," he says, smiling.

I wave a hand. "It's nothing."

"Mmm-hmmm." He makes a pouting face. "Not believing you right now."

I take a breath.

"OK. He said some stuff, at the Drag Night. And it was …" I shrug. "Obnoxious, I guess. Stuck up."

Sam nods, and waits for me to say more.

"You just – you sounded like him. I mean, I know you were joking, but …"

My friend grins. "So you're saying that Jez – he of the Angel Club Swoon – aspires to something better?"

I shake my head. "Unfortunately not." I'm tapping my fingers against the table, trying to explain. "He already *is* better. In his own head."

"Ah." Sam nods. "So Mr Swoon thinks he's All That? Better than the mere mortals around him?"

"Definitely. And he doesn't mind telling girls he's only just met exactly how much better he is."

Sam tilts his head and looks at me.

"I'm going to guess that he told you he thinks you're better, too."

My face heats up again, and Sam shakes his head.

"Uh-oh." He puts his half-eaten burrito down. "That's a creep move, Mel. Don't fall for it."

"He didn't … exactly … say that."

Sam rolls his eyes. "It's a classic move! Tell someone you're perfect, and then tell them they're perfect, too. Make out that you're the only two perfect people in a world of sad failures, and – oh, look! You'll have to end up together!"

"He didn't ..."

Sam gives me a glare. "So what did he say?"

I can't meet his eyes. "He asked me whether I'd ever felt that way. More ambitious than everyone else."

"And you said?"

"I didn't say anything."

He looks at my glowing face. "I bet you didn't need to."

I shrug, and try to wrap my hands round my dinner. I don't need a therapy session from Sam.

"Do you like him?" His voice is quiet. "I mean, I witnessed the swoon, but there were mitigating circumstances. You were in a club full of angels ..."

He stops when I kick his shin under the table.

"OK," he says. "I saw the swoon. And I'm hearing you talk, and I'm scared you're going to say you like him."

"And what if I do?"

Sam sighs. "He's playing you, Mel! No one is that full of themselves. Not really." He shakes his head. "It's an act. It has to be."

"Maybe," I say, taking a bite of bun and sauce.

"So do you?" My friend gives me a pleading look. "Like him?"

I shrug. "I don't know. He's ... confusing. And complicated."

"And swoon-worthy?"

I can't stop myself from smiling. "Definitely swoon-worthy."

"Ah-hah!" Sam points a finger at my flushed cheeks. "So you do like him!"

"He did make me feel special."

"Fake special." Sam takes a bite of his dinner and gives me a triumphant smile.

"It's not that simple." He gives me a disbelieving look, and I realise there's something I haven't told him.

"I threw a drink at him."

I think my friend might explode as he chokes on his mouthful of food. "You did what? At the Angel Club?" I nod. "Why?"

"He was mean. He said something really insensitive."

Sam spreads his hands, waving the last bite of his burrito at me. His eyes are wide.

"So why are we still talking about this?"

I shrug again. "He apologised. And he laughed after I threw the drink."

"OK," Sam says, nodding. "OK. So he's obnoxious, but swoon-worthy. He says horrible things, but apologises. And he doesn't mind provoking you to the point that you waste a perfectly good cocktail on his ... where did you throw it?"

I can't help smiling at Sam's wrap-up of our conversation. "His shirt."

"On his shirt." He nods. "Good. He deserved it."

I'm laughing when I answer. "He did."

Sam finishes his burrito and crumples the wrapper between his hands.

"Have you seen him since?"

I shake my head, trying to eat the remains of my meal.

"Huh." He looks surprised. "It's nearly a week, you know."

I'm glad I can't speak. I did know. I know exactly how many hours it has been since Georgie dragged me away from Jez, but I don't want to admit that to Sam. I give him an innocent look.

"Interesting," he says. "And are you planning on seeing him again?"

I shrug, but my face flares with heat. I finish my bun and attempt to clean my fingers on the tiny napkin. Sam laughs.

"Mel. Mel, Mel, Mel. This is some messy stuff, right here. Can you swoon at him from a distance?" He makes his fingers into binoculars and looks around the park.

"Because that's not weird and creepy!"

"I think it's already weird and creepy," he says. "And I don't think you can out-creepy this guy."

"Maybe," I say, and my voice is a whisper. "But he made me feel good."

Sam rolls the balled burrito wrapper between his hands.

"Except when he made you throw a drink at him."

I shrug, smiling. "That felt pretty good, too."

He stares, and then smiles.

"You're in deep with this one, aren't you?"

"Maybe," I say, standing up and collecting our trays and drink bottles.

"Watch out," he says, putting his hand on my arm. "I've seen you like this with Kane. All swoony and obsessed. I don't want you getting hurt again."

I give him a cold stare. "A little dramatic, don't you think, Mr West-End Stage? Whatever happens with Jez, it's hardly going to be prime-time news, is it?"

"God, I hope not."

We walk across the park, dropping our rubbish into the recycling bins next to the busy food trucks. At the main road I turn right towards my flat, and he turns left towards Faisal and the dance studio.

"See you tomorrow?"

Sam grins. "Sitting painfully still for hours while you mess around with paint? Wouldn't miss it for the world."

I wave my acrylic-stained fingers at him, and I'm expecting him to laugh. Instead he puts a gentle hand on my arm.

"Be careful," he says, watching my face. "And if you need a team of fake angels and a ninja in high heels to sort out another creepy guy, you know who to call."

"Thanks, Sam," I say as he turns away.

I settle my rucksack on my shoulders and head towards the flat. I check the time on the bus shelter's electric sign as I walk past, and I realise it's 93 hours since Georgie pulled me away from Jez. I wasn't sure what I thought about him, but talking to Sam has reminded me how he made me feel.

I know Sam wants me to steer clear, but there's a smile on my face and a bubble in my chest when I think about our conversation at the Angel Club.

And I know I want to see him again.

Chapter 16

"Keep still!"

I'm trying to finish Sam's portrait, but every time I darken one of the shadows on his face, the balance shifts and I pull the viewer's attention away from his eyes. I'm working on the final details, but I can't get this right. Maybe I was wrong to use exaggerated colours in this version of his image. Maybe I should have captured his true skin tone, and focused on the soft glow of the lights on his face.

"You're not the boss of me!" He says, grinning, and I give him a scowl. "OK," he mutters, and straightens his face. "Maybe you are."

"In my studio, I'm the boss of everyone," I say, using a tiny brush to correct the catchlight in his eyes.

"Careful," He says, trying to keep his face still. "You sound like your mother."

As much as I want to throw the paintbrush at him, he's right. I do.

"Are you calling me bossy, Sam? Or are you calling me a professional?" I give him a glare over the easel. "Take a moment to consider your answer."

He laughs. "So much like your mother," he says, shaking his head.

"Hey! Still, please. No head waggling." I realise too late that I'm waving my paintbrush at him.

Just like my mother.

He points a finger at me and waves it, mirroring my action. I have to force myself not to smile.

He's the only person outside my family and my mother's models who knows how she sounds when she's being bossy – and how she looks when she's waving her paintbrush. He knows how intensely she focuses on the artwork in front of her, and how she dismisses interruptions like a Victorian schoolmistress. You've done as you're told before you realise what she's said, and he's been witnessing that since we were both three years old.

I want to laugh. I want to tell him he's right, but I don't want to admit it.

And I want to keep painting. I don't want to waste time – I want to get this portrait right.

"OK." I hold my brush and palette in the air. "That's it. I don't need an insubordinate model. And I don't need comparisons with one of the most famous portrait painters of the century." He tries to look ashamed, but my reaction only makes him laugh harder.

And then I'm laughing, too. He's laughing at me, still waving his finger, and I'm laughing at him, gripping my paintbrush. Hidden behind the easel, bent double, gasping for breath. I end up lying on the floor, stomach muscles aching, tears in my eyes as Sam guffaws in the chair, hands clutching his stomach.

"Mel," he says eventually. "Mel – are you OK?"

His breathless voice sets off another round of giggles.

"OK," I say when I can breathe again. "I'm OK. You?"

"Great," he says, sitting up in the chair. "So much better for being able to *move*."

I sit up and wave a hand at him. "Go home, Sam."

"No, no – it's fine." He tries to arrange his arms in the pose I've used for the painting, but when he sets his face and stares at the wall behind me, he can't hold back the laughter.

"Honestly. Go home. I'm making final changes, and I don't need you for this. It's boring and frustrating, and you have better things to do."

"I'm not sure that's true," he says, suddenly serious.

"It's Friday night, Sam. Go find Fai. Do something fun." I point at the easel with my paintbrush. "I have a date with your portrait, so I'm fine."

He gives me a sad smile. "I would, but Fai's out with his dance class. They're celebrating the first dress rehearsal."

"Can't you join them?"

He frowns. "It's a bit of a dance-only clique. Drama students don't quite make the grade."

He sounds genuinely upset.

"I'm sorry, Sam." I push myself to my feet and make a useless attempt to brush the paint specks from my jeans. "What about the other actors? There must be some luvvies in your class you can hang out with tonight?"

He nods. "Maybe."

"Seriously, though. Go. I've got this from here."

"Thanks, Mel," he says, standing up and grabbing his jacket. He walks round the easel and stands with me, looking at the painting.

I start trying to explain the balance problem, pointing at the brown eyes, and the yellows, greens, and blues of his face.

"Mel," he says, one hand on my arm. "It's brilliant. It's balanced and it's eye-catching, and it shows off your very handsome model."

"Well, now you're just sucking up to the artist." I might sound grumpy, but inside I'm smiling. I'm thrilled that my best friend likes my work. That he approves of the version of him I've created with my brushes and paints.

He puts an arm round my shoulder and plants a kiss on the top of my head.

"Don't stay too late, Mel." He heads out into the corridor. "And don't forget to eat!

"Come out with us!"

Georgie stands at the door to my room, her phone in her hand. She's wearing a smart navy jacket, and fitted trousers that sparkle when she moves. I'm slumped on my bed, still wearing my paint-splattered jeans and work boots.

"Now?"

She shrugs. "Now-ish."

I've been standing at my easel for hours, tweaking the colours of Sam's portrait. My arms hurt, my feet hurt, my fingers ache. Everywhere I look, I see brushstrokes and colours, light and shadow. I can't get the painting out of my head, and I just want to lie here and close my eyes.

"Come on. Come out for a drink."

My brain catches up with my eyes.

"Wait – what are you wearing? Where are you going that needs fancy clothes?"

Georgie waves a dismissive hand.

"Oh, you know. Nothing special." She makes a face. "It's Patrick's birthday, and he's decided we all need to go to a wine bar." Before I can comment she crosses to my wardrobe and opens the door. "Put this on," she says, pulling out a short cowl-necked navy dress and tossing it over my chair. "And ..." She rattles the hangers as she searches through my clothes. "This."

A silver jacket lands on the dress. I cover my eyes with one arm, and groan.

"I need a shower, Georgie. I need to wash my hair."

"Of course you don't." She's standing next to me, holding out a hand. When I reach out to her she screws up her face. "I mean, you need to scrub your hands." She takes my fingers and turns them over, looking at the paint under my nails. "And brush your hair. Lipstick, maybe some dry shampoo, a messy up-do, and then we're good to go."

Her phone buzzes and she drops my hand to check her messages.

"Also, Sam's going." She holds out the screen to me.

I need a decent meal and an early night. I should stay here. Crawl into bed, let the others go out – but I know she's not going to let me say no.

"Who else will be there?" I pull myself up off the bed and let down my ponytail. Running my fingers through my hair only tightens the knots and tangles, and leaves flecks of dried paint in the blue-black dye.

Georgie pulls my charity-shop boots from the bottom of the wardrobe and starts looking through my basket of accessories.

"Oh, you know. The usual. Journalists. Both kinds." She hands me a navy blue clutch bag. "Sam. Some of his theatre mates."

I have to turn away to hide my smile. I'm glad Sam has found somewhere to be tonight, but that's not what inflates the bubble in my chest. Maybe I'll enjoy the evening after all.

I realise my hands are shaking. If Jez is there, will he want to talk to me? Will he buy me drinks and talk about wanting to be more, looking for his ambition reflected in my eyes? Or will he find another way to make me angry?

I'm breathless when I realise I don't know what I want him to do. I want him to make me feel special. And if he doesn't? If he triggers my anger?

I think I'll enjoy throwing another drink over him.

Georgie grimaces when she sees the mess I've made of my hair.

"Sit down," she says, pulling out my desk chair and throwing the clothes onto the bed. "And hand me your hairbrush."

I sit, and submit myself to Georgie's fast-track beauty therapy.

The wine bar is in a backstreet just off High Holborn. From the outside it's a small shop front with half-frosted windows, but inside it's all trendy rough-sanded wood, cast iron fittings, piano music and soft red-orange lighting. The walls are hung with Jackson Pollock-style abstract canvases in shades of red and black, but it's too dark to appreciate the designs.

"Georgie!" Patrick calls out as we walk in. "Welcome to Lawyer Land!"

He's sitting at a long, narrow table, and it's already crowded with student journalists. In spite of the dim lighting I recognise some of the faces from the Angel Club. We steal two chairs from another table and while everyone shuffles along to let us in, I take a look around. Judging by the smart suits and the prices on the wine list, he's not joking about the lawyers. This could be an expensive evening.

And that's when I notice him. Sitting at the far end of the table, wearing the same crumpled grey jacket, slumped back in his chair, hands folded across his chest.

140 hours since I left him at the club, Jez's eyes meet mine, and I'm glad I'm sitting down.

He raises an eyebrow, and sits up straight before looking up and down the table. There are no empty seats, and he's too far away to talk to. He shrugs at me, and I return the gesture.

Georgie nudges my arm.

"What are you drinking?" She points at the menu. "I fancy some bubbly. Join me?" I nod, and try not to notice the price.

"Mel?" She looks at me, and follows my gaze down the table. "Ah." She says, grinning as she stands up. "Distracted already. Stay here – I'll get the drinks."

Patrick's phone buzzes, and he picks it up from the table. There's a satisfied look on Jez's face when Patrick holds the screen out to me.

"I think this is for you?" He glances along the table as I read the message. No name for the sender – just a number, but it has to be Jez.

Give this to Mel. I need her number.

I'm glad it's dark in here. I'm glad no one will notice me blushing as I pull my phone from my bag and add Jez's details to my contacts.

"Thanks," I mutter to Patrick, who shrugs, deletes the text, and turns back to the person next to him.

So now I'm sitting in the red-lit bar, my face hot and my hands shaking, wondering what message to send to the man I can't talk to. The man who wants to know about ambition and human animals and what makes me cry. The man who might be dangerous, or exciting, or both.

If I send him a text, I'll give him my number. If I give him my number, am I giving him permission to call me?

I can't fake this. I can't send him made-up details. If I answer, I give him a way to keep in touch.

Is this what I want?

I think about the look on his face when he talked about ambition. About being *better*. And I think about throwing my drink over his shirt.

He made me angry, and he made me feel special. His focus on me, over everyone else in the Angel club – that was intoxicating.

I want to find out what happens next.

I take a breath, and start typing.

No pink cocktails tonight?

He smiles at the phone in his hand, types a response, then watches me as the message arrives.

No cute golden wings?

Interesting. I don't think we talked about my wings at the club. Just the wing envy ...

I make a show of looking around the bar, then reply.

Not really the place for wings, is it?

Jez raises an eyebrow and looks at me as he sends his answer.

I guess not. If there are any here, they're well hidden.

I didn't think it would be possible to blush harder, but my face is on fire. I can't believe I typed something so stupid.

I didn't mean ...

I stare at the phone for a moment, then delete the message. He thinks I meant real angels. He thinks I've said something awful – something I would never say, and something I could never mean.

I look around the bar again, trying to stop my heart from racing.

He's right. There are no angels here – not unless they're hiding their wings. But this is exactly the kind of place I imagine Kane hanging out in. Drinking champagne with his red-carpet companions. Posing for paparazzi photos, then turning his back on the photographers and focusing on his date. Making the bar staff smile, and leaving his legendary generous tips.

Of course this is a place for wings.

This is totally an Angel bar, I type. *Wear a Kane-style jacket, bring your own paparazzi, flash some cash. It's perfect.*

I'm holding my breath as I send the message.

Jez smiles. He looks up and nods at me down the table, and I feel as if I've passed some secret test.

I feel as if I'm glowing.

And then Georgie is standing next to him, handing him two glasses of bubbly and pointing down the table at me. He stands and takes the glasses, and Georgie slides into his seat. As Jez walks towards me, she holds her drink up to me and winks.

Before he can reach me, Patrick calls out to a group of people arriving at the bar. Sam waves back, I stand up to give him a hug, and in the confusion I lose my seat. Jez takes my elbow in the crowd, and when we've all found somewhere to sit we find ourselves on another table with most of Sam's theatre friends. I don't know anyone in this group, and they're happy to talk among themselves.

Sam mimes a swoon when he sees me from his seat next to Patrick, and I give him a smile before turning my attention to Jez.

"So," he says, handing me my drink. "Here we are again."

Chapter 17

"I've been thinking." Jez gives me a sly smile over his glass.

"About?" I take a sip of my bubbly, wondering where this is going.

"You," he says.

I can't help laughing. His gaze is intense, and his smile widens as he watches my response.

If this was anyone else, I'd assume they were messing with me. Seeing how far they could get with a cheesy chat-up line.

But this is Jez. 140 hours ago, I threw a drink at him and he was the one to apologise. He talked to me about ambition and observation. He understood about Kane and the Angel Club.

And I've been thinking about him, too.

"Get straight to the point, Jez!" I'm trying not to choke on my drink, and I hope he can hear the sarcasm. I know he can see my cheeks burning. "Don't bother with small talk. Just tell it how it is."

He pulls a fake confused face. "We did the small talk. With the phones?" He points a thumb behind him, at Patrick's table. "But now I've got you in person. Sitting next to me, in the flesh. Why waste time?"

His storm-grey eyes never leave my face. The bubble in my chest is back.

There's no way I can hide my smile.

"So. What's your passion?"

It's like a conversation with an alien, every time I talk to Jez. I can't work out whether I'm the subject of a convoluted experiment, or the latest candidate in his search for a soul mate.

"Passion?" I ask, keeping my voice as innocent as I can. "In or out of the bedroom?"

I can't believe I said that out loud. It's the kind of thing Georgie would say. I can't even claim to be drunk – I'm still nursing my first glass of bubbly. At this rate my face is going to be burning all night.

"Well," he says, starting to stand up. "I can see we're ready to move this date on."

I tug on the sleeve of his jacket. He sits down, grinning, and I'm very pleased to see that I've made him blush.

He raises an eyebrow, and gives me his best innocent look. "Too soon?"

"*So* soon," I say, shaking my head. "I haven't even finished the drink you didn't buy for me."

Jez gives me a serious look. "Right. Yes. Of course. Drinks." He clinks his glass against mine, and downs the rest of his wine.

"So?" He waves his empty glass at me. "What are you having, now that I'm buying?"

"The bubbly is nice," I say, and he nods, standing. "Makes less of a mess when I inevitably have to throw it over your shirt."

He looks at me for a moment, as if he's deciding whether I'm serious.

"True," he says eventually, and heads to the bar.

Sam catches my eye as Jez walks away. He's too far away for a conversation, but he raises an eyebrow and shrugs. I shrug back, and roll my eyes, hoping my friend understands. I'm as confused by this evening as I was at the Angel Club, and I still don't know what Jez wants from me. This feels too intense for a quick hook-up. When we talk, his focus is entirely on me. It's overwhelming. He makes me feel special, as if I'm the only other person in his world.

I've never felt this way before.

Is he hoping for a night in my bed, or a safe harbour for his ambitions and dreams?

Is he a whirlwind, or the ocean?

Sam mimes kicking with his heel, and smiles when I laugh and shake my head. If I need his help, I know he'll be there. For now, I want to see where this goes.

"Ready to spice things up?" Jez places four glasses on the table. Two bubbly glasses, and two shot glasses full of something dark and red.

"Living dangerously?" I point at the red liquid, and at his shirt. He shrugs, smiling, and hands me my shot.

"Better drink it quickly, before I give you a reason to ruin my outfit."

I raise an eyebrow. "Are you planning to?"

He shrugs again and sits down, raising his glass to mine.

We clink our glasses and down the shots together. It feels like drinking liquid fire. Jez glances at my scarlet face and smirks.

"What the hell was that?" I say when I can breathe again.

He gives me an innocent look. "I told you. Spicing things up."

I look at the glass in my hand. I swear my tongue has pins and needles.

"Chilli? You bought me a chilli liqueur?"

He shakes his head. "Spiced chilli vodka. Much more sophisticated."

I grab my bubbly from the table and drink half of it without stopping. He watches, a half-smile on his face.

"Something sweeter next time?"

"Yes, Jez. Definitely something sweeter. Or – better still?" I wave my half-empty glass. "Just stick with the bubbly."

"Noted," he says softly, as if I've just revealed a deep personal secret. "Bubbly it is."

I don't know what he's trying to do, but right now he's making me feel like the most important person in the room.

"So – now that we've turned up the heat, are you going to tell me?"

I roll my eyes at another cheesy chat-up line. "Tell you what?"

He leans towards me and lowers his voice. My breath catches. I can feel my hands shaking. This isn't cheesy. This is intense.

"Your passion," he whispers, his eyes fixed on mine. When I meet his gaze I feel myself falling. "The thing most important to you in the world."

I take a breath. This feels intimate. Naked. Far too personal for a crowded wine bar. But there's something about him – about the way he asks the question – that makes me feel as if the wine bar has disappeared. As if the chilli vodka is a distant memory. As if it's just the two of us, alone in the blood-red darkness.

I want to connect. I want to give him an answer. I want to keep his attention on me.

But I can't tell him. I can't talk about angels, and Kane, and my wall full of photos. That's too much. Too intimate. Last time I trusted him with my feelings he was cruel, and he ended up with my cocktail soaking into his shirt.

I have to say something – I don't want to lose this moment. I'm talking before I realise what I'm saying.

"I'm an artist." He nods, leaning into my words. "I paint." I wave a hand at the space around us. "It's how I see the world."

He nods. "And what does that mean? Seeing the world as a painter?"

I'm under his microscope again. He's watching me, waiting for my answer. I feel small, like something to be inspected – to be robbed of my secrets. To be understood and written up and filed neatly somewhere.

And I feel as if he's giving me the chance to be better. To be everything, to him.

I have to take a breath. A moment to line up my thoughts.

"Everything is colour," I say, and he tilts his head with a frown. I'm losing him, and I want to make him understand. "I look around at the world, and everything I see wants to be brushstrokes on a canvas. Colours. Textures. Patterns of light."

He nods, his eyes searching my face. I'm not sure he understands.

"It's like …" I begin, trying to find the words. "It's like speaking another language." I press a hand to my chest. "My language is paint and pigment and just the right colour in exactly the right place." He tilts his head again, but this time he's listening. "The world out there …" I wave my hand again, taking in the bar, and the street outside. "That's a language that doesn't care about beauty. It's chaos and mess and it looks different, depending on where you're standing."

He nods, and this time I think I'm making sense.

"What I do? What I'm always doing?" I take another breath. My hand is shaking round my glass. I've never explained this to anyone before, and I feel as if I'm revealing too much. "What I do is like translation. Taking the harsh, grey, mixed-up language of the world, and constantly translating it into images. Into colours. Into beauty."

I'm breathless when I finish my explanation. I've said more than I planned to say.

I feel as if I've shown him my soul.

"And are you good at painting, Mel-the-Artist?"

It's a brutal question. I feel as if he's misunderstood. As if what I can produce is more important than the language I speak, or the way I feel. From anyone else, I'd dodge the question. I'd think it was a trap, or someone mocking me.

I want to scream. I want to take it all back. I want to make a joke and move the conversation along.

I want to throw my drink over him.

But Jez is serious. And ambitious. He wants to know whether I am, too.

I think about Sam's comments. How much he liked the image of himself on my easel. *Brilliant ... balanced ... eye-catching ...*

I want to believe him. I want Jez to know. I want to shine for him.

I think of my mother's portraits, and all the years she's spent perfecting her art. All the years I have ahead of me, learning and growing and putting my visions on paper and canvas for everyone else to admire.

"Maybe," I breathe. "But I want to be better."

Jez holds my gaze for a moment, and nods.

"Ambition," he whispers, smiling. "I approve."

When he heads to the bar again, I make myself breathe. Another conversation with Jez, and another secret spilled. I feel as if he's testing my defences, wearing me down. Trying to work out what's inside.

Maybe Sam's right. Maybe it's creepy.

And maybe I want him to succeed.

Jez places a third glass of bubbly in my hand and takes his seat.

"So what about you, Mr Ambitious?"

He rests a hand on his chest and raises his eyebrows. I roll my eyes at his fake surprise. "Yes, you. What's your passion?"

There's a mischievous grin on his face, and I realise what he's going to say before he speaks.

"In or out of the bedroom?"

I raise my glass towards him, tipping it slightly, and his eyes widen.

"Wait!" He raises a hand to stop me. "My shirt doesn't deserve a soaking for that. I'm only quoting you! Plus this stuff is expensive."

I can't help returning his grin, and I'm relieved to see that we're both blushing.

"Let's stick with out of the bedroom for now," I whisper, emphasising the last two words. His blush deepens, but his eyes don't leave mine.

"For now," he agrees, nodding.

The promise of more, of *later*, hangs in the air between us. I feel as if I'm falling into his storm-grey eyes.

I make myself take a sip of my drink. "So?"

"Passion," he says, nodding.

"You're stalling," I say, waiting as he downs half his glass.

"I am." There's a smile in his voice, and for the first time he looks nervous.

"Not used to answering questions?"

He shrugs, not meeting my eyes. "I'm the journalist, remember? Asking questions is pretty much what I do."

"Ah. So it's OK when you want to find out my darkest secrets, but if I turn the tables and expect an answer from you, that's a step too far?"

His smile widens, and for a moment he looks completely unguarded, as if all his defences are down.

I'm falling again. There's no one else in the bar – there's no one else in the world.

"It's hard being the one being unwrapped," he says, and glances up at me.

"Unwrapped?" I say, and I think my voice might fail. The idea is surprisingly exciting. "Is that what you've been doing to me?"

He spreads his hands in a gesture of apology.

"It's what I do."

I lean in, close to his ear. "Buckle up", I whisper, running a finger down the collar of his jacket. "I'm going to do some unwrapping of my own."

I feel him shiver as I sit back, and I bite back a smile.

"Passion," I say again, and wait for him to speak.

He leans back in his seat and stares at the ceiling. When he finally speaks, his voice is quiet.

"I want to be the best," he says, and turns his gaze to me.

"That's it?"

He nods. "I want to ask better questions. I want to cover better stories. I want to write the insightful books people buy and keep and read over and over."

He sits up, lifting a hand to brush my hair back from my face. He leans close, his breath on my neck, whispering.

It's my turn to shiver.

"I want to know everything. I want to understand the world. I want to understand people and governments and greed and …" he takes my hand in his. "I want to understand artists, and emotions, and all the ways to be human."

I don't know what to say. I don't think I have a voice.

He answered my question. He told me his passion. He's next to me – real and warm and defenceless.

He's not playing games.

I should have told him about Kane. About the angels.

When he pulls back, we sit hand in hand. I can't pull my eyes away from his.

Chapter 18

The next table explodes into song – a drunken happy birthday for Patrick. I glance up, and the world crashes in with colour and light and noise.

The bar is crowded. Sam's friends are laughing at something only they understand. The moment with Jez passes and we both sit back, dragged into the noise and distraction. I feel disconnected. I feel shipwrecked.

The exhaustion of a day in the studio threatens to drown me.

I'm tired, I haven't eaten, and I've just finished my fourth drink. I lied to Jez, and I don't know how to fix it. I need to go home.

Sam waves at me from the other table, and I shake my head. He jumps out of his seat and pushes through the crowds around the door, glaring at Jez as he reaches me.

"Is everything OK?" He asks, loud enough for the whole table to hear. Jez smirks, but his usual confident swagger is gone.

"I forgot to eat," I say, my head starting to spin. Sam relaxes, and puts a hand on my arm.

"Mel! What did I tell you?"

"To eat?" I think I remember a conversation earlier, in the studio.

"OK." Sam pats my shoulder. "Wait here." And he pushes his way back to his table.

When he comes back, he's dragging Georgie behind him.

"Rescue mission?" She says, holding out a hand to me. I nod, and clasp her fingers in mine. "And is he coming?" She whispers as she pulls me upright.

I glance at Jez. He's leaning back in his chair, one hand on his chest, one holding the remains of his drink, watching the theatre students across the table as if they are cells under a microscope.

I still don't understand what he wants. I know I wasn't honest about my passion, and I know he liked what I said. I think he told the truth about his.

And I know he keeps making me feel good.

I nod, and Georgie rolls her eyes.

"Come on then," she says, kicking his foot until he stands up.

I stagger out of the bar with my friends, unsteady on my feet, and Jez follows. As we reach the street, he takes my hand and weaves his fingers between mine.

I don't know how we end up in a greasy kebab shop. There can't be many places like this in Lawyer Land, and I'm not sure how far we've walked. Between the bubbly and exhaustion and hunger, and Jez's hand in mine, I'm floating.

I told him what he wanted to hear, and he told me his passion.

He gave me something of himself, and I avoided his question. I didn't give him what he asked for.

I unwrapped him, and he thinks he unwrapped me.

The idea makes me stumble.

"Sit down, Mel." Sam sounds annoyed. "Jez – make her sit down."

His hand tugs me to a plastic chair and a plastic table, and I let myself fall into the seat. The lights are bright and blue-white. It feels like an operating theatre, and it smells of meat and hot oil. The lights are buzzing, louder than the TV in the corner. I don't know when it got dark outside.

Someone puts a bottle on the table in front of me. It's full of something orange and fizzy. The lid is off, and Georgie tells me to drink, wrapping my hand round the cold plastic.

It's horrible, but it's cold. I drink.

"Mel." Sam pushes my shoulder and rocks me against the table. "Mel," he says again. "Food."

I lift my head from my arm. I don't know when I fell asleep. Or when I dropped Jez's hand.

I sit up, heart thumping, desperate to know he's still with me. He's slumped back in the seat next to me, staring at his phone.

Sam slides a kebab across the table. "OK, Mel?" He sounds concerned, and his eyes flick to Jez.

I nod, and give him a tired smile.

"Eat," he says, pushing the kebab towards me and picking up his own. He grins. "I got you extra sauce."

"You booby-trapped my dinner?" I ask, reaching for the cardboard plate, and he hands me a pile of napkins. Georgie laughs.

"I thought it might help wake you up."

The spicy yoghurt sauce is all over my fingers before I've taken my first bite, but I don't care. I'm beyond hungry, and if Sam wants to amuse himself at my expense, that's fine. It's his advice I ignored. It's my fault I'm passing out and dragging everyone away from the party.

By the time I've finished, my hands look as if I've dipped them in thick white paint, and I'm sure my face is just as bad. I work my way through the napkins, soaking each one before moving on to the next. Georgie gestures to her face and points at mine, and I do my best to clean the sauce from my chin.

"Better?" Sam asks.

"Better. Thank you." I can feel the cold drink and the hot food hitting my bloodstream, waking me up. Reminding me what happened at the bar.

I turn to Jez. Unlike the rest of us, he's picking at a portion of chips and mayonnaise. He gives me a tight smile.

"Didn't fancy a kebab?"

He pulls a face. "Not really my thing," he says. Across the table, Georgie rolls her eyes.

"More of a fine dining person, Jez?" She says, and there's a catty note in her voice.

"Something like that." His smile is smoother now. More practised. Fake. She gives him a fake smile back.

Sam jumps as his phone buzzes in his pocket. He grins as he reads the text.

"Fai?" I ask, smiling with him.

He nods, and types a quick reply.

"It's been lovely – Georgie, Mel, Jez – but that's my signal to abandon you all." He gives me a stern look. "You OK to get home, Mel?"

"Sure", I say, as Georgie reassures him.

He stands up, grabs his jacket, and takes a bow as he steps back towards the door. "Then I go to meet the light of my life."

I give him a wave through the window, but he's already jogging to wherever he's meeting Faisal.

When I turn my attention to the table, Georgie and Jez are staring at each other. Georgie is wearing her *don't mess with me* scowl, and Jez is watching her, eyebrows raised. I feel like the referee at a boxing match.

"We should ..." I gesture at the remains of our meal, and start pulling our paper plates and bottles and napkins into a pile. Georgie nods, and gathers everything onto a tray.

"Shall we?" She asks, standing.

Jez holds the door for us both, and slips his hand into mine as we step into the street. I have no idea where we are, or how to get home from here, so I wait for Georgie to start walking. She picks a direction, and we follow.

"Back to the party? Or do you have something more ..." Jez lowers his voice to a whisper. "... intimate in mind?"

I catch my breath and grip his fingers more tightly as Georgie calls over her shoulder.

"We are very much going home, Lover Boy. No parties, and no ..." she waves a hand at the two of us, "... whatever this is. I don't know whether you noticed, but Mel just passed out on the kebab-shop table. That's a girl who needs a good night's sleep, not more stimulation."

Jez laughs, and I can feel my face burning.

"Defensive, isn't she?" He murmurs, and there's a smile in his voice.

I want to ditch my over-protective friend. I want to take this boy home and find out how it would feel to kiss him. I want to unwrap him – I want to find out everything about him. I want to discover his passions, in and out of the bedroom.

I can't help smiling at the thought.

But she's right. I'm exhausted. I've had too much to drink and not enough to eat, and I need to collapse and not wake up until lunchtime.

Georgie stops at a bus shelter and turns to Jez. "We've got this from here, thanks."

He smirks, and tightens his grip on my hand. Georgie rolls her eyes.

"I promised Sam I'd get Mel back OK, and that's what I'm doing. Just the two of us." She glances up at the electronic sign. "Say your goodbyes," she says, turning to the street. "Two minutes until the bus gets here."

"I should go," I whisper as he pulls me close for the first time, his body pressed against mine. His hair smells of something woody and spiced as I rest my head against his shoulder. The bubble is expanding in my chest, and I think my smile is wider than my face.

I don't want to leave him. I don't want to go with Georgie, but I know she's trying to keep me safe. And I still don't know what Jez wants.

One night, or forever? Whirlwind or ocean?

I'm too tired to figure this out. I need to go home.

I take an unsteady step back.

"Until next time," he whispers next to my ear, and the warmth of his breath on my skin makes me shiver. His hand falls away from mine, fingers brushing my palm. His storm-grey eyes catch mine, and I don't want to look away.

"Bye, Jez. Bye, now." Georgie shouts after him as he turns away, then holds out her hand to the approaching bus. I watch as he lifts his head and quickens his pace. He doesn't look back.

We climb on, and find seats at the back.

"What was that?" I ask as we pull away.

"Hmmm?" Georgie concentrates on sliding her Oyster Card into her wallet.

"Jez. What did he do to upset you?"

She lets out a sigh.

"Mel. I know you like him, but tonight is not the night." She waves a hand at my crumpled jacket. "Falling asleep on the table is not the beginning of a night of romance – it's the end of the date." She holds up a finger as I try to object. "No exceptions. If he's serious, he'll be right back. If he cares, he knows you need to call it a night. And if he doesn't? At least you get to find that out without some serious heartbreak."

I hate that she's right. I want to stop the bus and run after him, and I want to fall asleep where I am, my head pressed against the cold window.

"I've seen the way you look at him, Mel. And I've seen the way he looks at you. I don't know what that is – pretty fireworks or the full bonfire – but give yourself a moment. Take a breath. He's not going anywhere."

I nod. "So he didn't annoy you?"

She makes a face. "Well. There's that, too."

"What?" I ask, sitting up straight.

She turns to look at me, and reaches out to tug on my hand.

"He's just ..." She thinks for a moment. "He creeps me out."

I pull away from her. "You, too?" I shake my head. "Sam said the same thing."

"Ha!" She says, sounding relieved. "It's not just me. He's creepy, Mel!"

"He's just—"

She waves a finger at me. "No. No 'just this' or 'just that'. Haven't you noticed that his first move, both times you've met, is to isolate you from the rest of us?" I don't have an answer, and she doesn't give me the chance to reply. "And what was that, at the kebab shop? It wasn't his choice of food, and he didn't have you to himself, so he just ate chips and sulked. Who does that?"

Someone who wants to spend time with me, I think, but I know better than to argue with Georgie.

She sees my expression, and her face softens.

"OK. Get home, get plenty of sleep, and tell me how you feel tomorrow. Just – don't let him think he can do whatever he likes because you've had two drinks on a catastrophically empty stomach ..." I hold up four fingers and she rolls her eyes. "*Four* drinks, and fallen asleep while you wait for a kebab."

I could be with Jez now. We could be headed for his bed, or mine. I could be finding out about all his passions.

Georgie glances out of the window, and stands up to ring the bell.

"Our stop," she calls, and offers me her hand.

I stifle a yawn, and concentrate on keeping my eyes open as I stumble off the bus and onto the pavement outside our halls.

I hate that she's right.

Chapter 19

"You're coming, right?" Faisal fans out the tickets on our kitchen table as if he's performing a magic trick. "Next Saturday, seven o'clock. Smart dress code and up-dos." He sculpts his hair with both hands and strikes a pose.

"Sure," I say, laughing as I reach for my oversized mug of tea. "I wouldn't miss it."

It might be lunch time, and Faisal has clearly been up for hours, but I'm still in my pyjamas and fluffy dressing gown. I was trying to decide whether to give up on breakfast entirely and open a can of soup when Sam and Fai arrived at the door.

"Is Georgie coming?" Faisal glances over my shoulder. "Is she here?"

I stifle a yawn. "Georgie is either asleep or out, and as I've never known her to sleep past eight, I'm guessing it's the latter."

Sam rolls his eyes. "Tell me you slept in your own bed, Mel. Tell me Georgie brought you home."

"She did. And she made me leave Jez behind." I give him a sad pout, and he laughs.

"Poor Mel!" He mocks, dodging my kick under the table.

Faisal ignores us both. "And will you be bringing a plus-one?"

I shrug. I've had a great night's sleep. I know Georgie did the right thing, dragging me home on the bus – but

I haven't heard from Jez. I have no idea whether he'll want to come to a dance recital.

The thought of seeing him again makes me smile.

"That's a yes." Faisal grins, and slides two tickets towards me. "That's definitely a yes."

Sam gives me a stern look. "It doesn't have to be Mr Swoon, Mel."

"Fine." I say, picking up the tickets. "If Mr Swoon can't make it, I'll bring someone else. Deal?"

"Deal." Sam nods, his face serious.

"And Georgie? Plus-one, or not?" Fai waves his hands over the table, as if he's choosing a card from a deck.

"Leave her two tickets. I'm sure she'll find someone to bring."

As soon as my friends leave I pick up my phone. Still no messages from Jez, so I make myself another mug of tea and sit down to text him.

Hi, I write, and wait for his response.

I'm half way down my drink by the time he writes back.

Hi, he says. *Is it time for small talk again?*

I have to give myself a moment to smile before I type.

Didn't we do that already?

The bubble in my chest is back. Every part of me is waiting for his reply.

We did…

I wait for something else, but that's it.

It's tempting to write back, but I want more from him. I want him to keep me talking.

Eventually my phone buzzes.

I can see we're ready to move this date on.

I can't help laughing.

Speaking of… I type. *What are you doing next Saturday night?*

He must be thinking about his reply.

Moving things on?

I might be alone in the flat, but I'm blushing. I need to distract him.

I have tickets for my friend's dance performance. Posh do. Want to come?

I hate waiting so long for his texts. At least in the wine bar I could see his face between messages. This is torture.

You mean I have to share you?

If he was in front of me, I'd throw my drink at him. I take a calming breath.

I can always take someone else…

I can't believe I've hit send. That was unkind.

His response is lightning-fast.

I'll share.

My hands are shaking as I send him my address.

I'm drying my hair, still warm from my shower and wrapped in a towel, when my phone buzzes again. It's past lunchtime and I need to get dressed, but if it's Georgie trying to drag me out again tonight I want to know.

Show you something?

It takes a moment for me to catch my breath.

Jez is thinking about me. Jez is *texting* me. I didn't start this conversation, and I have no idea what he's going to suggest. My heart races and my mind throws up a thousand possibilities. I have to close my eyes and will myself to be calm.

I don't know how to respond. Is he flirting? Is he serious? Is he going to send me something very unsexy and prove Georgie right? I catch my look of horror in the mirror, and shudder.

Mysterious ... I send. Do I need to be sitting down?

I can feel my stomach twist as I wait for him to type.

The words flash up on the screen, and I'm no closer to an answer.

Nothing like that.

I stare at his response, trying to decide whether to laugh or throw the phone across the room. Nothing is straightforward with Jez, and I'm beginning to feel as if we're playing a game where only he knows the rules.

Give me a clue?

This time he makes me wait.

I've given up on the conversation and picked up the hairdryer again when his text arrives.

Meet me. One hour.

And he sends me his address.

He's waiting for me on the path outside his hall of residence. Where my building is old – all red brick, slate roof tiles, old-fashioned front doors and wooden windows – his might as well be a spacecraft. Silver-grey panels line the walls, interrupted by tall windows with black frames. White sunlight gleams from solar panels on the roof, and there's no colour beyond the gardens. Above the first floor, I could be looking at a black-and-white photo.

"So this is you," I say, looking around at the lawn and the newly planted flowerbeds. "It's—"

"Boring." He says, and I can't help laughing.

"A bit!"

He gives me a quick smile.

"Not exactly artist-worthy."

There's something awkward about his reaction. When we've met before, it's been at darkened bars and glamorous occasions. Jez and me, discovering each other, our whispered conversations kept private from the crowds around us. Just the two of us, in our own heart-stopping bubble.

But here, in his space, surrounded by daylight and grey walls and a hundred windows ... something is missing.

I remember catching his eyes at the Angel Club. And I remember his discomfort at the kebab shop. The way he sat under the bright lights, ignoring the others. The way he focused on his phone, and not on me or my friends.

He's like that now. It almost feels as if he doesn't want me here.

But I want to be here. And I want more from Jez. I want his full attention. I want to remember how he makes me feel.

I hold my hands up to frame the view. "I don't agree. You could use it as a low-res background for something urban and gritty. Collage, graffiti ..."

"Street art?"

"Yes!"

He gives me a thoughtful look, his eyes finally meeting mine.

"Just the right colour in exactly the right place?"

Something warm and terrifying slithers in my chest. He's quoting our conversation at Patrick's party. He's offering my words back to me.

He listened, when I told him about art.

When I almost told him about Kane.

He looked after my words, and now he's handing them back.

I nod. I don't think I can speak.

This is what I want from him. I feel as if I'm flying.

"Well, Mel-the-Artist," he says, holding out his hand. "As colourful as this is inside your head, I have something much better to show you." He glances down at my paint-covered work boots and jeans. "I'm glad you wore sensible shoes."

The black metal rungs of the ladder are cold against my fingers as we climb the four floors to the roof. We're hidden behind the building, shaded from the street by trees that have stood here for decades. I'm following Jez up the side of his space-age home, and I have no idea what we're doing here.

He used a key to unlock a metal gate at the side of the building, and we followed a narrow path between grey cladding and a tall brick wall topped with spikes. The ladder is enclosed, so we're climbing inside a circular cage. There are windows and rooms an arm's reach away, and he warned me to stay quiet.

We're not supposed to be here.

I should have refused to follow him. I should be afraid, but instead I feel light. Excited. As if the bubble in my chest is lifting me into the air.

I'm here with Jez. Just the two of us.

I glance up as he reaches the top of the ladder, pulling himself out of sight onto the roof. All I can see is the deep autumn blue of the sky and the yellowing leaves of the trees.

And then he reappears, leaning out from the roof, and waves at me to follow.

"So? What do you think?"

I stop to catch my breath, pushing my frozen fingers into the pockets of my coat.

We're on top of the world.

There's coarse gravel, crunching under our feet. A flimsy-looking black metal handrail set back from the edge of the building. Solar panels angled against black metal frames, each one facing south to catch the sun. The tops of the trees, their gently stirring leaves level with my waist, blocking the view of the road.

Jez reaches out and touches my elbow, gently, with his fingertips.

"Look up," he says, and turns me slowly towards the road.

And there is London, sparkling in the autumn sunshine. Buildings and parks and skyscrapers and golden leaves. There's a church spire rising above the trees, just to our left. The art college buildings I walked past to get here. Across our horizon, there's a string of high-rise buildings, like beads on a necklace. Elephant and Castle, the City of London – the Shard, the Cheesegrater, the Walkie-Talkie – and off to our right, Canary Wharf, glass towers glinting in the sun.

"It's …" I've run out of words. The colours, the light, the landmarks – I can't take my eyes from the view.

He nods. "I thought you might like it."

I turn to face him, and over his shoulder I can see hills to the South. A line of dark clouds massing over the Crystal Palace TV transmitter like a bruise against the sky.

I want to stare at the city until it gets dark. I want to open my paintbox and put it all onto paper. I want to stand here and breathe it all in.

"Wow," I say, shaking my head and meeting his eyes. "It's ... wow."

He smiles, and the awkwardness is gone.

"I know."

Chapter 20

He sits down, cross-legged, a little way back from the handrail, and holds out a hand to me. After a moment I take it, and sit next to him. We're off the gravel, sharing space on a concrete pad behind one of the solar panels. The panel feels like a tent, bringing us together and sheltering us from the sky. From here the trees block the view to the west, but we can still see the City, and Canary Wharf. The sunlight glitters as it touches the glass in the towers – green, blue, and gold. The autumn leaves look like stained glass – a glowing green tapestry shot through with the first hints of red and yellow, reaching from the edge of the roof to the skyscrapers. I feel as if I could stand up and walk on the treetops to the Shard.

I feel as if I could fly.

His fingers are warm against mine, and he takes my hand in both of his. I can feel my fingers glowing under his touch.

"So," he says, leaning close to my ear. "How would Mel-the-Artist capture this?"

There isn't an easy answer to his question, and I'm not going to give him a simple reply. I'm going to make him think. I'm going to make him understand.

"That depends," I say, quietly. I don't look away from the view, but I know he's watching me. Waiting for something he can challenge, or twist.

"Does it?" I can feel his breath, soft against my cheek.

"The obvious choice would be acrylics, or oils." I sound like the lecturer from the History of Art course – cold analysis, and no feeling. It's the only way I can concentrate on what I'm trying to say. "The colours ..." I wave my free hand at the horizon. "They're bright and vibrant. Opaque paint would make them pop and shout on the canvas. Show off the autumn trees."

"But ...?" He turns my hand over between his palms, his skin slipping against mine.

"But ..." I point at the skyscrapers. "That would put all the focus on the leaves. And that's not what this view is about."

"Hmmm." He's stroking my hand, his fingers brushing my wrist. I'm having trouble concentrating on my lecture, and I have to force myself not to smile.

"What are we looking at?" I give his ribs a nudge with my elbow. I want him to hear what I'm saying. "What's the point of this trip to the roof?"

"I can think of several," he says, and I dig my elbow in harder.

"Hey! Concentrate. You asked me a question."

He nods, and clasps my hand more tightly. "I did."

"So? What are we looking at? What's special about this place?"

He glances out at the carpet of leaves, the towers, the sky – and shrugs.

I roll my eyes.

"London," I say, pulling my hand from his and waving at the view. "This is London! This is the most amazing city in the world."

He's looking at me now, a smile playing at the corner of his lips. He nods.

"Careful," he whispers. "The other cities might get jealous."

I give him a hard glare. "Do you actually want to know what I think, or are you just trying to see what makes me tick?"

He shrugs. "Would that be so bad?"

If I had a drink, I'd throw it at him. I stare at him, and he straightens his shoulders, shifting away from me.

"Okay," he says, sitting up straight. "I'm listening."

"Good. Because I'm going to explain how watercolours, or a pen-and-ink sketch, would give you a completely different image. Pull the buildings out from the background, and emphasise their shapes against the sky." I'm waving my hands again, and he's actually watching the city as I talk. He's giving me his attention, and the bubble in my chest is back. He's listening, and it feels good. I feel honoured. I feel important.

I feel as if I'm made of gold.

We're still discussing the skyline when the first fat drops of rain start drumming on the solar panels. The dark clouds have rolled over us from the south, and the blue sky is vanishing behind the storm. I tug my hood over my head, watching the light changing as the clouds spread.

Jez shuffles backwards, under the metal frame, and I follow. He's not wearing a coat, and the solar panels are the only shelter on the roof. We sit, hunched under the sloping metal, his shoulder pressed against mine.

It's cold, and wet, and all I can hear is the harsh beating of the rain above our heads. I push my hands back into my pockets, and steal a glance at Jez as he stares out at the view.

He's smiling.

"So did you know?" I have to raise my voice to be heard over the noise.

He turns to look at me, shifting his body away. "Know what?"

I wave a hand at the grey clouds and driving rain. "That this would happen? That we'd be stuck up here?"

A smile steals across his face, and he shrugs. "Is it so bad?"

I shrug back. "I'm dressed for it. I can sit here all day. You, on the other hand ..." I nod at his sweatshirt, and he grins.

"All day?" he says, raising an eyebrow and ignoring my dig at his clothing. I can't help smiling back.

"Unless you have something better to do."

He leans his shoulder against mine, and looks out at the grey city.

"All day sounds good," he says.

He holds out his hand, and I take his fingers in mine.

"So how would you paint this, Mel-the-Artist?"

The rain has settled to a gentle, steady downpour. A veil of grey, draining the colours from the scene in front of us. With every gust of wind, the curtain of water dances sideways, catching what's left of the light. The skyscrapers have all but disappeared.

"This?" I ask, nodding at the view, and he tilts his head, waiting for an answer.

"Easy," I say, after a moment's thought. I lift my hands and trace out a square in the space in front of us. "A Rothko-style canvas. Dark grey at the top, fading to a mid-grey, maybe blue-grey in the middle, and a pale grey section at the bottom to frame the view. Plenty of vertical brush strokes to merge the light and dark elements."

"Just grey?" He asks, eyebrow raised. "You're ignoring the colours? No just-right colour in just the right place?"

I frown, squinting at the edge of the roof. "Maybe some muddy green smudged in to suggest the trees." I stare into the rain, willing myself to see more than falling water. I shake my head.

"No. No green. This …" I wave my hand. "This would be much more powerful in shades of grey. Cold, wet, moody."

"Depressing," he says, mimicking my tone of voice.

"Hey!" He's smirking, and I want to explain. I want him to understand. "It's hard to paint rain! It sounds like something a sadistic art teacher would make you do, just to make you think."

"So – depressing." He's trying to hide a smile as he repeats his accusation, and I can't tell whether he means it, or whether he's testing my reaction. I bite back a shout of frustration and fold my arms over my chest.

"You want happy rain?" He makes a face, as if he's considering my offer. "I'll tell you how to paint happy rain."

"OK." He waits for me to continue, and I give him a smile.

"Give me a streetscape. Big city. Rainy night." I can't help waving my hands to set the scene. "Streetlights, shop signs, neon, headlights. People with umbrellas." He's nodding, so I keep talking. I want him to see what I see. "Everything is grey, except the lights. The rain makes the roads shine, and the lights are reflected in the surface water. White, red, yellow, green – entire rainbows thrown from ordinary things. A dull, depressing day transformed into something wonderful."

He tilts his head, considering, and I wait for his comment.

"So you're saying my secret rooftop hideaway isn't colourful enough for you?"

I want to shout at him. I want to ask what's wrong with him, but I don't want him to see that he's getting under my skin.

"Yes, Jez," I say, trying to sound serious. "That's exactly what I'm saying."

He holds a hand out, pointing at the corner of the building. "So – a neon sign on the edge, there? Maybe a streetlamp over the ladder? Something fancy, maybe Art Deco."

"Right. Yes." I'm smiling now. He understands.

"And what about a car, parked just over there? Headlights, tail lights …" He sculpts the scene with his fingers.

"Small car," I say, eyeing the space on the roof.

"Small car," he agrees. "Bright red, to catch the light."

"And hire some people to walk around with umbrellas?"

He grins. "Of course! Colourful umbrellas. And big, bright wellington boots."

"Perfect," I say, smiling at him.

And I mean it. He listened. He pictured my suggestions. He understood.

He leans his shoulder into mine as we both look out at the imagined rooftop. He's done it again. He's tested me and provoked me, and here we are, creating something better, together.

The rain slows, the clouds thinning as they roll north over the city. The drumming dwindles and stops. I can hear the wind shifting leaves in the trees. Traffic in the street below us, the rushing of water and tyres, and Jez's gentle breathing next to me.

"Are you ready to go down?"

He gives me a look of mock surprise. "What happened to sitting here all day?"

"The rain stopped." I stretch my hand out from under the shelter to prove my point. "We're not trapped here any more."

He nods, his face serious. "Fair enough. My plan to imprison you on the roof has failed. Might as well give up."

I push his shoulder with mine. "You're cold, Jez. You've got to be. Let's go and warm up."

He hangs his head, takes a deep breath, and shuffles out from under the solar panel. He holds a hand out and helps me to stand. His fingers are like ice.

"You're freezing!"

He shrugs, and leads the way to the ladder.

"I'd say 'ladies first', but ..." He looks down at the rungs. "It's wet and dangerous, and if you'll allow me to lead I can at least break your fall."

I can't help laughing at his exaggerated chivalry, but when I catch the expression on his face I realise he's serious. I smother my laughter, nodding, and he turns to take the first step.

He's right. The ladder is cold and wet and there's nothing to stop me from falling – to stop both of us from falling. My feet slip more than once, and I'm glad of the cage around us. More than once I reach out for a handhold and find the safety bars instead of the rungs. By the time I reach the ground I'm shaking, and I'm glad when he takes my elbow and steadies my final step.

It's gloomy under the trees, and the wet concrete path reflects the glow of security light further along the building. Water drips from the branches, splashing onto the path, and thudding into my coat and hood. By the time we reach the gate, the shoulders of Jez's sweatshirt are wet through, his hair plastered to his forehead. He locks the gate behind us and takes my hand, walking me to the door.

The sky is brightening, and the people walking past us are dodging puddles and shaking out umbrellas before heading indoors. The lights are on in the lobby, highlighting vending machines and fake-leather couches on the polished concrete floor. It looks warm and welcoming, and I wait for Jez to ask me inside.

To ask me to his room.

My heart skips. After this afternoon – after our conversation on the roof – is this where I find out what Jez wants? Where we finally unwrap each other? Anticipation steals my breath, and I close my eyes.

When I look up, he's watching me, his eyes the colour of the sky over London, and I have to make myself breathe. He runs a hand over the back of his neck, and it comes away slick with rain.

"You're soaked!" I take his hand, water dripping from his fingers. "You need to change."

I move to open the door, but he tightens his fingers around mine. The awkwardness is back, and he looks away. He doesn't want me here.

"Jez?"

He nods. "You're right," he says. "I need to warm up." He rubs a hand over the sleeve of his sweatshirt. "Dry out."

I step back from the door, and his fingers slip from mine.

I don't understand. I don't know what I've done wrong.

I don't want to stand here, waiting for him to turn away. I want to walk away before he can tell me to leave.

"Go," I say, pushing his shoulder. "You need a hot shower and a hot drink."

He nods, and I make myself step back. I make myself turn, and walk across the garden to the road. It feels like a thousand-mile walk, my throat tight and my hands shaking.

When I look back, he's gone.

Chapter 21

"He did *what*?"

Georgie flops down next to me on her bed and grips my elbow. "Tell me everything," she says, and sits back to listen.

I shrug. "We went to the roof."

Georgie shakes her head. "You went where?"

I can't help smiling. "He has a key. There's a ladder round the back of his building." I lean closer to her and whisper, "I think it's supposed to be a secret."

She grins. "The mysterious man has mysterious secrets. Go on."

"We watched the rain. We talked about painting." I take a breath. "It was nice."

"You talked about painting." Georgie frowns. "Painting ... rain?"

"Actually, yes ..." I say, watching her frown deepen. There's a charge in my spine as I remember our conversation. Jez, listening. Picturing the scene together.

"Well." She shrugs. "You do you, Mel."

"But ..."

"Mm-hmmm?" She gives me a stern look, and waits for me to explain.

"When we came down ..." I shake my head. "It's as if he didn't want me there."

"Jez, as in the person who invited you over, didn't want you there?" I nod, and she shakes a finger at me.

"That boy is no good, Mel. Don't let him treat you like that."

"He didn't ..." I don't know how to explain what happened. "He wasn't ..." I take another breath. "He was perfectly nice on the roof. He was a complete gentleman, actually. It's just, when we got down. When we got to the door ..."

"When you stopped being alone?"

My stomach sinks. "Yes."

She throws her hands up in frustration. "I told you! All he ever wants to do is get you alone. It's as if he can't relate to you when there are other people around."

"Alone's not so bad." There's a smile twitching the corner of my mouth.

"Ha!" She says, pointing. "That's what you want, isn't it? More alone time with creepy Jez?"

I can feel myself blushing. "Why not?"

She sighs, and takes my hands in hers.

"I know you like him. Like I said, you do you. But just ... be careful, OK? What he's doing? It's not normal. It's ..." she stops, searching for the right word. "It's weird and creepy and I don't like him manipulating you."

I nod. "I know. Thank you."

"So you'll leave him alone? Let him be weird by himself?"

I can't help laughing. "I didn't say that."

She tightens her grip on my fingers.

"At least promise me that you won't go chasing after him? Let him come to you, if he wants to. He needs to figure out what he wants, so he doesn't invite you over and push you away again. That's not OK, Mel."

I shrug. "Sure," I say. "I'll let him come to me."

But I don't think I mean it.

"What do you think?"

I stand back from the painting, waiting for Sam to comment. I can't believe how nervous I am.

Fai nudges me. "So this is what you've been stealing my man for?"

I shrug, and I'm relieved when he flashes me a grin. "It's amazing, Mel. Really."

Sam still hasn't said anything. This is the first time he's seen the completed portrait, and I wanted to show it off. I've tidied my studio space, cleared my sketches from one white wall, and hung the canvas gallery-style. We're standing in front of it, all three of us, as Sam's image stares back in a rainbow of acrylic brushstrokes.

"There's something ..." Fai makes a face as he tries to find the right word. "... regal about it. Isn't there?" He turns to me, and I notice Sam's shoulders tighten.

"Bold?" I say, smiling. "Brave? Superior? Looking down on the rest of us?" I can't tell whether Fai is winding Sam up, or pushing him to comment, but I can't help joining in. I want to know what he thinks.

Fai nods. "Like – I don't know. Black Panther, or something. T'Challa, defending his people."

Sam raises a hand, eyes still on the painting. "I can live with that," he says, nodding.

"So," I say, hands clasped tightly in front of me to steady my nerves. "Do you like it?"

There's a pause, and I realise I'm holding my breath.

"Mel," Sam says, turning to me. "I love it." He holds up a hand. "I didn't love all the sitting still and being painted, but this?" He looks back at the painting. "This is …" He nods. "Wow."

Fai laughs as I punch the air, and offers me a high five. He grins at Sam as our palms meet.

"I thought you were chatting like a pair of old ladies," he says. "Not sitting in silence."

I nod. "There was chatting. Lots of chatting."

"And so much sitting!" Sam throws his arms in the air. "I've never sat so still for so long in my life!"

"Drama Queen," says Fai, and we're both laughing as Sam takes a bow.

"Seriously, though." Sam takes my hands in his. "I don't have to like it."

My stomach clenches. "But I want you to …"

He shakes his head. "I'm just the model, Mel. You're the artist." He looks back at the portrait. "Do *you* like it?"

I stare at the brightly coloured canvas. There are places I'd still like to change, colours I'd like to brighten, but I know I've got the balance right. If I start tweaking things now, I'll upset the composition, and I'll end up changing everything.

It's done. It's as good as it's going to get.

"Yes," I say, folding my arms and trying to sound confident.

"That's what matters." Sam nods. "And for the record, this belongs in a gallery. A proper, posh gallery."

I know we're both thinking about the angel exhibition, and I'm grateful that Sam is kind enough not to say that out loud. He knows I don't need reminding.

But I can imagine my painting hanging in that church-like space, viewed by people in their best clothes, drinking champagne.

I think my smile is too big for my face.

"So. Is it lunch time?" Sam stretches his arms above his head and takes a step towards the corridor.

"What is it with you and food?" I straighten a layer of protective paper over the painting. Fai grips my elbow as I step down from the tall stool, and we both stand back to make sure it's covered.

"Fast metabolism," Sam says, patting his tight stomach.

Fai nods. "We should probably feed him," he whispers, trying to hide a smile.

Sam is already in the corridor when I pick up my bag and coat, Fai striding after him towards the stairs.

"Burgers?" Sam calls over his shoulder.

We settle for hot dogs from a van in the car park of the leisure centre, sitting on the front steps to eat them. I'm cleaning mustard and ketchup from my fingers with a handful of paper napkins when my phone buzzes in my pocket.

It's been three days since my trip to the roof with Jez – 73 hours – and I've kept my promise to Georgie. I haven't texted him. I haven't called. I've waited for him to come to me.

I pull out my phone and check my messages.

You, me, and the solar panels?

My smile draws a scowl from Sam as the phone buzzes again.

Rooftop with a view?

Another buzz.

Look down on the greatest city in the world?

"Is that …" Sam waves a finger at me. "… you-know-who?"

"That," I say as I drop my napkins into the cardboard hot dog tray, "is my signal to leave you two to whatever you have planned for today."

"Mel—"

"Sam. I'm going to meet Jez. I know what you think, and I know what you're going to say, so don't." I give him a stern look, and he rolls his eyes. "Fai, thank you for your help with the painting, and thank you for coming to see it. I will see you both soon."

I don't wait for an answer. I pick up my bag, dump my rubbish in the bin, and send Jez a text as I reach the road.

On my way.

Chapter 22

"So where have you been?"

Jez raises an eyebrow. "You missed me?"

I shrug, checking that there's no one around as he pulls the key from his pocket and unlocks the gate. We slip through and make our way round the building.

"After you," he says, his voice hushed as he waves me towards the ladder.

"Don't you want to lead the way?"

He smirks, and looks up at the roof. "I think you can figure out where we're going."

I have to stop myself from rolling my eyes.

"And if I slip, you get to be the hero?"

It's his turn to shrug. "It's my roof. It's up to me to keep you safe."

There's no point arguing, and I don't have a drink to throw at him, so I step onto the ladder and start climbing.

When I reach the roof, I have to catch my breath. It looks as if someone has repainted the view. Most of the green leaves have slipped towards yellow and red, and between me and the glass towers lies a carpet of flame. Sunlight splashes across the skyscrapers, and paints the trees with gold.

I wish I'd brought a sketch book.

"This is ..." I stare out at London, waiting for Jez to cross the roof behind me. "Wow."

"Better than last time?" I can tell he's smiling before I turn round.

I pretend to consider his question. "It'll do."

We sit together on the cold concrete pad, watching wisps of cloud shred across the autumn sky.

"So," I say, leaning into his shoulder. "Where were you?"

He shrugs, and looks away. "Family thing. I had to go home for a couple of days."

"The ambitious journalist has a family? That sounds inconvenient." I'm grinning, and I'm relieved when he laughs, and nods.

"It can be."

"Let me guess. Mother's birthday? Brother's trombone recital? Some sort of cat-related emergency?"

"Something like that." He shrugs. "Can we talk about something else?"

There's an edge to his voice, and I don't want to push him.

"Sure."

We sit for a moment. He stares at his hands in his lap.

"Last time we were up here, I told you how I would paint the view." I spread my hands to take in the city in front of us. Trees, skyscrapers, landmarks. "So, soon-to-be star journalist – tell me. How would you describe the view? How would you compose the best possible journalistic take on this?"

He gives me an approving look, and I feel the familiar jolt as my eyes meet his.

"An intriguing question, Mel-the-Artist," he says, and looks out over the carpet of leaves. "I think I'd start with a description. Maybe suggest a painting in acrylics, to set the scene for my readers."

I nudge his shoulder. "Hey! No stealing my ideas!"

"No – it's good. It's a great hook, to get people reading. Maybe you could paint the picture to illustrate the article."

I'm not sure whether to laugh or roll my eyes. "Carry on."

"I'd talk about the city. What's hiding behind the trees, and away from the gleaming towers. The things you don't see when you're standing on a rooftop in the sunshine."

I lean in, excited. "Organised crime? Shady gang stuff? Dramatic murders? Or hidden gems? Historical stories?"

"More like deprivation. Child poverty. Inequality. Domestic violence. Human trafficking."

I nod. "Very noble. Very important. Very serious."

He stares at me, as if he's trying to decide whether I'm joking.

"Ambition," he says, eventually. "There's no point churning out another touristy column on London's hidden treasures, or lurid gangland murders. Too obvious. Too easy. Everyone's writing those." He shrugs. "I'd want to unpack the city. Tell some personal stories. Contrast privilege with poverty, freedom with slavery. Make people think."

"So – zooming in on small parts of the image to tell the story of the whole?"

"Exactly," he says. "And I'd end with your lecture on different styles of drawing. How a watercolour image would show a different city, even though you're painting the same view."

"And I suppose I get to draw that image, too?"

"Of course."

I roll my eyes, but I can't keep the smile from my face.

He was listening.

"My mother would love you," he says, suddenly, and I'm caught off-guard by the change in subject.

"What?"

"Nothing." He shakes his head. "Just – nothing."

"Jez—"

"What would your family think of me?" He turns to face me, and his gaze is intense.

I stare back at him. I don't know what my mother would think, but I have the uncomfortable feeling that she'd agree with Georgie and tell me to ditch Jez. Tell me he's creepy.

This is creepy. He's just asked not to talk about his family, and now he's talking about his mother, and asking after mine.

I concentrate on the colour of his eyes. On the warm feeling in my stomach when he looks at me.

"Well, my mother ..." I shrug. "No idea." He raises an eyebrow and waits for me to continue. "My father – that's a toss-up. On balance, I think he'd light up a joint and start asking you questions. See if he could figure out what makes you tick."

"Do I get a joint, in this scenario?"

"Oh, definitely. Basic hospitality! Plus he'd want to know your answers were genuine."

He makes a face. "Interesting."

"And my grandfather ..."

"There's a grandfather in the mix?"

I nod. "He lives with us – with my family. He would ... I think he would roll another joint, and give you the talk about dating me, and not hurting me."

"Ah," he says. "So he's the one I need to worry about."

I shrug. "I guess. What's this about, Jez?"

"Nothing." He looks away again. "It's not important."

I can't believe I'm sitting here, letting him control this conversation. I thought he was opening up to me. Describing the view, talking about his family – that's more than he's shared before. But now? Now he's pulling away. Pushing me out.

I didn't come here for this.

"Jez", I say, gently, and he turns back to me. I put a hand on his shoulder, and I feel him shiver at my touch.

He looks at me, and for a moment there are no barriers. I see pain and hurt and longing. I see *him*, storm-grey and real.

I want to fall into his eyes.

He takes my hand and pulls me close, until we're kneeling face to face, my hand on his shoulder, his arms round my waist.

I lean into a kiss as soft and hesitant as sunlight. I'm falling and floating, his arms locked around me. Every sense – sight, smell, taste, touch, sound – is full of him. The woody scent of his hair. The soft touch of his lips against mine. The contented sound he makes as he pulls back and smiles.

"I didn't think you …" he breathes. "I wasn't sure. Is this what you want?"

I roll my eyes and pull him into another kiss, and I can tell he's still smiling.

I don't care that we're on the roof. I don't care that I'm kneeling on cold concrete under a solar panel. I want to unwrap him and find out what his passions are.

I slide my hands round his waist and his arms tighten around me. His soft kiss gives way to something harder, more urgent, and I can feel my heart, stomping in my chest. He slides one hand down, into the back pocket of my jeans and I have to take a breath. I think I'm on fire.

I think I'm flying.

Gently I slip one hand under the hem of his sweatshirt, gripping his T-shirt and sliding it out from his jeans. My fingers touch the skin of his back and it's like connecting a circuit. Light and sparks.

He flinches, and I'm smiling as the charge runs through us both. I push my hand higher, following the line of his spine—

—and he freezes.

Every muscle tenses. It's like hitting the stop button on this amazing kiss, and he lets go of me, pushing my hand away, twisting his body out of my arms.

"No," he says. "Stop."

I lift my hands and shift away from him, putting space between us.

"What ... what's wrong?"

He closes his eyes. "Stop."

He's shaking his head and tucking his T-shirt back into his jeans and I don't know what I've done wrong.

"Jez?"

"You should go," he says. He won't meet my eyes.

I'm breathless. I'm shaking. I'm still on fire. I don't want to stop.

"What happened to passions, Jez? What happened to in and out of the bedroom?"

"Don't ..." He holds a hand up to stop me. "Please."

"You've been trying to get me to come home with you every time we've met. Was it always going to end like this?"

He sits back on the concrete and hangs his head. "Please, Mel. Just go."

I make myself stand up. I move my shaking legs and my trembling hands, and make myself walk across the roof. I step onto the ladder, close my eyes, and take a calming breath.

Jez is sitting, arms around his knees, staring out at the treetops.

I leave him, and begin the long climb down.

Chapter 23

"I can't believe I'm here again." Sam shifts in his seat, trying to find a comfortable pose. "Remind me why I'm here?"

"Because you love me, because I need you, and because under that grumpy act you desperately want to be the centre of attention."

I wave a hand at him and he gives me a grudging smile.

"How long am I sitting for this one?"

I shrug. "A few sketches. Some sessions for me to get the colours right." I can't help laughing at the expression on his face. "Don't worry. Watercolour is easy compared to the acrylic. I'll make a series of sketches and work from those. I'll invite you back at the end, just to make sure I've captured the real you."

He grins. "Capturing me, are you? I think Fai might object to that."

"Don't worry," I say, grinning back. "He'd be storming in here like a knight in shining armour if he thought I was stealing your soul."

Sam makes a thinking face. "More like a graceful ninja," he says, and there's reverence in his voice.

"Dance ninja?" I pick up my pencil and hold it up, measuring the proportions of Sam's face and making the first marks on my sketch. The graphite slides across the cartridge paper, and I'm smiling as the image appears on the page, one pencil stroke at a time.

Sam nods, smiling, and I have to remind him to stay still.

"Speaking of ..." he says when I give him permission to move again. "Dance recital tomorrow. You're still coming?"

"Wouldn't miss it," I say, my attention on the shape of his shoulder and the curve of his upper arm.

"And your plus-one?"

The pencil slips in my fingers and I roll my eyes, reaching for the eraser.

"Mel?"

I close my eyes and take a breath.

"I don't know, Sam."

"Uh-oh. Trouble with creepy guy?"

"Trouble. Domestic disaster. Personal crisis." I shrug. "I really don't know."

"Did something happen? Do I need to track him down and extract an apology?"

"Nothing like that. He just ..." I shake my head. "He had a moment. Asked me to leave. He broke off a really hot kiss, too."

I can feel my face warming, and Sam grins.

"So there was kissing?"

I nod. "There was. And then there wasn't."

"And has he explained? Apologised?" I shake my head, and Sam sighs. "Not good enough, Mel," he says. "You deserve better."

I pick up my pencil and try to concentrate, but I'm thinking about Jez, on the roof. About the conversation.

He seemed real. He seemed relaxed. I felt less like a specimen to be examined, and more like a friend. I felt trusted.

He seemed warmer. Less guarded, when he was talking about writing. And that kiss ...

I turn my attention to Sam, and try to pretend my face isn't the colour of a beetroot.

"It's Friday night, and I do not want to hear another word about your tragic love life."

"But ..." I start to protest. I've only given Georgie the outline of what happened on the roof.

She turns from the kitchen sink and waves a bubble-covered hand at me.

"Something about going away, something about his mother, blah blah kiss, blah blah you need to leave, and you've been moping since Tuesday. Is that the shape of it?"

"Yes, but ..."

"But nothing." She dries her hands on the towel I've been using to dry the dishes, then tugs it from my hands and hangs it in front of the oven. She grabs me by the shoulders, and peers into my eyes. "Get dressed," she says. "We're going out."

"I'll ask Sam," I say as I turn towards my room, but she pulls me back.

"Absolutely not." She waves a finger at me. "No boys. No man-friends. You need to forget that they exist, just for one night."

"Georgie …"

"Just you, me, and the music. Girls, booze, dancing."

The Student Union bar is crowded, the floor is sticky with spilled drinks, and beer is on two-for-one. Georgie pushes her way through the crowd until we find a spot by the speakers. The DJ is playing cheesy 80s anthems and it's so loud we can't hear ourselves as we sing along. Georgie says no to every approach – boys, girls, groups wanting to join our fun – and we dance and drink and sing until we can hardly stand up.

It's impossible to think about anything beyond the noise and the beer and the grins on our faces.

She's right. It's exactly what I need.

There's a message waiting on my phone when I sit down to a hungover breakfast.

Dance recital. Am I still welcome?

I stare at the phone screen. I've heard nothing from Jez since I left him on the roof four days ago, and I'd started to assume he wasn't coming back.

My head hurts. My feet are sore from dancing.

And now this.

Georgie puts a mug of coffee down next to my half-eaten toast, glancing at the phone over my shoulder.

"He has got to be joking." She gives me a stern look. "You're not thinking of answering that, are you?"

"No." I put the phone down on the table, but I can't take my eyes off the screen. "Yes? Maybe."

Georgie rolls her eyes, and sits down opposite me.

"We need to talk about your taste in men," she says, and I can't help laughing.

"Just because you don't like him—"

"Mel! Wake up! He's messed you around twice now. What's left to like?"

I shrug. "There's something going on with him. He's … I don't know. Distracted."

"Then let him be distracted on his own time. He can figure it out on his own. You don't need this."

She's right. I should walk away. But I can't stop thinking about the way he makes me feel, when we're together. About being the focus of his attention.

About that kiss.

I pick up my phone, and Georgie puts her head in her hands, her red curls spilling over the table.

"Mel …"

I read his message, over and over, and think about what I want from him.

I want more of the thrill of his attention. More of the way he makes me feel special. I want to lose myself in his eyes.

I want another kiss.

I start typing, and Georgie groans.

Do you want to tell me what happened?

I want an answer. I want to hear his side of that kiss – what made him stop, what upset him.

But nothing happens. There's no response. Just my sent text, waiting.

After a minute or so, Georgie takes my phone and places it on the table between us, checking my messages.

"I can't wait for this," she says gleefully, sipping her coffee and watching the screen.

The expression on her face makes me laugh. "I'm not a soap opera, you know!"

She grins. "If you're going to do this to yourself, at least let the rest of us watch."

"Fine," I say. "Great. Would you like me to make you popcorn as well?"

She makes an approving face. "That would be—"

The phone buzzes, and I grab it before she can put down her coffee.

And there's his answer.

No.

Nothing else. Just *No.*

Georgie is watching me, and I'm staring at his message. My jaw drops.

She snatches the phone, her eyes wide.

"Did he ...?" She looks at me. "Did he just refuse to explain?"

Before I can do more than nod, the phone buzzes again and Georgie holds it out to me.

You just ...

"Just what?" I'm shouting at the phone. "Just what, Jez?"

... caught me by surprise.

Before I can take it from her, Georgie flips the phone round and starts typing.

"Don't you dare!" I reach out and she pulls the phone away, still tapping on the screen. "Georgie!"

My heart is crashing, my face is burning, and I can't believe my friend is replying to a private conversation.

When she returns the phone to my shaking hands, I take a deep breath before I read what she's sent.

You've been chasing me for weeks, and I caught you by surprise when I kissed you?

Relief hits me in an icy wave. Georgie folds her arms on the table and gives me a smug smile.

"It's what you wanted to say."

As much as I want to argue, she's right. She's said what I needed to say.

We sit and wait for the phone to buzz.

Let me make it up to you, Mel.

Georgie makes a face. "It's not an explanation." She shrugs. "Or an apology. What are you going to do?"

"I don't know." I shake my head. "I don't know."

I want him to come back. I want him to look at me as if I'm the only person in the room. I want him to kiss me again.

But he hasn't apologised, and he hasn't let me in to whatever is going on.

"He wants to make it up to me," I say, pointing at the phone.

"Whatever that means." Georgie takes my hand in hers. "Do you trust him? Do you want to give him another chance?"

I'm saved from answering by another message.

I don't want to lose you.

Georgie treats me to a dramatic eyeroll. "Oh, that's just emotional blackmail, Mel. Do not answer that."

I'm tempted to agree. If he didn't want to lose me, why ask me to leave?

"This isn't your problem, Mel. If he doesn't want to lose you, he needs to put the work in."

I nod, but my mind is replaying that kiss. The feeling of being swept away when I look into his eyes.

Mel?

Georgie groans again as I pick up the phone.

Sure, I type. *Meet here at 7. Don't forget there's a dress code. Smart dresses and sharp suits.*

His response is fast, and efficient.

Noted.

He's got what he wanted.

Chapter 24

Jez is waiting outside when we pile out of the flat just after seven. He raises an eyebrow at my ankle-length Chinese-style dress, and smiles as he offers me his arm. I'm relieved to see that he's ditched his usual grey jacket, and he's wearing a smart black suit with a Kane-style red shirt. Not the best match for my turquoise faux silk, but at least we both look as if we've made an effort. Georgie worked her magic on my hair with a posh-messy bun and a charity-shop diamanté clip. We left her hair loose, her red curls tumbling over a dark green velvet jacket and matching dress. The effect is undermined by the large black camera bag over her shoulder, but she's determined to get some shots for her portfolio tonight. Beside her, Sam wears a very flattering suit in midnight blue.

It's a short walk to the theatre, and Jez steps back to let Sam and Georgie lead. When we reach the pavement, he turns to face me. He drops my arm, takes my hand, and moves me to his opposite side. Satisfied, he tucks my hand round his elbow, and returns to following the others.

"What was that?" I say, laughing.

He gives me a serious look. "Always walk between a lady and the road," he says. "You never know when a rogue driver might ..."

I stop, closing my eyes against the flashbulb vision in my head. An SUV, tearing through a crowd.

Spotlights. Cameras. An angel, falling. I shake my hand from Jez's arm and press my hand to my mouth, stifling a scream.

My heart is clattering like a thousand camera shutters. My palms are cold and damp. I can't get enough air.

Spotlights. Cameras. Kane's feathers, scattering around me.

Blood. Shouting. My hands on his chest.

I don't know when I knelt down, but when I open my eyes, Jez is crouching beside me. The pavement is cold and hard.

"Breathe." He sounds panicked. "Breathe," he says again.

I'm safe. There is no SUV. There is no Kane, dying in my arms again.

I'm safe. I'm kneeling in the street. There are no cameras.

I make myself take a slow breath.

"What the hell did you do?" Georgie's voice carries along the street and I can hear her running footsteps. "What the *hell*, Jez?"

I try to stand up, but my legs won't move. I try to explain, but my voice is gone.

Jez is shaking his head, one hand on my arm. Georgie is shouting. Sam looks ready to explode.

"It's fine." I say. No one hears.

"Hey!" I hold up a hand, and Georgie finally stops to listen. "It's fine. He said something … he doesn't know … it's fine." I give her a pleading look.

Understanding dawns on her face, and she holds out a hand to help me stand. She gives me a quick, fierce hug.

"Tell him, then," she whispers. "He'll only do it again."

I nod, and she lets me go. My heartbeat is slowing. There's air in my lungs. I've knelt in a puddle, and the front of my dress is cold and wet but undamaged.

Georgie glares at Jez, and Sam flexes his fists.

"I'm fine," I say to both of them. "I'm fine. Thank you."

My hands are shaking as Jez offers me his elbow, and he's looking at me as if I've just turned purple, or sprouted a second head.

"What did I do?" He asks, careful to keep his voice down.

I shake my head. "Later." I say. "I'll explain later."

I suppose I should have been flattered by his concern. I can't decide whether putting himself next to the road is romantic, or insulting. Whether he's being adorably chivalrous, or desperately old-fashioned.

Either way, he didn't deserve my reaction. He didn't mean to throw me into my worst memory.

And it does make me feel good, having someone to watch out for me. Georgie's right – I do spend too much time focusing on the thoughts in my head, rather than the ground under my feet.

I didn't frighten him away. He saw my reaction, and he stayed with me.

I clasp my hand more tightly round his arm, and allow myself a smile.

Patrick meets us at the theatre door. He's wearing a suit, but it looks as if he borrowed it from someone wider and taller. He smiles when he sees Georgie, but rolls his eyes at me and Jez.

"See," Georgie says, turning to Sam. "I told you I'd bring a journalist." Patrick pulls a notepad and pen from his pocket, grinning. "We'll get Fai into the papers. I promise." She pats her camera bag. Sam shakes Patrick's hand and thanks him for coming.

Beside me, Jez coughs, and Georgie turns.

"Oh, right," she says. "Jez is here, too. I don't think your attention is going to be on the stage tonight, is it?" She snaps, and he shrugs. "Besides, isn't writing up a dance show a little *beneath you*, Jez?"

Patrick scowls, and Georgie turns back to him. Jez laughs under his breath.

"Good luck to him," he says, quietly.

The theatre lobby is gorgeous – deep red carpet, gold fittings and enormous chandeliers. I'd love to sit here and paint the crowd as they wait for the show to begin. There's a rainbow of dresses and some gorgeous hairstyles. The light is bright, but soft, and there are mirrors along the walls, expanding the space. It's beautiful, like a crowd scene by Renoir or Toulouse-Lautrec.

"Hey." Georgie snaps her fingers in front of my face. "Mel. I have to go and sweet-talk the Stage Manager." She swings her camera bag out from behind her back. "Can you make sure this lot don't kill each other?"

I glance at the rest of our party. Patrick is scowling at Jez. Sam looks as if he's standing in his own private thunder storm. And Jez is ignoring both of them, watching the people around us as if they are here solely to keep him entertained.

"I'll do my best," I say with a shrug.

"With any luck, I won't see you inside. If I can get stage-side access, I'll be down there with the camera." She grins. "So keep them safe from each other, OK? We don't want to spoil the show for Fai."

"Sure," I say, wondering what I can do.

I make sure Patrick sits as far away from Jez as possible with our tickets, and sit myself between Sam and my plus-one. Georgie's seat is empty as the curtain rises, and I'm hoping she's in the shadows with her camera.

The show is fantastic. The sets and costumes are vibrant and full of colour. Faisal is one of the star performers, and he moves as if he's made of silk, or water, flowing across the stage. In the seat next to me, Sam is glowing.

"See?" He whispers as the first dance ends. "Boy-tights. I told you." I can see his grin, even in the dark auditorium.

"You did," I whisper back, "and there they are."

"Everywhere," he says, and it sounds like a prayer. I can't help laughing.

"You're a lucky man, Sam," I say. "Fai is something special."

Sam places one hand on his heart. "Yes." He nods. "Yes he is."

Chapter 25

"There he is!" Georgie punches the air with her fist. "Star of the show!"

Sam leaps up from our corner of the theatre bar, a smile lighting up his face as Faisal weaves his way between the tables towards us. There's a moment when they hesitate, grinning at each other, and then Fai takes Sam in his arms. Their movie-star kiss earns cheers and applause from across the bar, and they're laughing as they stand, foreheads pressed together, enjoying the attention.

Georgie kicks a chair out from the table. "Get down here, you two. You're making the rest of us feel inadequate. Untangle yourselves, and have a drink." She winks at me. "Your round, Mel," she says with a grin.

The bar staff put a bottle of bubbly on ice for me when we arrived, and a girl with dip-dyed rainbow hair is already loading glasses onto a tray when I reach the bar. She waves me away, and points at the table, so I head back and sit down.

"Drinks?" Patrick asks, giving me a sarcastic shrug.

"Coming," I say, and he nods.

It takes two staff members to bring the bubbly and the tray, and they make a huge fuss of Faisal as they open the bottle and empty it into six glasses.

"Toasting the lord of the dance?" The girl asks, and Georgie nods. "He deserves it," she says, giving Fai a shy smile.

"We caught the dress rehearsal yesterday." The man passing out the drinks smiles. "You'll get used to this," he says, looking round the table. "Your friend here is a star in the making." He holds up the empty bottle as he turns to leave. "Cheers!"

We raise our glasses and drink. Georgie lifts hers above her head with a whoop, while Jez barely moves his from the table.

"Woah!" Faisal grins. "Someone bought the good stuff!"

"Thank Mel." Georgie waves a hand at me. "She finally decided to buy a round, and if this is what she chooses, she can buy more often."

It cost the same as a week's worth of food, but this is a special occasion. It's worth it to see the look on my friend's face.

"Cheers, Mel," he says. "Thank you."

"So ..." Georgie slaps a hand down on the table. "Now we've drunk to your dancing genius, you need to answer a question."

Faisal puts down his glass and takes Sam's hand in his. "OK," he says. "This sounds serious."

"I get that you've been working hard on ..." She waves a hand towards the auditorium. "All this. And it's great – well done and all that – but the question is – why have you been abandoning Sam?"

The question hangs in the air. There's a flash of discomfort on Fai's face, but I wonder whether I've imagined it when he grins and plants a kiss on Sam's lips.

"What can I say," he says to Sam. "I'm married to the dance!"

Sam smiles, and kisses him back.

Georgie gives them a moment, then pulls a face as if she's considering the idea. "I can see the appeal," she says. "The dance gives you all the glory with none of the annoying stuff." She counts on her fingers. "Snoring, farting, not doing the washing up." Patrick laughs, and Faisal raises an eyebrow. "Plus," she says, waving her hand, "Sam gets to be the exciting mistress!" She sits back in her chair and takes a sip of her drink. "Win – win."

Sam nods. "Well – he does come back to me every night." He gives Fai's hand a gentle tug. "Eventually."

"There you are, then." Georgie raises her glass. "Abandoned for a good cause, but not completely left out."

"Anyway," Patrick says, pointing at Georgie. "You can talk. I've never seen someone more married to their camera. What's the word?" He thinks for a moment. "Photo-sexual? Camera-sexual? There's no room for someone else in that relationship."

"Me?" She presses a hand to her chest. "Really? Says the man who is surgically joined to his notebook and pen?" She shakes her head, her red curls bouncing over her shoulders. "I swear I could get you naked, and you'd turn out to have some sort of journalistic stationery pouch. Like a hairless, skinny kangaroo." I'm trying not to choke on my drink as she holds out a hand and mimes pulling out a notepad. "Before we continue," she says in a mocking boring-man voice, "I notice you have a nipple ring. Could I just get your views on intimate piercings and the modern woman? It's for an article."

He shrugs, a smile tugging at his lips. "So I never want to miss a story. I think that makes me a good journalist." He leans closer and lowers his voice to a stage whisper. "And I'm always up for naked conversations about nipple rings."

Georgie stares at him for a moment, and then gives in to laughter. "In your dreams", she says, shaking her head. "This is exactly why I've sworn off men. None of you can handle a woman with a passion that doesn't involve you." She holds out a hand to Sam and Faisal. "Good for both of you. You have your passions, and you have each other. You're making it work. Good for you."

I'm still laughing at Georgie's vicious takedown when Patrick turns to me.

"And what about you? You're spending all your time flirting with Know-It-All here, but you're not about to give up your art for someone else."

Beside me, Jez tenses in his chair. I promised Georgie we wouldn't spoil this evening for Faisal, but right now I don't know how to stop Patrick from annoying everyone at the table.

I shrug. "I think I can handle more than one passion at a time." I wave a hand. "Art. A love interest. Supporting my amazing dance-sexual friends."

Fai grins. "Don't get any ideas, Patrick. Mel's an angel-sexual." He mimes a swoon. "You should have seen her when we met Kane."

My breath freezes in my throat. I can feel the blood draining from my skin.

My heart is a tight knot. I don't know where to look.

I can't believe he said that.

Sam drops Fai's hand, and there's a look of horror on his face as he tries to catch my eyes.

Georgie takes a sharp breath, and stares at me across the table.

Patrick smirks, and then his face falls. I can see him putting the pieces together.

I want to run. I want to disappear. I want to take back the drinks and the dance and the evening.

I want to scream.

I glance at Jez, and he's looking at me. He sits back slowly in his chair and raises an eyebrow, folding his hands over his chest.

I'm under his microscope again. He's studying my reaction.

His storm-grey eyes are fixed on mine.

I haven't had a chance to tell him – to explain what happened earlier. He doesn't know, and he's about to work it out. Here, in front of everyone.

I feel like a butterfly, pinned to a board. There's nothing I can do to take this back, and now he's watching everything I do. Every breath, every expression, every word I say.

I feel like a glass, shattering. Pieces of myself catching the light as they fall.

I can't hide from this.

"Oh, shit." Patrick's voice is like a prayer behind me. "Oh, *shit*. Mel Abbott. *Melodie Abbott*. You're the girl in the photo."

Jez's eyes widen, and he tilts his head, never breaking his gaze.

I can't breathe.

I can hear Patrick, tapping on his phone screen, and I know he's searching for my image. Pulling up the worst moment of my life for a cheap thrill. I can hear Georgie's harsh whisper – *Not now.*

I can hear Sam's shallow breathing, and I know his fists are clenched tight.

But I can't look away from Jez.

He holds my gaze, and gives me the briefest nod, as if he's listened to a speech I've made, or my side of an argument.

"Well," he says, looking away and reaching for the jacket on the back of his chair. "This has been an interesting evening."

"Wait–" Georgie begins, but she has nothing else to say.

"Sam, Faisal," Jez says as he stands. "Thank you for the invitation." He looks round the table. "Don't stand up. I'll see myself out."

And he's gone.

I feel as if I'm drowning. I feel as if an ocean is swallowing me, dragging me down into the dark. There are hands on my shoulders and people shouting and someone is saying *sorry, sorry,* over and over and I am choking on tears, my fingers streaked black with mascara.

Jez is gone.

Chapter 26

"He's not worth it, you know."

Georgie's voice cuts through my spiralling thoughts. I can't stop thinking about this evening.

About Jez.

"You're awake, right?" She taps quietly on my door. "Your light's on. Can I come in?"

"Sure," I say, without shifting my gaze from the ceiling. My voice is flat. Emotionless. I don't know what else to say. I shuffle sideways on the bed to give her space to sit down, and the high collar of my dress pulls tight against my neck. It takes a moment to tug it loose.

"Mel," she says. "That can't be comfortable. At least put your PJs on."

I shake my head, my eyes fixed on a crack in the paintwork above my pillow. I'm not ready to give up on tonight.

I'm not ready to give in.

Georgie kicks off her slippers and curls up on the bed beside me. Her white fleecy pyjamas are soft against my arm, and it's comforting to know she's here.

"I'm so sorry," she says. "About Patrick. He shouldn't have said anything."

I shrug. There's a rough pebble in my throat and my eyes are puffy and sore from crying. "Patrick didn't know. Faisal, on the other hand ..."

I run out of words. I can't believe Fai told everyone about Kane.

Georgie nods. "He was distracted. He had other things on his mind."

Something shatters in my chest.

"Dance moves? *Boy tights*?" I'm shouting, and I can't stop. "Just because he's the star – that doesn't make it OK."

"It's not an excuse. He shouldn't have done that."

Georgie sounds tired, as if she's been replaying the conversation. As if she's trying to see everyone's side. I can't believe she's being so calm.

"He was there, Georgie. He saw everything. Me, Kane, the crash …" I shake my head and try to swallow the lump in my throat. "He came to the hospital with me and Mum and Sam. He was *right there*."

Tears burn across my skin. Fai is the one who picked me up when the paramedics stepped in. He was my life raft in all the chaos. He's the one who told me about Mum.

He was with me. He saw … everything.

I thought he understood. I thought he knew.

"How could he? How could he laugh about it like that?"

Georgie takes my hand in hers, her face pale. "I don't think he meant to. It was just a throwaway comment."

"But—"

She clasps my fingers more tightly. "Did you hear him apologising? He wouldn't stop!" She takes a breath. "He's really sorry, Mel. He knows what he did, and he feels horrible about it.

"Good." I say, with more venom than I feel.

Because she's right. Of course she's right. He didn't mean to tell everyone who I am. He didn't mean to crash me back into Kane's final moments – blood, cameras, shouting. I know he was talking about the gallery, and the swoon, and Sam keeping me on my feet.

But that didn't stop Patrick from joining the dots. And it didn't stop Jez from walking out.

My stomach twists. I can see him reaching for his jacket. Turning his back. Weaving between the tight-packed tables as he left me behind.

I take another jagged breath.

"I know you don't care …" I begin, and Georgie groans.

"This isn't about Jez, is it?"

I nod. "What *happened*?"

"What – you mean apart from him taking your true identity very badly, for no good reason, and then ditching us all in a really passive-aggressive strop?" She squeezes my fingers. "You mean apart from that?"

Her sarcasm is almost enough to make me laugh, but she's missing something. Something about the conversation.

I shake my head, willing myself to remember.

"Before that," I say, thinking it through. "Before Patrick, and the photo." Georgie nods, listening.

"When Fai mentioned Kane. When he called me an angel-sexual ..."

"For which he also apologised. Lots."

"I know he did. But this isn't about him." I close my eyes, trying to bring back Jez's face. His reactions. "Something changed, with Jez. Right when Fai ..."

My breath catches. When Fai made his comments, Jez was watching me. He slouched back in his chair, folded his hands over his chest, and watched my response.

I felt examined. I felt like the subject of an experiment. He sat back, raised an eyebrow, and let everything play out in front of him as if he wasn't involved.

It felt like something breaking between us. Something important.

"He didn't know." I think I'm piecing this together.

Georgie laughs. "I think that's a safe bet."

"No – not about Kane." My heart hammers against my ribs. I can feel his eyes on me. His look of detached interest. "About the angels. About swooning and angel paintings and how I'm the resident angel fan."

It wasn't just Kane. It wasn't just that he didn't know about me, and the photo – and he hadn't guessed.

My hands are shaking. My lungs are frozen.

"It was the angel-sexual comment." My voice is a whisper. I turn to look at Georgie, and she's frowning at me. "That's when he checked out of the conversation."

Her frown deepens. "What do you mean?"

I can't find the words to explain. "Just ... the way he looked at me. As if that was the big secret. As if *that's* the thing I hadn't told him."

She makes a face. "What? Why?"

I shrug, my heart still pounding. "No idea. I mean – he saw me crying at the Angel Club. He teased me about having wing envy, and he was really surprised when that upset me. I thought ..." I shake my head. "I thought he understood."

"Nope." It's Georgie's turn to stare at the ceiling. "I think we can be certain he did not."

There's a headache building behind my eyes. I feel sick and dizzy and breathless. I want to stop thinking about tonight. I want to forget everything that happened and go to sleep. I want to wake up tomorrow, wash the tears from my face, and start over.

And then she grips my hand.

"You know what this means, right?" There's excitement in her voice, as if she's just solved a mystery.

I don't want to know what she's going to say.

"Mel!" Georgie nudges my shoulder. "You know what this means?"

She's not going to leave me alone. I make myself answer.

"What?"

She sits up, and bounces my hand against the sheets.

"Either he's admitted defeat, because he knows he doesn't stand a chance with you – and good riddance, by the way."

I give her a scowl, and she laughs.

"Or?"

"Or ..." She grins. "He's an angel. He's an angel, and *he* hasn't told *you*."

I stare at my friend. I can't take a breath. My lungs stop. My heart forgets to beat.

The room spins. The mattress sinks. I'm glad I'm lying down.

It's not possible. Jez is ... many things. But not this.

He's an angel, and he hasn't told you.

"No." I'm shaking my head. "No. He's not. He can't be ..."

"Think about it." Georgie's grip on my fingers tightens. "It makes sense."

"No ..."

But even as I'm protesting, my thoughts are racing.

Jez, selling himself as better than everyone else.

Jez at the angel club – being there, being part of it, but never joining in.

The two of us on the roof. The way he pulled back when I lifted his T-shirt.

Jez at the theatre bar. The look on his face when Fai told everyone my secret.

Don't get any ideas. Mel's an angel-sexual.

He looked as if he was inspecting me. He looked ... interested.

And then Patrick jumped in with the photo and the evening shattered into a thousand shards and Jez pretended I didn't exist.

He left, and he couldn't even say my name.

It felt as if he'd punched me.

"It doesn't make sense. If he's an angel, why did he leave? Why did he blank me, and say goodnight to the rest of you? Why not stay, and hear my side of the story?"

She shrugs. "It wasn't the right time. And you weren't exactly wowing him with your angelic desire." I open my mouth to protest, but she talks over me. "You looked as if someone had put you in front of a firing squad, Mel. You looked like a ghost – no colour in your cheeks, desperation in your eyes – you didn't have anything to say for yourself." She waves a hand to stop me interrupting. "I know why. I understand. The PTSD is real, and I know it does a number on you when you're not expecting to hear about Kane. I know." She takes a breath. "But he doesn't. He doesn't know, and he doesn't get it. He doesn't understand."

There's a sinking feeling in my stomach. "Because I haven't told him."

She nods. "He saw what happened to you in the street before the performance – god knows what he said to trigger that, and I'll give him a black eye if he does it again – but he doesn't understand. You haven't given him a chance to understand."

I close my eyes and take a breath.

She's right. I can't expect Jez to be there for me if I haven't told him what I need. I can't expect him to avoid my triggers if he doesn't know what they are. And I can't expect him to keep landing in situations he doesn't understand, and come back for more.

I did this. I pushed him away. When I had the chance, I told him about art, not angels. I wasn't honest about my passion.

I run a hand over my face. "I need to talk to him."

Georgie shrugs again. "Talk to him, don't talk to him. I know which one I'd prefer – but if you want to see him again, you need to explain." She gives me a stern look. "And don't forget that he needs to explain. He owes you an explanation for whatever tipped him off his perch at the theatre."

"I guess …"

"For real, Mel. Don't let him treat you like that." She gives me a flirty smile "And …"

"What?"

"He might be an angel." Georgie pokes a finger at my shoulder. "He might be *your* angel."

My breath catches. My heart kicks. She winks at me, and I wish I wasn't blushing like a neon sign.

"He might be my angel," I whisper, and it feels like a prayer.

"So what should I do?"

I'm not sure Georgie is still awake. We've been lying here for ages. It's quiet in my room, and I can hear her steady breathing. I'm not sure whether I'm asking her, or me.

I'm not sure I want her to answer.

"Hmmm?"

"Jez." I'm whispering. "What should I do?"

Georgie stirs, and I think I feel her shrug.

"What ..." She stifles a yawn, and her voice is thick with sleep. "What do you want to do?"

It's my turn to shrug.

She shuffles onto her side, so she's facing me.

"What do you want from him? Because that's going to decide what you do." She yawns again, and waits for my answer.

I can't stop thinking about him. I can't stop thinking about what I want. My mind is running in circles, and I wish I had an answer.

I want him to understand. I want him to know who I am, and I want him to be OK with ... all of it. Kane, the photo, the memories.

I want to understand him. I want to know what drives him. What makes him ... him.

Why he's interested in me.

I close my eyes. I have my answer – I just don't know how to make it happen.

I want him to want me. I want him to be my angel.

"Mel?"

I take a breath. "I don't know."

"This is up to you, now," she says. "After tonight. After he walked away. What happens next is in your hands, so you have to choose."

I give her a sideways glance. "And you think I should let him go."

There's a sad smile on her face as she shakes her head.

"Yes, but ..." She waves a hand. "What if ...?"

My breath stalls. There's a warm glow in my chest.

I can't help smiling. "What if he's an angel?"

"What if he's an angel."

I shake my head. "But you don't like him. You've been trying to make me ditch him since we met."

She nods. "I don't have to like him, Mel. I'm not the one losing sleep over him."

"You're not losing sleep over anyone." I regret my comment the moment I've spoken, but Georgie is laughing.

"It's easy to sleep when there's no one to lose it for."

I don't want to be pushing Georgie away, but there's something about her attitude that's getting under my skin. As if there's a switch I can flip and walk away. As if I can decide not to care.

"Right." I give her a slow nod. "You've sworn off men, so none of this affects you."

She shrugs. "Works for me."

"Have you sworn off women and all the other genders as well, or is it just the men who are beneath you?"

She grins. "I've sworn off anything that doesn't run on batteries. Much easier that way."

I'm choking back a laugh, but I know she's serious. I pull my pillow over my face as my skin floods with heat.

"Too much information, Georgie!"

She tugs at the pillow, and we're both laughing. I tighten my grip.

"I'm serious, though", she says quietly. "No trying to understand the other person. None of this 'what did he mean?' and 'why doesn't he like me?'. None of whatever you're going through right now, with the tears and running mascara and the 'what do I do?' drama. Just me, and everything I like."

I think back to her comments at the theatre. "No snoring and farting, and you're not waiting for someone else to do the washing up." I push the pillow away and nod in approval. "That's actually pretty smart."

She bobs her head from side to side, considering my comment.

"Well – not that smart. I still share a kitchen with you, and I'm not sure you're fully domesticated."

"Hey!" I'm trying to sound indignant, but she's making me laugh again. "I do the washing up! Just … not always on the same day."

"What can I say, Mel? You don't run on batteries."

There's no answer to that. "Point made", I say, still laughing.

"So what are you going to do?"

She sounds serious. I stare at the crack in the ceiling.

"I don't know." She gives me a stern look, and I know she's waiting for my answer. I let out a frustrated, strangled scream.

"OK," she says, nodding. "Let's think this through. What if he doesn't come back?"

My stomach feels like ice. I hadn't thought about what happens if this is over. If I never see him again.

I brush a stinging tear from the corner of my eye, and Georgie raises an eyebrow.

"OK. We don't like that scenario. Good to know."

I nod. "We absolutely do not like that scenario."

"Right. So if he doesn't come back we do tears and get drunk and move on. I'll make a note to buy the booze."

"Hey! Don't sound so happy about it!"

She shrugs, and grins.

"And if he does come back?" My voice is a whisper around the lump in my throat.

"Does he apologise? Do you want him to apologise?"

"I guess," I say, still trying to gather my thoughts.

"Do you want him to explain?" I nod. "Is this a great excuse to get to know him better?"

"I suppose."

"Then there's your plan. Apologies, explanations." She waves a finger at me. "Make sure you ask, though. Make sure he knows what you want from him."

I take a moment to breathe.

"Ask, accept apologies, listen to explanations. Got it."

"And when you've done all that, and had a nice smooch – or whatever it is you two are going to get up to behind closed doors – what then?" She takes my hand. "Is this a forever thing, or do you just want to get close enough to find out what colour his feathers are?"

The thought of Jez with wings is enough to make my heart race. I feel as if I'm sinking into the mattress.

"If he's an angel," I whisper.

"If he's an angel." She pokes my shoulder. "And how are you going to find out?"

I cover my face with my hands. My cheeks are burning. "Ask him?"

She laughs. "Sure. Or – more fun idea, seeing as you're so desperate to know – tempt him to take his clothes off."

"Georgie …" I'm squeaking now. I'm begging her to stop.

"Yes?" She sounds completely calm.

I take a breath. Wait for my pulse to slow.

"What if you're wrong? What if he's not?"

"Not an angel? Not the answer to all your hopes and dreams? Not your very own objectified minority?"

I don't have an answer for her.

She claps her hands. "Well, then. I suggest you stand up, pick up his clothes, hand them to him, and point to the door. No need to actually speak to him – he didn't say anything to you at the theatre, so I think he's earned that."

I stare at her. "That's …"

"Awful? Yes. And so is how he treated you tonight." She frowns. "Don't let him get away with it, Mel. You're worth more than that."

"I guess."

"I'm serious." She takes my hand again. "Chase him if you want, if you're enjoying the attention. Find out what's going on with him. Find out what his problem is. Find out what's under that awful jacket he wears. But don't let him mess you around. It's time you two had an honest conversation, and figured out what you both want."

She's right. If he comes back, if he apologises, if we can figure each other out …

My hands are shaking when I think about what could happen.

"Thanks, Georgie." I give her fingers a squeeze. "I'm glad you're on my team."

Chapter 27

The bright lights and hushed whispering of the National Portrait Gallery are comforting as I make my way through the exhibition rooms to the paintings I've come to sketch. It's been 88 hours. Four days since Jez walked out without a word to me, and I badly need a distraction.

Every time I close my eyes, he's there. Standing up, saying goodbye to everyone but me. Watching me, hands folded on his chest as he sits back in his chair.

Inspecting me.

And Fai, joking about the worst night of my life. Patrick, calling up my photo on his phone. Jez piecing everything together.

I couldn't control what happened. I couldn't stop any of it. It's my fault I hadn't told Jez. It's Fai's fault for talking about it. It's Patrick's fault for treating me like public property.

I shake my head, trying to derail my thoughts. There's nothing I can do about it now.

Georgie is right. Either Jez explains and apologises, or we're done. I can't tiptoe around, waiting for him to react.

I reach the contemporary galleries and find a seat in front of a head-and-shoulders watercolour. I need some inspiration for Sam's portrait – colours, composition, background. I pull my sketchbook and pencils from my bag and start mapping the image onto the blank page.

I want to see how the artist put this painting together. How they emphasised the subject's eyes and expression. I want to lose myself in their lines and brushstrokes, and I don't want to think about anything else.

But as I fill in the detail of the sketch, I can't ignore the ache in my chest. The empty, lost feeling when I think about Jez.

How much I want to see him again.

I close my eyes and take a breath, concentrating on the velvet touch of my pencil against the paper.

"You're back!" Georgie's voice echoes down the corridor from her room as I close the door to the flat. "Kettle's just boiled. I was about to make tea."

"I can take a hint!" I'm smiling as I dump my bag on a chair and grab two mugs from the cupboard.

"Did you get what you wanted?" Georgie sounds distracted. "Did you find your inspiration?"

I shrug, even though she can't see me. "I guess. I made some sketches." I drop tea bags into the mugs and switch the kettle back on.

"That's good, right?"

"I hope so," I say, pouring the water. "I'm not sure how helpful they're going to be."

There's silence from Georgie's room as I fish out the tea bags and add milk.

She closes her laptop as I step through the door and hand her a mug.

"Cheers," she says, and digs out a coaster from the piles of books and paper on her desk.

I nod at the laptop. "Secret project?"

"No ... I just ..." She rolls her eyes. "I didn't know whether you'd want to see. I know you're not OK with what happened on Saturday."

"Your photos from the dance recital?"

She nods. "Backstage and on stage. I'm trying to pick a couple to send to the newspapers."

"You're kidding." I nudge her chair with my hip. "Of course I want to see. Show me."

It's harder than I expect to look through photos of Faisal. I can still hear him calling me an angel-sexual. Joking about meeting Kane. His voice as he apologised again and again.

I swallow my hurt and try to pretend I'm looking at photos of a stranger.

"They're beautiful, Georgie."

She flashes me a smile. "Thanks. That means a lot, from a star portrait painter."

We scroll through the images. Fai, his body like a sculpture on the stage. Groups of dancers, their limbs creating abstract shapes on the screen. Solo performers, high in contrast, stark shadows offsetting their movements in the spotlights. And everywhere, colour. Flashes of red from sashes around the dancers' waists. Iridescent greens and blues from feathers woven into hair and headbands. A high-energy piece where everyone on stage is wearing bright yellow work boots and gloves. A woman in a long fuchsia-pink tutu leaping towards the camera, her skirt flaring behind her, head back, arms outstretched.

"You caught all this from the wings?"

Georgie nods. "All while being trampled and shoved out of the way by dancers trying to meet their cues."

The idea of Georgie fighting for space with her camera makes me laugh. "Make sure you put that on your CV. You'll be top of the list for covering riots and battlefields."

She makes a thinking face. "True. If I can survive when these muscle-bound athletes have it in for me, I can survive anything." She lowers her voice to a whisper. "Of course, what I won't tell anyone is how many terrible photos I took." She mimes being thrown out of the way. "Blurred dancers. Someone's elbow knocking the camera. Somewhere there's a great close-up of the back of the curtains."

I hold a finger to my lips. "No one needs to know!"

"These are the ones I liked enough to edit – crop, tweak the contrast, boost the colours."

"I shall assume that you're an infallible genius. The other photos don't exist." I give her a conspiratorial wink, and she grins.

"OK." She opens a new folder. "Backstage. These are different. I was aiming for candid documentary."

She's taken a series of informal portraits. Most of her subjects seem to be ignoring the camera, or unaware of her attention. There are chaotic scenes in full colour – dancers rushing past to the stage, racks of costumes in rainbow tones. Some are colour-popped – black and white, but with a single costume element picked out in bright red or green, turquoise, yellow, and pink. My favourite are her black and white pictures, mostly moments of contact or conversation between dancers. The body language projects emotion, exhaustion, elation. The monochrome gives them a quiet energy, turning my focus fully towards her subjects at the moment the shutter clicked.

One of them is an image of a muscular dancer, stripped to the waist, with a man in a T-shirt and jeans, their foreheads pressed together. The dancer's skin glistens with sweat, and the other man has his hand on the back of the half-naked man's neck.

With a jolt, I realise the dancer is Fai.

I reach out and stop Georgie from clicking to the next image. I can't take my eyes from the screen.

The pose exactly echoes Faisal and Sam in the theatre bar, after the show. Except Fai and Sam were laughing, and in this photo both men are staring intensely into each other's eyes.

"Who ...?" I say, pointing at the photo. "Who is that?"

Georgie tilts her head. "That's Kyle. The director."

"They seem ... friendly." I can't think of another word. I don't want to suggest something worse, but my stomach is knotted and my chest is tight. I don't want to think about Fai hurting Sam like this.

She leans her shoulder against mine. "Don't worry," she says. "I know people think that the camera never lies, but sometimes it exaggerates."

"What do you mean?"

"He'd just come offstage after one of his solo pieces. The director was completely thrilled, and Fai was on a high. I caught a fraction of a second between them, and now it looks like a major emotional event."

The photo sits on the screen. Fai, and another man, locked together.

"It does," I say slowly. I feel sick.

"Honestly." She waves a hand at the image. "It wasn't. A couple of seconds at most. I just got lucky."

I make myself nod. "Lucky."

She clicks to the next image, but all I can see is my friend, forehead-to-forehead with someone who isn't Sam.

I want to ask Fai about the photo. I want to hear his side of the story.

"Maybe don't publish that one?" I have to push the words past the lump in my throat. "Maybe don't show anyone? Don't mention it?"

Georgie gives me a long look. I can feel the colour draining from my face. I know she wants to protest, and I know it's a good image, but I can't stand the idea of hurting my oldest friend.

"Yeah," she says, slowly. "OK. I'll take it out of the running."

I let out a tight breath. "Thank you."

"It's honestly nothing," she says as she moves the file out of the backstage folder. "I promise."

I nod. But if I'm reading more into it, then so will Sam. I'm happier with it safely out of the way.

Chapter 28

"You need a distraction."

"Hmmm?" I'm concentrating on my sketch. There's something wrong with Sam's pose, and I'm not sure whether it's me or him. Whether I've messed up my drawing, or whether he's shifted in the chair.

"Come with us tonight, Mel." He takes a breath and I give him a frown. "I know you're mad with Fai, but just come out with us. I really need you two to be talking to each other."

I shrug.

"Please, Mel. You've been moping for a week. You need to cheer up."

I place my pencil carefully in the pocket of my apron, and look up at Sam, hands on hips. He puts his hands up, palms out, as if he's calming a wild animal, and I can't help laughing.

"Your studio," he says quickly, before I can open my mouth. "You're the boss. Just ..." He clasps his hands together. "... Please come and talk to Faisal. Please come and have some fun with us. Please make this normal again."

My smile fades.

"Hang on," I say, pointing a finger at him. "Fai makes a joke, in public, about the worst day of my life ..."

"He didn't mean to. You know he didn't mean to."

"... which leads to Patrick doing some journalistic connection-making ..."

"I know. I know."

" ... which leads to Jez walking out on us without even saying my name."

"Yup."

"And disappearing. No one's seen him since last week. Patrick told Georgie he hasn't been to lectures. And no texts, no calls – nothing."

Sam nods, his shoulders slumped.

"And you want *me* to make this normal again?"

He spreads his hands in a shrug. "Fai apologised. He feels horrible about it."

"I know. I was there." I throw my hands in the air. "Doesn't change anything, though, does it?"

He shakes his head.

"I'm really sorry it happened, Mel," he says. "Fai wasn't thinking. You know he was talking about the exhibition, not ..." He waves a hand, and I nod, closing my eyes against the flashbulb images in my head. "And I know that tipped Patrick off, and I know Jez lost it, but Fai didn't mean for any of that to happen. He's really worried about you, you know."

"He's worried about me, you're worried about me. Is anyone worried about Jez? It's been a week."

Sam shrugs. "He's ghosted you before. He'll be back. You'll be up on your secret rooftop together, forgetting any of this happened."

"Not for seven whole days! And no, I don't think we'll be forgetting about this. He's found out who I am, and I'm guessing he's offended I didn't tell him, and he's probably livid that Patrick the sub-standard journalist worked it out before he did."

Sam raises an eyebrow. "You've been thinking about this."

I nod. "It's kind of hard not to."

He smothers a laugh. "It is pretty funny – Patrick getting there first. Jez must be choking on that."

I bite back a smile. "He must be." I strike a dramatic pose. "Ambition!" I shout. "The scaling of great journalistic heights!"

Sam smirks. "He said that?"

"Oh, yes he did. About sixty seconds after we met."

He's laughing now. Shaking his head. "And this is the relationship you want to save?" He gives me a stern look. "The arrogant not-very-good journalist who walked out on you, instead of your friend who – did I mention this? – Is really, really sorry?"

I close my eyes and let out a yell of frustration. When I open them, Sam is grinning at me.

"So you'll come?"

I make myself take a breath. "Fine. Fine, I'll come."

"Thank you, Mel," he says, quietly.

I realise I'm looking forward to seeing Sam and Fai together. To convincing myself that Georgie's photo is a lie.

"Where are we going?" The expression on his face is impossible to read. "Sam?"

"Promise you won't back out?" I shrug, and he waits for me to say something.

"Fine."

"It's another Angel Drag Night," he says, eventually. "Sparkly wings, cocktails, singing."

I feel as if he's knocked the floor out from under my feet.

"Of course it is," I say, and he grins.

"Sam says you're coming!"

Georgie waves her phone at me as I walk through the door. She's wearing her dressing gown, and her hair is wrapped in a towel. I don't have the chance to take off my jacket or drop my bag on the kitchen table before she's grabbed my hands. She inspects my nails and holds my fingers up to the kitchen light.

"Not too bad," she says, nodding. "No painting today?"

"Sketching," I say, pulling my hands back and shrugging out of my jacket. "For a watercolour."

She screws up her nose and inspects her own hands. "That explains the grey smudges."

I pull out a chair and try to sit down, but Georgie drags me to my feet.

"No time," she says. "You – shower. Now. Wash the artist off your hands. Wash the studio out of your hair. We need to be ready when the boys get here."

"Georgie ..." I know I'm whining, but I just want to sit down. "I've been on my feet all day. All I want is five minutes ..."

She shakes her head. "We're on the clock. There are pizzas in the oven – I know you need to eat before drinking – and then we need to get dressed."

I can't help smiling. She's thought of everything.

"You're wearing the serious wings again?"

She grins. "Of course I am. Wings, catsuit, boots. And you're wearing yours."

By the time the boys arrive, we're ready to go. Georgie looks fantastic in her silver catsuit and theatrical feathers. I'm wearing the cute golden wings we bought for last time, but I've swapped my red outfit for a little black dress and a black jacket, straightened my hair, and gone full goth with my makeup. Fai gives us an appreciative whistle as he steps into the flat, and we both strike fashion-shoot poses while he pulls out his phone for photos.

"Wait ..." Georgie holds up a hand. "Wings, boys. Where are your wings?"

Sam and Fai exchange a smile. They're wearing matching black suit jackets over skinny jeans and smart black shirts, open at the neck. There's no sign of the Kane-inspired outfit or the leather from last time, and I can't see any feathers. They turn away, still smiling, and the backs of their jackets glitter in the light.

They both have sparkling golden wings, stitched into the fabric. Hundreds of tiny golden feather-shaped sequins flutter as they turn, the wings flexing and following their movements.

They are breathtaking.

Georgie gives them a round of applause.

"Walk with you?"

Fai taps my shoulder as we step out into the cold. Ahead of us Sam offers Georgie his arm, and they set out towards the road. Sam throws me a glance over his shoulder, and I realise I've been set up.

This is where I'm supposed to talk to Fai. Listen to him. Forgive him.

I'm tired. I'm worried. It's been 165 hours since Jez walked out and I still haven't heard from him. I don't want to do this now, but my friends aren't giving me a choice.

And I know this means a lot to Sam.

"Sure," I say, forcing a smile, and Fai gives me a nervous smile back.

We walk in silence to the road. Our shadows grow and shrink as we follow Sam and Georgie under streetlights and past brightly lit shop windows.

I'm not starting this conversation, whatever Sam wants. I'm going to wait for Fai to explain himself.

He takes a breath.

"So, about what I said."

I nod, and wait for him to continue. He puts both hands on the back of his head and looks up, as if he's asking the streetlights for inspiration.

"I'm really, really, spectacularly sorry, Mel," he says, dropping his hands and giving me a pleading look. "I wasn't thinking, it was unbelievably stupid of me, and I am so, so, so sorry."

"OK," I say. "You said that before."

"I know. But I'm still sorry."

"You understand what happened? That Jez has ..." I wave a hand. "Vanished. Ghosted me. Disappeared."

He gives me a sideways glance. "Is that such a bad thing?"

I roll my eyes. "Yes, Fai. I know you're with the others on this, and I know none of you gets what I like about Jez, but honestly? I don't care. I don't care what you think. I want to get to know Jez, and I wanted to tell him what happened in my own time."

"You hadn't told him anything? About Kane, or the ..." He holds out a hand, filling in for his own lack of words.

"The attack? The murder? The whole dying-in-my-arms thing?" I shake my head. "No, Fai. I hadn't. I decided that 'Hi, I'm Mel, and a famous angel died right in front of me – you may remember my photo in *all the papers*' wasn't the best chat-up line, actually."

He nods, and I'm surprised at my own anger. I didn't mean to be so hard on him, but I'm realising how much he upset me.

"And," I say, before I can stop myself, "does this look like the face of a girl who wants to be recognised?" I stop walking and point at my dyed hair and goth makeup. Fai turns back, his shoulders slumping as he meets my gaze.

"No." He shrugs.

"It was humiliating. The way Patrick looked me up on his phone, as if I'm some plastic celebrity. The way Jez just … left." There are tears pricking my eyes, and I'm annoyed at myself for letting this get under my skin. "I've tried really hard not to get stuck as the girl in the photo, Fai. My heart rate doubles when I hear a revving engine or squealing tyres. People taking photos make me nervous. I had a proper panic attack on the way to your recital because Jez wanted to walk between me and the road to protect me from the traffic. And I still didn't tell him." I close my eyes and take a breath. "I didn't explain, because it wasn't the right time. And then you …" I shake my head and blink away the tears.

"I get it, Mel. I'm really sorry."

I make myself take a step, and another, past Fai, following Sam and Georgie. "You know the horrible part?" I glance back to make sure he's with me. To make sure he's listening. "You were there. You know all the details. You're the one who picked me up and made me feel safe when the worst thing in my life had just happened." I turn towards him, and he nods. "We were all there. We all went through that together."

"I know," he whispers.

"I thought I could trust you, Fai. You and Sam. I thought you understood."

He blinks, and I realise there are tears in his eyes, too.

"That's why I feel so bad, Mel. That's why I wish I could take it back." He tips his head back again, his hands over his face, then he turns to me. "You know I was talking about the gallery? About you swooning in front of your mother?" He takes another breath. "You know I would never joke about … what happened. You know that, right?"

His voice is quiet, and he sounds defeated. He sounds exhausted. "I never meant …"

I put a hand on his arm, and he looks at me.

"I know, Fai," I say. "I get that you didn't mean … any of what happened." He nods. "But it still hurts. OK?"

"Yeah." He runs a hand over his face. "I screwed up. And I'm really, really sorry."

I can feel my stomach sinking. I'm hurting, but so is Fai. This happened to both of us, and we're both stuck with the memories. We're both still dealing with the aftermath. We're both making mistakes. I press my fingers against my eyelids, and they come away stained with mascara.

"I'm sorry too." I feel as if there's a stone in my throat, blocking my words. "It's not all on you. I should have told Jez. I should have told him about me and Kane and angels and …" I shrug, remembering

Patrick's party. Jez, asking about my passion. "I had the chance, and I didn't tell him. That's on me."

We walk for a while in silence.

Fai frowns. "This is going to keep happening, isn't it?"

"What?"

He points a finger at me. "You, me, Sam. We're going to keep circling that night. Like a dance we can't step out of."

I nod, thinking about what he's said. "I think that's how it works. Something as big as that ... I think it stays with you."

"In which case ..." He straightens his shoulders and adjusts his jacket as we walk, as if he's about to make an important announcement. "I'm sorry in advance, because this will happen again. Misunderstandings, accidental comments – and I want you to know that I never, ever mean it. Anything I say is stupid, not deliberate. I'd never use that to try and hurt you, Mel."

For a moment I can't take a breath. I think that's one of the kindest things anyone has ever said to me. He's right that this isn't going away, but he understands. He's reminding me that he cares. He knows how powerful these memories are, and how easy it will be to hurt each other.

He's reminding me that I'm not alone – that all three of us are in this together. That we need each other's support.

I push away the memory of Georgie's photo. Fai with his director, her explanation.

It's honestly nothing. I promise.

I realise I'm smiling.

"Right back at you, Fai."

He returns the smile, and lowers his voice. "For what it's worth, I hope Jez comes back. I know you like him." He holds up one hand and gives me a guilty glance. "Do not tell Sam I said that!"

The panic in his voice makes me laugh.

"Our secret," I whisper, hooking my arm through his. "And I hope he does, too."

Chapter 29

We join Sam and Georgie in the queue outside the Angel Club, and this time no one bothers us. Standing in the street are four muscular angels in black jeans and matching sleeveless leather biker jackets, the shoulders slashed to show off their gorgeous wings: brown, grey, black, and gold.

"Security?" Sam raises an eyebrow.

I grin at Georgie. "I guess your stiletto self-defence moves earned us some protection."

"Maybe they're here to protect the local idiots from me." She smiles and purposefully taps the pavement with her boot heel, her dove-grey wings shivering with the movement.

"If I was a local idiot, I definitely wouldn't try anything." Fai says, staring at the nearest angel. "Look at his arms. You'd have to be a proper idiot to go up against that."

"Hey!" Sam waves a hand in front of Fai's face. "Enough drooling. I'm standing right here!"

Fai gives the angel a final dreamy gaze. "Can I swoon instead?"

Sam laughs. "I think that's Mel's department," he says, giving me a nervous glance. "I don't think I can handle two of you throwing yourselves at the floor."

Fai throws the back of one hand to his forehead and fakes a dramatic stagger. Sam catches his elbow, and slips an arm round his waist.

And the angel looks over at us.

His tanned, tattooed arms are crossed over his chest, the muscles standing out like coils of rope. On the front of his jacket is a black patch with a logo. *Guardian Angels*, it says, over a pair of silver wings. He has long, grey hair in a neat ponytail, and his eyes are a shocking shade of green. When he sees me looking, he smiles, and I can feel the world tilting.

"Careful," Georgie whispers, pushing her hand against my back. "Stay on your feet."

I nod, taking half a step back to keep my balance. I can't take my eyes from his wings. They shimmer as he moves, the streetlights picking out each golden feather.

They're beautiful. Mesmerising.

They're just like Kane's.

Patrick and the other journalists have claimed the same table they chose last time. I know Jez isn't coming, but I find myself looking for him. Someone else is sitting in his spot on the velvet bench, and I'm not ready for the jolt of disappointment.

Georgie tugs on my hand. "Come and sit with us," she whispers, and gives the bench a meaningful glance. "And don't forget – we're here to have a good time, not mope over boys who don't know what they want. OK?" She gives my fingers a squeeze, and I can't help smiling.

Sam raises an eyebrow as I sit down next to Fai. "Good conversation?"

I pull a disapproving face. "We have agreed never to speak of it again."

Sam looks at both of us, confusion on his face. "So you are talking again?"

I can see Fai trying not to laugh, and I can't stop myself from smiling.

Sam breathes a relieved sigh. "Good," he says. "Thank you."

Georgie watches the conversation, nods to Sam, and picks up a menu from the table.

"Drinks?"

"Sure," I say, remembering last time, and an evening of pink alcohol. "Just ... no cocktails. Not this time."

"So ..." she says, running a finger over the list. "That'll be posh craft beer or bubbly, then. Any preference?"

We settle on beer, and Georgie waves a waiter over to take our order.

Our drinks arrive just in time. The lights dim, the music starts, and the crowd erupts with clapping and cheering as the red velvet curtains draw back. Georgie grins and raises her glass.

"To angels," she shouts over the noise.

The first act is a young singer in cute shorts and fishnets with a bright pink T-shirt knotted at the waist.

She absolutely nails the first lines of Little Mix's 'Wings', and before long most of the audience is on their feet and dancing. With each new section of the song, another performer joins her on stage until there are four of them, dancing in the tiny space. When the volume kicks up, they all turn their backs to reveal neon-coloured butterfly wings, and the cheering nearly drowns out the music.

Georgie is dancing, Fai and Sam are singing along – Sam clapping and Fai drumming on the table. I'm tapping my foot to the beat, and it feels amazing to lose myself in the music. I'm not thinking about the person next to me, and what they're going to think if I dance. I'm letting myself sink into the energy of the club, and it feels good.

The song ends, the crowd cheers, and the singers take a bow. They file offstage, kissing their fingertips and touching the photo of Kane. As they leave, Angelica sweeps onto the stage to welcome us to the club, her signature sequined black dress and silver wings glittering in the spotlights. I settle back in my seat and wait for the music.

There are songs about wings, and songs about flying. Real wings and gorgeous fakes. We dance, we sing, and we cheer.

When a tall angel with long blond hair sings the first words of Sam Ryder's 'Spaceman', I'm squealing and gripping Fai's arm before I can stop myself. It's another Angel Club Eurovision moment, and we're on our feet before anyone else. The angel gives us a smile as he sings, and I feel as I'm floating.

Angelica's number is a sultry rendition of 'Fly Me To The Moon' that has everyone joining in. There's a slow, acoustic duet of 'Up Where We Belong' sung by two young women that almost brings me to tears, and I realise I'm waiting for someone to make fun of me for crying. I glance over at Jez's spot on the bench, but the people sitting there are watching the stage and smiling. No one throws a drink – no one comments at all. We're all listening, and enjoying the performance. I make myself pay attention to the song.

By the time all the singers are gathering on the stage for the finale, I've watched at least twenty acts give their salute to Kane's image. And this time, I'm convinced they mean it. I'm sure it's a show of respect, and I feel as if they all understand – who he was, how he opened the way for other angels to show their wings. What he meant to me.

It feels safe. It feels familiar.

It feels like coming home.

Georgie drapes an arm round my shoulders and Fai takes my hand as Angelica calls on everyone to stand up and join in, and 'Angels' by Robbie Williams comes belting out of the speakers. The performers pass the microphone between them, and we all sing along as loudly as we can.

Chapter 30

"Where next?" Georgie slaps her hands onto the table. "I don't feel like going home. Let's find more beer!"

Sam smiles, and wraps his arm found Fai's shoulders.

"As fun as that sounds, I think we're ready to call it a night."

Fai reaches up and puts his hand over Sam's.

"My boyfriend has plans, ladies," he says, and plants a kiss on Sam's cheek.

Sam grins, standing up and returning the kiss. "I'm taking my angel home now".

Georgie spreads her hands in defeat.

"I can't compete with your boyfriend, Fai. I know when I'm beaten."

It's only when they walk away, hand in hand, that I realise I didn't ask Fai about the photo. I still don't know what was going on between him and the director at the recital.

Georgie presses a hand to her heart.

"They are so perfect," She breathes. "I told you there's nothing to worry about."

"You did." Her expression makes me laugh, and I watch as they walk away. Hands clasped, their matching golden wings shimmering as they move, they make a beautiful couple. "I think I believe you."

Sam turns back to us and waves a hand.

"Go!" He says, walking backwards through the crowd. "Drink! Enjoy yourselves!"

Georgie pushes her chair back, picks up her clutch bag and turns to me. "Coming?"

Jez is leaning against the wall of the alleyway where it joins the street. He's wearing his usual grey jacket and jeans, and there's a scowl on his face. One of the Guardian Angels is watching him.

My heart slams in my chest. It's been 170 hours.

"I wasn't expecting ..." I stutter. "What are you doing here?"

He shrugs. "I figured I'd find you with the angels." There's a hard edge to his voice, and he's not smiling.

Georgie takes my hand and leans in to whisper. "Is this OK?"

Jez gives her an unfriendly look and she laces her fingers through mine.

He turns to me. "Walk you home?"

His eyes are dark, lit with flecks of gold under the streetlights. They're beautiful, and I can feel myself falling.

I grip Georgie's fingers and make myself stand up straight. The cartoon wings tug against my shoulders. "That depends."

He raises an eyebrow. "On?"

"Are you going to tell me what happened the other night? On the roof?"

His folds his arms over his chest. His gaze never leaves mine.

"I could say the same to you. Are you going to tell me what happened at the theatre?" He pretends to think for a moment. "And on the way to the theatre. Oh – and every time before that when you didn't tell me who you were?"

"Jez ..." Georgie holds up a hand and steps towards him. "This is not—"

I pull her back. "It's OK," I say, keeping my voice calm. "It's time we talked about all this."

She stares at me. "It's not OK. *He's* not OK!"

Jez smirks. The Guardian Angel takes a step towards us and I wave him away.

"You're not walking home with him."

I look past her to Jez, lounging against the wall. I haven't seen him for a week. I haven't heard from him. I don't know where he's been, and I don't know what he wants to say to me.

"He wants answers, and so do I." I shrug. "This feels like a good time to get them."

"But—"

I tighten my fingers. "He's here, Georgie," I whisper. "He's come back, he's come to find me, and he wants to talk."

"Yes, but—"

I shake my head. "I think I want to talk. Before he disappears again."

"I'll come with you." It's not a question, or an offer. Over her shoulder I see Jez roll his eyes.

"No. Honestly. It's fine."

She nods, unlacing her fingers from mine.

"If you're sure?"

"I'm sure."

She takes her phone from her bag, and makes a show of taking it off silent.

"This is on," she says, waving it at me and making sure Jez can hear. "My stilettos are on call, if you need them."

I can't help laughing. "If I need a terrifying angelic defender, I promise I'll call you."

The rest of the journalism crowd push past us in the narrow alley.

"And that's my cue to take Patrick for a drink. The flat's all yours." She leans in close to my ear. "I know you want to find out what's under that awful jacket, and believe me, I don't want to be there when you do. Be safe, OK?" She gives me a quick grin and hurries after the journalists.

"Patrick? It's your lucky night. You're taking me out. Bubbly in a wine bar, or shall we slum it at the Student Union?"

I don't hear the answer. She's already dragging him away, and Jez is still watching me.

I can't look away.

"Shall we?" He says, pushing his hands into his pockets and giving the Guardian Angel a hard stare.

I take a slow breath. I have no idea whether this is a good idea. I don't know how this ends. Maybe Georgie is right – maybe I shouldn't trust him.

But I want answers, and so does he.

I straighten my wings, and start walking.

"So – where were you?"

He shrugs.

"Jez. You disappeared. No one has seen you for a week. Where were you?"

"Thinking," he says, eventually.

"Thinking ..." I wait for him to explain, but he keeps walking. "Thinking in your room? Thinking at home? Thinking on some desert island?" He barks a laugh. "Where do you go, to think? I feel as if this is something I should know about you."

He shrugs again. "It doesn't really matter, does it? I'm here now."

I stifle a scream. "Not the point, but yes. You're here. Are you going to tell me what happened?"

"I don't understand," he says, stopping in the street and holding out a hand to catch my arm.

I shrug him away. "What?"

"You're Melodie Abbott. You're famous. You're the subject of one of the most iconic photos in history. And I had to find out because one of your friends made a joke, and someone else Googled you."

"Jez ..."

He shakes his head. "I asked about your passion. I told you about mine. I thought you understood. Ambition, being better. I thought you got it."

I think back to our conversation at the Angel Club. To sketching through a lecture where everyone else was taking notes. The way Jez put all that into words.

"I get it."

"But no mention of your angel fascination? No reference to being there when Kane died. To being *that* girl, in *that* photo?"

I hold up a hand to stop him. I know he wants to understand me, to unwrap me, but I can't believe we're having this conversation. I can't believe I have to explain.

"That's not who I am, Jez. I'm Mel. I'm an artist and a painter and a friend. My life didn't stop at that moment, when the camera flashed and that one photographer got the shot of a lifetime." I make myself slow down. Take a breath. Stay calm. "That photo? That's not me. That's a picture of the worst moment of my life, and I am never allowed to forget it. Whatever happens, whatever I do, I'm still that girl, crying over a dying angel."

"So you dyed your hair and moved on?"

He wants me to argue. He wants me to deny it.

I stare at him. "Yes! That's exactly what I did!"

He shakes his head. "That was your moment of greatness."

"What?" I can't help snapping at him. I can't believe he doesn't understand.

"For a few hours, you had the attention of the entire world. The entire planet."

I nod. "I know." There's nothing else I can say.

He holds out his hands. "Do you know what I would give to have even a tiny part of that? For people to know who I am?"

He's still not getting it. He's not listening.

"It's not like that." He raises an eyebrow. "It's horrible, Jez. It's an invasion of privacy. It's completely out of my control, and I hate it."

He shrugs. "I'll have to take your word for that."

I feel like screaming. I can't believe anyone would want this.

"It's not glamorous. It's awful." I roll my eyes. "I get … flashbacks. Something sets me off, and I'm back there. Kane is dying, the cameras are flashing, the noise …" I can feel my panic rising, and I make myself take a slow breath.

"That's what happened." He looks at me, and his eyes are the colour of the sea at dawn. "On the way to the theatre. That's what happened."

For a moment I can't speak. My heart kicks against my ribcage. I nod, keeping my eyes on his. The grey is calming, his gaze slowing my pulse.

He swears under his breath. "Your friends knew. Why didn't you tell me?"

I focus on his eyes, amazed at the way my heart slows. The way the panic evaporates. I feel connected – with Jez, and with something else. Something vast and protective. I'm not swooning. I'm not tripping over my feet – but I'm not crashing back into the flashbulbs and noise.

I feel as if I'm balanced on a tightrope. As if his gaze is the only thing keeping me from falling, keeping me safe.

I take a breath. My hands are shaking. The scream of a siren in a neighbouring street makes my heart race again, and I know if I close my eyes I'll see the cameras. I'll see Kane. I keep my eyes fixed on his.

"What do you want from me, Jez?" My voice is a whisper. He's upset, and I can't see a way to make this OK.

He frowns, and looks away. I force myself to keep breathing.

"Your friend called you 'angel-sexual'. What was he talking about?"

"Faisal. His name is Faisal, and yes. He called me an angel-sexual."

Jez shrugs, and looks at me again. "Why?"

I can't help rolling my eyes.

"OK," I say. "Fine. I'll tell you. But this is important to me, so just listen."

He nods, and pushes his hands back into his pockets. "Listening," he says.

"Since I was five, I've been fascinated by angels." He raises an eyebrow, but waits for me to say more. "Well – mostly by Kane. I saw his billboard, in London. I was there, in the crowd."

"And you remember?"

I let out a breath. "How could I forget? It was ... beautiful. Big and brave and miraculous."

He smiles. "It changed the world."

"Right." I nod. "So I maybe developed a bit of a crush. A bit of an obsession."

"With angels?"

"With Kane."

He nods, as if this explains everything. As if I've just revealed the final piece of a jigsaw.

I close my eyes and make myself breathe. I'm going to have to tell him everything.

"So I may have hundreds of photos of Kane on my bedroom wall. At home," I say quickly. "Not here."

"Hundreds?" He says, and there's a smile playing over his lips.

"Mmmm." I can feel my face burning.

"The Angel Exhibition." He tilts his head, looking into my eyes. "Why were you there?"

"I was my mother's plus-one. She painted Kane, and she invited me to the opening night."

"And Kane was ... admiring his painting?"

I nod, my cheeks glowing. "Oh, yes. And talking to people. And being charming."

"Of course he was."

"And Sam and Fai were there, and they saw me ..." I cover my eyes. This is embarrassing. "They saw me swoon."

He laughs. "Swoon? Like, fainting?"

"Sam had to catch me."

He nods. "OK," he says. "Wow."

"Not a full faint," I say, quickly. "More of a temporary inability to use my feet."

"So you were head-over-heels in love with Kane," he says, still smiling. I nod. "Well – I guess we've established that you're a Kane-sexual."

I cover my eyes again. "Not exactly."

"Oh?" His voice is gentle. It's as if he's waiting for me to confess. To show him who I am.

I have to tell him. This is my chance to make things right.

"The swooning …" My voice fails. My skin feels like fire under my fingers. "It's … it's an angel thing."

"What do you mean?"

I keep my hands pressed against my face. I can't look at him. "It's not just Kane. It's any angel."

There's a long pause. I think my heart might break out of my chest.

"Any angel? *Every* angel?"

I nod. "As far as I know."

"So what happens?" He asks, quietly.

I shrug, and drop my hands. I make myself look at him.

"I … I stop feeling the floor. I forget how to stand up. I forget to breathe. I'm floating and I can't …" I shrug again. "I can't explain it. I just … swoon."

"Is it a good feeling?" His smile has gone, and he's not frowning or smirking. He's not playing games. He's asking, and he's listening.

"Yes," I say, giving him his answer. "It's a wonderful feeling."

He takes a quick breath, his grey eyes reflecting the golden streetlights.

"Do you feel that when you look at me?"

My breath catches. Did he just tell me he's an angel?

My heart is a drum.

Is this real? Is he testing me? Is he afraid he won't live up to my feelings for Kane?

There's a bubble expanding in my chest. I feel as if I'm floating.

"Yes," I whisper, my voice failing.

He steps towards me, and I can feel the pavement tilting as my eyes meet his. He takes my hands and steadies me, his gaze like storm clouds and thunder. Our breath mingles in the cold air.

"And do you feel it now?" He asks, gently. His fingers grip mine.

"Yes."

He drops one hand, and reaches up to cradle my face. I lean in to his touch. I can't feel the ground under my feet.

"May I kiss you, Melodie Abbott?"

I have to remember to breathe.

"Yes."

And he does.

I want this. I want him. I want the feeling when he looks into my eyes. The way his gaze calmed my body as it tried to throw me back to cameras and feathers and blood. I want him to want me. I want him to understand me.

I need to find out. I need to know who he is.

I take his hand, and start walking home.

Chapter 31

He's here. Jez is here, in my room.

He seems nervous as I close the door behind us and turn the lock as quietly as I can. He's standing in the middle of the space, hands in his pockets, shoulders hunched.

I have no idea what he's thinking.

My heart is pounding, and my hands are shaking as I shrug out of the angel wings and place my bag carefully on my desk.

Jez is here.

He hasn't apologised. He hasn't explained.

And right now, I don't care about any of that.

When I turn back to him, his eyes are on me. He takes his hands from his pockets and stands up straight, losing the slouch. His gaze never leaves my face.

I step towards him, and lift my hand to his cheek. I want nothing more than to kiss him. To lose myself in his eyes.

He's trembling. Tense, like a drawn bowstring, waiting for release.

"Jez," I say, gently, my hand cupping his cheek.

And it's like a dam breaking. The arrow, flying from the bow. He pulls me to him, one hand steady against my back and the other against my neck, and this kiss is urgent, breathless. Bruising.

I kiss him back, hard, reaching under his jacket to pull him closer, and he shudders at the touch of my hands.

When we break apart, I'm gasping for air, and his arms are locked around me. He buries his head in my hair.

"I thought I'd lost you," he breathes.

I should be talking. I should be asking him what happened, but this isn't the time for words.

There's pain in his eyes when he pulls away. Hurt. Desire.

"I didn't mean ..."

I shake my head, and tighten my arms around his waist.

"I don't care."

I kiss him again, my heart racing against his. I can't think. I can't speak. There is nothing in the world outside this kiss.

My hands snake up his back, and there's a roughness under his shirt.

I can't feel his skin through the fabric. I can't feel the muscles of his back.

I can't catch my breath.

He moves against me, breaking the kiss and arching his back as my hands find his shoulders, and the shape of something hidden.

Something bound.

"Jez," I whisper, my fingertips playing over thin cotton. He makes a soft sound in his throat, his eyes closed, then leans to press his forehead against mine.

"Jez," I say again, and this feels like the most intimate moment of my life. I'm shaking as I trace my fingers down his spine. I need to know. I need to find out. "Will you show me your wings?"

He makes a sound like a sob, and drops his head to my shoulder. His arms are strong against my back, but I can feel him shaking.

"How did you ...?" His voice sounds broken.

"It doesn't matter."

He takes a long, trembling breath and lifts his head to look at me.

"I don't know if I can do this," he says, and I think my heart might shatter.

His arms surround me. He holds me close, as if I might disappear. His gaze is intense.

"I don't understand."

"I've never ..." He takes a moment to breathe. "I was taught to be ashamed."

I push away from him, my fingers gripping his arms. His hands find my waist.

"You ... what?"

"My wings. I was taught to hide them."

My fingers are creasing his jacket, bruising his arms, but I can't let go. I think I might fall.

I think we'll both fall.

"Why? Who ...?" I can feel tears in my eyes. I can't make sense of his words.

"My mother," he whispers, blinking away his own tears. "She ... she used to bind them. Keep them out of sight."

I lift a hand to his face, and he presses his cheek against my palm.

"I didn't think it would be this hard." He shakes his head. "I'm sorry."

I take his face in both hands and kiss him, and this time it's gentle. Tender.

Real.

I step back.

"Show me."

He nods, his eyes on mine, his voice fractured.

"You won't judge me, Melodie Abbott?"

I want to speak. I want to reassure him, but all I can do is kiss him again. Nothing I can say matters.

He nods as I step away, and begins to slip his jacket from his shoulders. I step forward to help, but he shakes his head. His jacket falls, and I make myself meet his gaze. His eyes, storm-grey, fixed on mine.

He moves his hands to his shirt, and takes a breath. His fingers shake as he undoes his buttons, his eyes searching mine for a reaction. He tugs his shirt from his belt, and that's when he looks away.

"Jez ..." I step up to him, cradling his face in one hand. "I'm here."

He breathes, slowly, and guides my hands to his shoulders.

"Can I take off your shirt?" It's hardly a whisper, but he nods, waiting.

I slide my hands under the fabric, and gently push it back, over his shoulders and down his arms. My fingers brush the muscles, taut under his skin, and he shivers as I press the cuffs over his hands. The shirt drops, and I see his bindings for the first time.

They're tight, like skin-tone bandages. Over his shoulders, under his arms. I can see where the edges have pressed into his skin. Years and years of shame, marking his chest and back. I run my fingers over the rough surface and his shoulders shake under my touch.

"How do I ...?"

He shakes his head. "Let me."

Slowly, carefully, he drags the bindings across his skin, shrugging his shoulders one at a time as he slips the bandages back. He reaches behind his back and tugs, and the harness drops behind him.

"OK?" I ask, as he rolls his shoulders. His eyes are closed, and he takes one, two, deep breaths.

He takes my hands in his.

"Don't judge me," he says, and releases his wings.

For a moment I forget how to breathe.

His wings unfold, reaching up and spreading behind him like a flower unfurling in the sun. There's a rustling, like a bird in flight as he shakes the feathers and stretches the delicate bones and muscles. His eyes are closed as he moves his neck and shoulders, standing tall, reaching his wings out towards the walls of my narrow room.

He is beautiful.

His wings, like his eyes, are a hundred shades of grey. They rise like thunder clouds from his back, and there's an iridescence on the feathers that makes them gleam in the light as they move, flashing rainbows through the storm.

There's nothing I can say that will tell him how I feel. I trace one hand over his chest, up to his neck, and run the other through his hair, pulling him into another deep kiss. He stands, unmoving for a moment, then wraps his arms around me and returns the caress.

My heart is drumming as he pulls me close.

Georgie was right. Jez is an angel. An abused, bound, hidden angel.

And his wings are utterly gorgeous.

"Can I ... touch them?"

I reach up, out of his embrace, out of my first kiss with a half-naked angel, and he nods.

"Be gentle," he says, smiling.

I realise I'm smiling, too. I couldn't stop if I wanted to.

He slides his arms from my back, releasing me, and I stretch out my hand. Over his shoulder, and up to the grey, rainbow-streaked wings.

The feathers are soft under my fingertips. Warm. They twitch and shiver as I stroke my hand softly across them. He takes a sharp breath as I run my hand lower, following the feathers to the edge of the wing.

"Sorry," I breathe, pulling my hand away, but he shakes his head.

"You didn't hurt me."

"Can I touch them again?"

He nods, and I reach out, running my hand so gently along the top of his wing, down to where it joins his shoulder blade.

His entire body shakes against mine as I stroke the tiny, down-like feathers against the skin of his back.

When I kiss him again, I realise his cheeks are wet with tears.

My stomach tenses. I don't want to hurt him.

"What did I do?"

He shakes his head, holding me close. It's a long time before he speaks.

"You were kind," he says, eventually. "You understand."

I don't know how long we stand, wrapped in each other's arms in the middle of my room. Jez clings to me, shivering when I run my fingers across his back. I can feel the imprints of the harness where it cut into his skin, the rough dimpling of the binding written on his body, and I don't know what to say to him. I can't imagine teaching someone – teaching a *child* – that wings like his are shameful. Ugly. Fit only to be hidden and bound and kept secret from the world.

I think about Kane. His golden feathers, uncovered and unfurled on his billboard. The outfits he wore, slashed and tailored to show off his shining wings. The light, scattering across the walls of my mother's studio as he moved.

Jez deserves all of that. He deserves tailored jackets and famous paintings. He deserves admiration.

He deserves to be himself.

"How could she, Jez? How could she hide your wings away?"

His body stiffens in my arms and he shrugs, gently.

"She couldn't understand," he says, his voice quiet. "She wasn't …" He takes a shuddering breath.

"She wasn't an angel?"

"Isn't." He corrects himself. "Isn't an angel."

"So what? What does that have to do with … *anything*?"

He straightens, pulling out of our embrace.

"I thought you'd understand," he says, disbelief in his voice. "I'm a random. My mother wasn't expecting an angel. My father … my father *left* when I was born." He closes his eyes and takes a breath. "I thought you'd understand."

I'm lost. I'm holding an angel in my arms. I should be happy, but he's pulling away.

I don't know what's happening. Something doesn't make sense. There's a look of pain on his face.

I'm starting to panic, colour rising in my skin.

He takes my hands, his storm-grey eyes searching my face.

"Melodie," he whispers, and my heart jumps in my chest. "I've shown you mine." He drops my hands and runs his fingers over my shoulders. "Will you show me yours?"

Chapter 32

"Show you ... what?"

I know the answer. I know what he's going to say, but it doesn't make sense.

His hands pause at the tops of my arms, and he touches my shoulders again. I realise I'm still wearing my jacket. He's half naked, his beautiful, impossible wings spread out behind him, and I'm still dressed for going out.

I'm wearing a jacket, and he can't tell that I don't have wings.

He can't tell that I don't have anything to hide.

He slips his hands down my arms, and I shiver at the touch. He takes both my hands in his.

"Show me your wings, Melodie Abbott," he says, his voice low and gentle, and I feel as if the world has split in two.

I feel as if I'm watching this conversation from a distance. From the sky, or through a window.

I feel as if I've lied, or tricked him. As if I've made this happen.

I feel as if I'm tumbling through the air. As if I'm falling, and screaming, and out of control.

I don't understand.

"Mel?" he says, and his fingers tighten against mine.

I'm shaking my head. I'm stepping back, but he won't let go of my hands. All I can hear is my panicked heartbeat, drowning out the small sounds of his wings, the loud rasp of my breathing.

He won't let go of my hands.

"No," I hear myself say. "No … no …"

The look on his face is deep, unfathomable hurt. He's shaking his head. Lifting his wings like some terrible biblical revenge.

I'm scared, and I'm hurting, and his hands grip my fingers.

The storm in his eyes is real.

I'm shaking. I'm gasping for breath.

Rainbows flash across his feathers as he holds me still, and it takes everything I have to snatch my hands away and step backwards. To pull myself to safety.

"I …" My voice cracks and I have to start again. He stares at me, anger and hurt on his face, and I don't know what's going to happen. I don't know what he's going to do to me.

I choke on my words. I make myself shout. I plant my feet and stand tall, and I tell him.

"I don't have wings, Jez. I don't have wings."

He steps back. He tips his head as if I've slapped him. He stares at me, a look of horror dawning on his face. He opens his mouth to say something, then shakes his head as if he's shaking his thoughts loose.

"What?"

He sounds angry and confused and broken and … I don't know what else. I wrap my arms across my chest, making myself small. Making myself safe. There are tears on my cheeks and my throat feels as if I've swallowed broken glass.

"I'm so sorry, Jez," I say, hugging my arms and stepping further away. "I'm sorry."

"But at the Angel club ... you ..." He stops and takes a breath. "That song ..." His eyes are closed, shut tight against the truth. "You cried. You cried about not showing your wings."

"I cried about not *having* wings, Jez. I cried because of Kane, and all the people who couldn't be themselves. I cried for angels like you, and people like me. I wanted more."

He watches me, and I can see him reasoning this out. Calculating our next moves. I feel as if I'm under his microscope again, but this time we're alone. This time he's undressed and unbound, and he's waiting for me to share the same secret – but I have no secret to share. I can't give him what he wants.

He nods, eventually. Crosses his arms over his chest in a mirror of my body.

"I screwed that one up, didn't I?" He says, but he's not smiling. It's not like the Angel Club – that first night when I threw a drink at him and he laughed. He made a joke out of his mistake.

He's not joking now.

"Jez," I say, stepping towards him. "You're ..." I glance at his wings. At the rainbows playing across every feather. "You're beautiful."

His mouth twists in a sneer and his wings rustle as he settles them against his shoulders.

"I can't accept that," he whispers. "I can't believe that from someone like you."

"Someone like—"

"A *human*." He spits the word at me. "A normal, wingless, basic, unremarkable *person*."

I gasp as if he's hit me.

"Jez." I reach out a hand towards him, but he doesn't respond. "Your wings – they're stunning." I ignore his humourless laugh. "You shouldn't be hiding them. You shouldn't be binding them and hurting yourself." I stare at him. "You're an *angel*, Jez! You're … amazing."

"And what would you know about that, Melodie Abbott? Just because a famous angel died in front of you. Just because the whole world thinks of you and Kane together in that terrible photo. What would you know about wings?"

I shake my head, tears spilling down my cheeks.

"*What would you know about wings*?" This time, he shouts his question at me, his wings raised and his fists clenched.

"Nothing," I whisper. "Nothing. I'm sorry."

He stares at me, his fists shaking, and I make myself look back at him. He's hurting, and he's angry, and I can't tell how much of that is because of me, and how much is about his mother, and his father's rejection, and I realise that it doesn't matter.

"You should go," I say, forcing my voice to stay calm.

He takes a deep breath, then reaches down to pick up his clothes. I have my first glimpse of his back, and the wings growing from his shoulders. There are muscles, under the harness-scarred skin, flexing as he moves, keeping his wings steady.

He really is beautiful. I wish I could convince him of that.

He drags the harness over his shoulders, not bothering to fold his wings. It pulls them close to his back, but the feathers are visible below his waist. He throws his shirt on, covering the binding, and then his jacket, without buttoning his shirt.

"I should have known," he says. "I should have guessed."

And he turns, unlocks my door, and walks out.

When I step into the corridor behind him, there's a single storm-grey feather on the floor, rainbows playing across it in the light from my doorway. The front door slams as he leaves the flat, and I bend to pick up the feather.

It feels soft and warm in my hands.

I dream of Jez. Of what might have happened. Of exploring his body as he explores mine. Of being sheltered and protected, wrapped in his beautiful wings.

But when I wake in tears, I'm alone, and all I can think about is Kane. His face, repeated over and over on my bedroom wall at home. His confidence. His smile. The way he shared himself with everyone, and let everyone see who he was.

Golden feathers, falling around me.
His blood on my hands.

Chapter 33

It's dark, and I can't tell what time it is. I brush away tears and reach for my phone, and find a screen full of missed calls and messages. Georgie, Sam, Georgie again ... I scroll through them, and choose one from Sam to open.

Where are you? I need you, Mel.

I sit up, dragging myself awake, and scroll back to the top of the list.

I know you're busy with lover boy, but call me. OK?

I feel as if someone has plunged me into Arctic water. My breath freezes. If Georgie is interrupting what she thinks is my night with Jez, if Sam is trying to track me down ... what's happening?

I scroll again, but there are no messages from Fai, and none from Jez.

Fai.

I remember the siren, as I stood on the street with Jez. Before ...

... before we came back here.

The memory of his wings crashes through my slowly waking mind. The way he looked at me. His raw anger. The way he left.

And I'm crying. Terrifying sobs that shake my body. I feel sick. I feel as if I'm drowning.

I don't know how I was so calm, after he walked out. How I got myself into pyjamas. Washed off my makeup. Brushed my hair. Cleaned my teeth.

How I slept.

It all feels robotic, as if I stopped feeling anything when he realised I didn't have wings. When I realised I couldn't be who he needs me to be. I remember feeling empty, as if I had expected it to end this way. I remember feeling nothing. Nothing at all.

And now I'm hurting. Burning and freezing and choking, gripping the duvet in my fists as the hot tears bleed over my skin.

What would you know about wings?

I can hear his voice – the pain and anger and betrayal.

I screwed that one up, didn't I?

I can feel our connection splintering. Breaking. Shattering like glass.

I can't believe that from someone like you.

I draw my knees up to my chest and curl into myself, my fingers snarled in my hair, tugging at my scalp.

Someone like you.

Georgie was right. Sam was right.

I have to make myself breathe.

Fai. I have to find out about Fai.

My hands are shaking as I pick up my phone. My face is wet with tears, and my eyes are stinging. Everything hurts. My throat is raw and I feel as if someone is hammering inside my skull.

It's half past four. The last message was an hour ago. I close my eyes and count slowly to ten, my breath catching as I try to focus.

I scroll to one of Georgie's missed calls, and call her back.

She answers after two rings.

"Mel—"

"What's happened?" My voice is broken. Cracked. It hurts to speak.

I want her to say it's nothing. I want her to laugh, and tell me to go back to sleep. That she's checking on me and Jez.

"Are you decent?" She says, and she sounds exhausted. "Can you get here?"

I haven't read all the messages. I don't know what she's talking about. My stomach knots.

"Where's here? What's happening?"

I hear her take a breath.

"It's Fai. He's been ... he's in hospital. King's – Emergency Department. Can you get here?"

There's an iceberg in my chest. Sharp slivers of ice in my throat. I can't speak.

"Mel?"

I untangle myself from the duvet and push myself to my feet.

"On my way."

It takes me five minutes to throw cold water on my face, tug my hair into a pony tail and pull underwear, jeans and a jumper from my laundry pile. Socks and shoes take longer, and I'm squinting in the bright light as I try to find shoes I can run in. I grab my coat, and on a whim I head to Georgie's room and throw a pair of jeans and a shirt and jacket into a bag. If she hasn't been back here, she'll be sitting in a hospital waiting room in her silver catsuit and feathered wings. I remember her stilettos, and add socks and trainers to the bundle.

And then I'm running. Down the stairs, across the grass, along the pavement. It's cold, and every breath feels like knives in my chest.

There are grey figures, curled and hunched in doorways. A drunk couple holding each other up as they weave across the pavement. A Night Bus, pale faces staring from the brightly lit windows. Someone shouts as I run past, but I don't stop.

Jez is forgotten. I have to get to my friends.

The Emergency Department is all white lights and bright surfaces. It's Saturday night, so the waiting area is full of people who drank too much and fell over or got into fights. There's a constant buzz of voices, and a line of ambulances outside.

Georgie is slumped in the corner, her silver boots beside her on the floor and her wings tucked over the back of her chair. Sam sits next to her, his head in his hands.

"Mel!" She stands up slowly, her wings dragging the chair forward. She gives me a tight hug, her hair spilling over my shoulder.

"What happened?" I hold her hands as she steps back.

"Idiots. They were waiting."

"The guys from last time?"

She nods. "They couldn't get near the club – not with the angel security. Too chicken to take on big scary guys with wings."

"So?"

"So they waited round the corner for the audience to leave."

I glance at Sam. He hasn't moved, and I realise his knuckles are bandaged. I can see the edge of a dressing on his forehead. His jacket and shirt are torn.

"How did they overpower Fai and Sam?" I think about the boys stepping in when the idiots attacked Georgie. Fai's an athlete – a dance ninja, and Sam can defend himself.

"There were more of them. A whole gang, Sam said."

My stomach twists. I feel sick. A gang of idiots, waiting for my friends. Beating them up, because they wore wings on their jackets.

Gorgeous, beautiful, golden wings.

Georgie grips my fingers as I close my eyes. I'm fighting the vision of golden feathers falling around me. Cameras flashing. The roar of an engine, too fast and too close. The shouts of protesters in the crowd.

"Breathe," she says. "Breathe, Mel. I've got you."

Chapter 34

I concentrate on the sound of Georgie's voice, and take a slow breath. My pulse steadies. I open my eyes.

"OK?" She's watching my face, still holding my hands. I nod.

And remember why I'm here. Sam. Fai. The clothes.

"I brought you something to wear," I say, slipping the bag from my shoulder and pushing it into her arms.

A smile dawns across her face. She looks as if I've handed her the most precious thing in the world.

She wraps me in another tight hug, the bag dangling from her fingers as she pulls away.

"You're an angel, Mel."

I stare at her, and I feel as if I've forgotten how to speak. It's such a ridiculous thing to say, after what happened tonight. After Jez and feathers and shouting.

My giggle catches me by surprise, and so do the tears.

I shake my head. "No," I whisper, and for the first time I feel the absence of wings as a wound. Flashes of pain across my back. "No, I'm not."

"Mel?" She's looking at me, her smile fading. "What—?"

"It doesn't matter." I swipe tears from my face with the back of my hand.

"But—"

"Honestly." I make myself smile. "You're looking pretty angelic yourself. Go and get changed. I'll sit with Sam."

She hesitates, watching me, then nods. "Thank you," she says, her feathers rustling as she turns away.

I push Georgie's chair back against the wall. Sam finally looks up when I sit down next to him, his face grey and bruised and swollen. The dressing covers most of his forehead and one eyebrow. He has a split lip, and I think his nose is broken. I can see grazes on his shoulder through the tear in his jacket.

My fingers curl into fists. I can feel anger boiling my stomach.

Seeing him like this is like looking in a mirror and finding his injuries on myself. His face is so familiar, and so damaged. The shock takes my breath away.

I can't believe anyone would do this.

"You came," he says, his voice like sandpaper.

I give him a quick smile. "Sorry I'm late. I left my phone on silent. Missed all your messages. I came as soon as I could."

He nods. I wonder whether he knows I was with Jez.

I wonder whether he cares.

"What happened, Sam? How's Fai?"

He takes a long breath and lets it out slowly.

"Big gang of them. Anti-angel guys. They waited for us – for the first people to leave the club." He takes another breath. "Cornered us. And then they all started kicking and punching and I tried to save him, Mel. I tried to get them off him, but …"

"Hey." I put a hand on his arm. "You didn't do this. This isn't your fault."

"I couldn't stop them."

He sounds empty. Defeated.

"And Fai?" My voice almost fails. I'm not sure I want to hear the answer.

He shuts his eyes tight and covers his face with his hands.

"Broken arm. Needs pins. Face like mine."

I move my hand to his shoulder. "I'm so sorry."

He shakes his head. "It's worse than that. They're checking him for internal bleeding, and …." He snatches a sharp breath, "… they're trying to work out whether his ankle is broken."

I think about Fai, star of the dance recital. His strength and grace and skill on stage. My stomach twists.

"That could mean the end of—"

"Dancing. Yeah." Sam drags a hand across his eyes, brushing away tears.

"Shit."

There's rage, catching fire in my chest. I want to hurt the people who did this.

"Why you two?" I sit back and look at Sam's jacket. The back is torn and scuffed, and most of the sequins are missing. "There were plenty of people there with more extravagant wings. There were actual angels.

And last time they picked on Georgie and her proper feathers. So why you?"

He shrugs. "We were the first people who walked into their trap. We were dressed as angels. We were two men holding hands. I'm black and he looks Middle Eastern." Another shrug. "Take your pick."

I feel as if he's thrown a punch. I have to catch my breath. Angelism, homophobia, racism, and being in the wrong place at the wrong time, and Fai may lose everything he's worked for.

I feel as if my blood is boiling.

"How dare they? How dare they decide that you guys deserve this?"

Sam rests his elbows on his knees and stares at the floor, tears shining on his cheeks. His voice is quiet, but edged with steel. "No one deserves this, Mel. No one."

I wrap my arms round his shoulders and he leans into me. Sam-and-Mel in another hospital waiting room, on another horrible day. I close my eyes and pretend we're somewhere else. Somewhere safe.

Somewhere far away.

"They say we can see him."

Georgie stands over us, her catsuit exchanged for skinny jeans and a brightly coloured floral shirt. She's holding the back brace of her costume, and the wings sit over her arm like a shield. She looks majestic, like an angelic superhero trying out a new look.

"Now?" Sam pushes himself out of the chair.

"Fai's dad says it's OK."

I hold my hand out for Georgie's bag, and carefully stuff her boots inside. She smiles when I tuck it over my shoulder.

"Thank you," she says, and lifts her wings. "These are heavy enough, without extra baggage."

Sam snorts. "If I didn't know you better I'd think that was some kind of metaphor." He doesn't smile, and Georgie touches his shoulder gently as he walks past her towards the reception desk.

"You got him talking, then?" She keeps her voice quiet while Sam strides ahead of us.

I nod. "I think he was waiting for me. I know you both left me messages. I'm sorry it took so long to find them."

"Right." She nudges my elbow. "Jez. Do I want to know?'""

I find myself crossing my arms over my chest, shrinking into myself, trying not to think about what happened.

I shake my head. "Can we not talk about it?"

She raises an eyebrow, but keeps walking. "We can not talk about it *now*, but sometime you're going to tell me exactly how much I need to hurt him."

I think about her stilettos in the bag. About Sam, and how much Fai's injuries are hurting him.

No one deserves this, Mel. No one.

I shrug. "I think it's more complicated than that."

She clears her throat. "Did he upset you? Did he mess you around? Did he do something weird and bottle out on you?"

I can feel my face turning scarlet. "OK, yes, but—"

She rolls her eyes. "Oh, enough with the 'yes, but', Mel! He keeps hurting you, and he's going to keep on hurting you. Walk away. Leave him to play whatever games he wants to on his own."

In front of us Sam gives our names to a nurse, and he waves us to follow. We have to hurry to keep up with Sam and his escort as we walk down a noisy corridor lined with curtained cubicles and busy medical staff.

I think about the look on Jez's face when I told him I didn't have wings.

I need to tell Georgie. This feels like a confession, but I need her to understand.

"I think ..." I feel as if there's a pebble in my throat. I can barely whisper. "I think I hurt him first."

Georgie glares at me, eyes narrowed.

"Good," she says, eventually. "Good for you."

Chapter 35

Fai looks a lot worse than Sam, and I have to close my eyes and take a breath before I step into his room. This feels too much like the night we waited together for news of my mother's injuries. The dark sky outside the window, the disinfected hospital smell. Bright lights, humming machines.

I feel disconnected. Outside time. Sleeplessness and hurt and anger catching up with me as I watch Sam cross to Fai's bed.

Fai wears a hospital gown, his right arm and right ankle bandaged and immobilised in plastic emergency splints. His face is so swollen he can hardly open his eyes.

There's a painkiller drip in his left arm, and I can see bruises and dressings across his exposed skin.

His dad sits in a chair next to the bed, and gives us a tight smile.

"Thank you for coming," he says, and he sounds as if he's been awake for days.

Sam strokes Fai's hair, then leans down and rests his head on Fai's shoulder. Fai stirs, and whispers something, and Sam's shoulders shake with sobs, his fingers gripping the front of Fai's hospital gown.

I drop the bag by the door, and Georgie props her wings carefully against the wall.

"Is there anything we can get for you, Mr Khalid?"

Fai's dad gives her a smile and shakes his head. "That's kind," he says. "But no, thank you." And he turns back to Fai and Sam.

I can't believe how much damage the attackers have done to my friends. How quickly everything turned from fun and drinks and sequined wings to violence and hate and a hospital bed. They're bleeding and broken, just because they dressed as angels.

It's the same hate that killed Kane. That broke Mila's wings.

And it's pointless. They weren't harming the men who threw the kicks and punches. They were just being themselves, and together, and proud, and the idiots who hurt them chose to take offence. Chose to take their hate out on two young men walking home together.

I want to scream. I want to cry. I want to find those men and make them understand what they've done.

"Have they spoken to the police?"

I'm surprised by my own question, but Fai's dad looks up and nods.

"They came by earlier. Sam gave a statement. Fai told them what he could, but he was ..." A look of anguish crosses his face. "... he was in too much pain."

My stomach turns to ice at the thought of my friend's broken bones. The bruises on his face.

"I'm so sorry," I say, and he nods. "Did they find the people responsible?"

"Not yet. They said they'd come back in the morning and update us."

I check my phone. It's nearly six, so they shouldn't have long to wait.

Georgie touches my elbow. "We should give them some time together," she whispers. "There are vending machines at the end of the corridor. I have a sudden need for crisps and chocolate, and I know you do, too."

I open my mouth to protest. I don't want to leave Fai and Sam, but she digs her fingers in and steers me towards the door.

"Are you OK?" she asks when we're half way down the hallway. "I was worried. You looked ... you know. Wobbly."

I shrug. "I'm not flashing back, if that's what you mean." I glance around at the bright lights and polished floors. "Not yet."

"OK," she says. "Good."

I take a breath and tighten my fists. "I'm really, really angry."

She nods, still walking. "Yeah," she says quietly. "Me too."

"Fai might not be able to dance again."

She looks up. "Shit. Sam said that?"

"He didn't tell you?"

"I could barely get him to talk. He called me when he couldn't get hold of you, and by the time I got here Fai was being treated, and Sam was sitting in the waiting room, bleeding, with a dressing pressed against his head. They took him off and patched him up, and he's been texting you and waiting to see Fai ever since."

She glances at me. "You know he has stitches under that dressing? On his forehead?"

I shake my head.

"He'll have a scar." She stabs a finger at her head. "Right there on his face. He wants to act. He wants to be on stage and screen, and his gorgeous face will have a scar."

I can't breathe. First Fai, and now Sam.

I've seen Sam's casting calls, and the actors he'll be up against. He's been checking out auditions and agencies since we were ten. He had a good chance, before. He can act, he can sing, and Georgie's right – he's gorgeous. He's the perfect model for my portraits, and I know he wants to be in the spotlight.

But now?

I feel hollowed out. I feel as if I'm drifting in the dark.

I stumble, and I'm on my knees in the corridor, Georgie's arms round my shoulders. My face is a river of silent tears.

"Come on, Mel," she whispers. "We need to be the strong ones. We need to be here for the boys."

I nod, and wipe my face with my hands, but the tears keep coming.

"Come on," she says again, taking my hand and pulling me to my feet. "Let's find somewhere to sit."

There's a small seating area next to the vending machines, and Georgie guides me to a chair.

"Wait here," she says, and pulls a wallet from her pocket.

I lean back, resting my head against the wall. I'm cold and uncomfortable, but I'm so tired I feel as if I could sleep forever.

The last twelve hours have been ... unexpected. Disastrous. Painful. I've lost Jez. Fai might have lost everything. Sam will always have a scar.

I can feel rage building again in my chest. Fear for my friends, and what this means for them.

And an empty space, where Jez should be.

I can't stop the tears.

Georgie kicks my foot, then drops a pile of crisp packets and chocolate bars into my lap.

"Here you go," she says, holding out a disposable cup. "You look like a girl who could use a hot chocolate." She pulls a handful of napkins from her pocket. "And something for all this." She points at my face.

I sit up and take the drink and the napkins. She sits down next to me, her hands wrapped round her own cup. From the colour, I'm guessing it's very black coffee. She reaches over and pulls a bar of dark chocolate from the pile on my knees.

"Careful," I say. "That's a caffeine overdose. You'll be bouncing off the walls."

She grins. "No such thing. This is my sleep replacement therapy. Turns out it's hard work, sitting around being angelic all night."

I can't help smiling at that.

"Thanks," I say. "For being here for Sam when I ..." I close my eyes, blocking out the last few hours. "When I wasn't answering the phone."

"Mmmm." She sips her coffee and gives me a long look. "About that. Jez, weirdness, disaster – care to elaborate?"

I shrug. I'm going to have to tell her sometime. "Short version?"

"Go on ..."

I wonder whether my voice will work. I wonder whether I can speak at all. But when I think about Jez, I realise I'm feeling numb. Empty.

I feel as if last night happened to someone else. As if I'm telling a ridiculous story – a fiction that has nothing to do with me.

I think about how to explain. How to make Georgie understand.

"So." I take a breath. "Turns out, he is an angel."

"Ha! I knew it." She nudges my shoulder. "What's he like? What are his wings like? Oh my god, I can't imagine Jez Priestly with wings. I bet they're dull and brown and boring."

I blink away a vision of rainbows, flashing across his stormcloud feathers. My chest feels tight, and I make myself take slow breaths. I'm not ready to tell her everything.

"Short version, remember?"

"Yes. Sorry." She waves a hand. "Continue."

"That's the good news. The bad news ..." My voice cracks, and I have to clear my throat. "He thought I was an angel, too."

"Oh." Georgie shakes her head. "Oh, no."

"Oh yes. And when I wasn't ..." I shrug. "Game over, I guess."

"So – what? He dumped you? He left?" She grips my arm with her fingertips. "What happened?"

I take another breath, and I can feel the tears returning. "He said some really mean things. Really, truly awful. And then he left."

She slumps back in her chair. "Wow."

"Yeah."

"I'm sorry, Mel. I know you liked him." She takes a sip of coffee. "I mean, god alone knows why, but I know you wanted things to work out between you."

I nod, and try my hot chocolate. It's watery and too sweet, but it's warm. I can feel it glowing in my stomach.

"Hold on," She says, gesturing with her cup. "You actually saw his wings." I nod. "So one of you was getting naked."

I roll my eyes. I thought this conversation was over. "Georgie ..."

"So he's – what? Half-dressed? Full-on birthday suit? Come on – fill me in here."

She's not going to stop asking.

"Fine," I say, trying not to think about it. "He's topless. I'm still wearing my jacket."

"OK," she says, slowly. "So there must have been kissing. Some hands-on action."

I want to walk away. I want to finish the story. I want to talk about something else.

"Yes – and before you ask, yes, it was hot. And then he asked to see my wings, and he was sure I was lying when I said I wasn't ... I didn't ..." There are tears pricking my eyes again. "He got angry. He said some stuff." I shrug. "He left."

"That's it? He just ... wanted an angel?"

I make myself take a calming breath. "It's more complicated than that, but this is the short version, Georgie." She makes a face, but stops talking. "And anyway – I wanted the same thing. I can't judge him for that."

She laughs. "You can judge him for literally everything else, though."

I take another sip of my drink, and feel the warmth spreading through my body.

"One day," I say, leaning back against the wall. "For now it just hurts."

She rests her head on my shoulder.

"I know," she says. "I'm sorry."

The chime of a text message sends us both scrambling for our phones. There's nothing on my screen, and I realise the sound came from further down the hallway.

There's a young man in loose navy sweatpants and a hoodie standing next to the vending machine, checking a map of the hospital on the wall. He glances at his phone, and then back at the map. I'm just realising that there's something familiar about him when Georgie jumps up from her seat.

"Kyle?"

He jumps, and turns to us.

"You're that photographer," he says, shaking his head in confusion. "What are you doing here?"

"I could ask you the same thing."

And now I see it. This is the man from Georgie's photo. The man with his hand on Fai's neck, their foreheads pressed together.

He shrugs. "Looking for Faisal," he says, and shows us his phone. "I got a text."

I feel as if he's punched me. I'm out of my seat, scattering the remains of our vending-machine breakfast on the floor.

"No." I'm shouting, and walking towards him. I don't know what I'm going to do, but I'm not letting him barge in on Fai and Sam. I can feel hot tears on my cheeks, and Kyle is staring at me as if I've just appeared from nowhere.

He steps back, pushing his phone behind his back and holding out a hand to stop me.

"Wait!" He sounds panicked. "I'm just ... I want to see Faisal."

I step right up to Kyle. He's taller than me, but he looks terrified.

"Listen," I say, trying to keep my voice calm. "Fai is my friend. He's hurt. He's really hurt. And he's with his dad and his boyfriend right now." I take a breath, and Kyle takes another step back. "I have had the shittiest day. So has Fai, so has his dad, so has Sam. There is *no way* it's OK for you to disturb them right now."

He keeps his hand up, keeping me back, and holds out his phone.

"Boyfriend ..." he says, sounding confused. "Faisal asked me to come. He sent me a message."

I think about Fai, broken and bleeding, and I think about Sam. He was bleeding and hurting, but I don't think he cared about himself. The pain I saw was all for Fai.

And I remember Georgie's photo. Kyle and Fai, and how much it would hurt Sam to see it.

All the rage, all the anger, all the frustration of the last few hours rushes through me and I throw myself forward, pushing Kyle hard in the chest.

"Get out." I'm shouting as he staggers backwards. "Get away from my friends."

"OK, OK." He holds up both hands, and looks over my shoulder to Georgie.

"You heard the lady," she says, arms folded. "I'd leave now, while she's still calm. She's not joking about her bad day."

He points past us, along the corridor, away from Fai's room. I nod, and step back, waving him through.

"Good decision," Georgie mutters as he hurries away.

I head back to my chair, collecting the remaining snacks from the floor, trying to pretend my hands aren't shaking. "Still think there's nothing going on with him and Fai?"

She sits down and rests her elbows on her knees.

"I really, really want to think that, but ..." She shakes her head. "What's Fai playing at?"

I think about our conversation in the theatre bar. "*Married to the dance*, he said. What if that means ..." I wave a hand at the corridor.

"Kyle?"

"Yeah."

She hangs her head, her hair falling over her face. "Good luck to Fai, but Sam really doesn't need this right now."

Chapter 36

"How bad is it?"

Sam peers at his reflection in my bathroom mirror, gently prodding the dressing on his face. The white gauze glows against his dark skin.

"Pretty bad," he says. "I don't know what they hit me with, but it looks as if someone's sliced me with a knife."

"Go on." I lean towards the mirror, and he presses his shoulder against mine. "Impress me. How many stitches?"

He's trying not to smile. "Eight," he says.

I give him an appreciative nod. "Proper war wound."

"Yeah." He smooths the dressing with his finger, wincing as he touches the cut.

I pull his arm down. "Leave it. Stop poking it."

He rests his hands on the edge of the basin and hangs his head.

"Go home, Sam." I lift a hand to his shoulder. "Let your mum look after you for a few days."

He runs his fingers over his hair. "They're away, Mum and Dad. Ghana. I told them not to come back."

"And they're going to listen?"

He shrugs. "I'm not the one in hospital."

"Ah," I say, smiling. "You didn't tell them the bad stuff."

He smiles back. "They didn't need to know. And I'm not leaving Fai. Thanks for ... all this," he says, waving at the room, "and for keeping me company ..."

I shake my head. "Didn't want you to be home alone."

"... but I need to get back to him as soon as they'll let me."

"The hospital?"

He nods, and his voice shakes as he answers. "Surgery, visiting hours – you know what it's like. His dad's going to call me."

I give his shoulder a squeeze and step back, my hand running over the tear in his shirt. He's ditched the jacket and the worst of the damage, but his jeans are stained with mud, and I can't tell where the dirt and stubble on his face end and the cuts and bruises begin.

"Do you need a hand?"

My spare towels are stacked on the edge of the basin along with a pack of antiseptic wipes. It's the best I can do until Georgie gets back from Sam's flat with clean clothes and toiletries.

"If you can figure out how to use the shower without getting the dressings wet, you're welcome to try. Or if you need a nurse to dab at your brow, just ask."

He gives me a sad smile. "I think I can manage."

"My dressing gown is on the back of the door. Borrow it until Georgie gets back." He glances over his shoulder and raises an eyebrow. "Yes, it's the pink fluffy one. We both know you'll look fabulous in it."

He grins, and takes a bow.

"Thanks, Mel," he says.

"I hope I've got what he needs."

Georgie drops a black gym bag onto the kitchen table. I hand her a mug of tea, and she sinks into a chair.

"Clothes? Razor? Shoes? Whatever potions he keeps in his bathroom?"

She nods. "How is he?"

"OK, I think. Cleaning up."

"I'm claiming the bathroom next." She sniffs her shirt. "I smell like old socks."

"You and me both," I say, wrinkling my nose, and Georgie shrugs.

I'm laughing as I carry the bag to Sam and leave it outside the door.

"Laundry service!" I shout, knocking. "Fresh threads!"

"Thank you, ladies," he calls back, and I can hear the relief in his voice.

Sam and Georgie are dressed and busy in the kitchen when I make it out of the bathroom. I've pulled on fresh clothes and wrapped my wet hair in a towel, and I finally feel clean. I've never been so grateful for a long, hot shower in my life. Sam is wearing my dressing gown over his black jeans and T-shirt like a smoking jacket, and somehow he makes it look edgy and cool. I can't help smiling. If it wasn't for the cuts and bruises, and the dressings on his face and knuckles, he'd look like a model at a fashion shoot.

"Hey, bathing beauty." Georgie waves. "The breakfast buffet is open!"

I stifle a yawn. "Didn't we do this already? Vending machines?"

Sam pats his stomach. "Speak for yourself. Some of us haven't eaten since last night."

"Sam is hungry?" I give him a look of mock surprise. "Then it's definitely breakfast time!"

He flashes me a quick half-smile, and points at the crowded worksurface. "We've got cereal, milk, toast, butter, jam, honey, hard-boiled eggs ..."

"Ah," I say, nodding. "Real food."

"... juice, tea, coffee, hot chocolate ..." He pulls open a cupboard. "Tortilla chips, salsa, ginger cake, popcorn ..."

Georgie frowns. "Not exactly breakfast—"

"Shhhh." I press a finger to my lips. "He's hungry. Don't argue."

They've brought an extra chair from Georgie's room, and we crowd round the tiny kitchen table to eat. Sam wolfs down three bowls of cereal before I've finished my first. I keep almost falling asleep, and even strong coffee isn't helping. My brain is a mess – a jumble of thoughts about Jez, Fai, Kyle, and Sam.

Angels and fake wings and violence. I'm having trouble following the conversation.

I can see Jez in my room, his wings spreading behind him. Fai in his hospital gown, his face bruised and swollen. Kyle, holding his phone out to me in the corridor. Everything feels wrong. Broken.

"Mel." Georgie pours a glass of orange juice and holds it out to me. "Vitamin C. Fixes everything."

I don't mean to laugh, but I'm too tired to stop. "I don't think so," I say, and Sam freezes.

"Shit." I press my fingers into my forehead, hiding my face. "Sorry, Sam. I just ... I feel as if I can't fix anything. You, Fai, Jez ..." I stop myself before I mention Kyle. I don't want to hurt my friend again.

Sam nods, his face solemn. Georgie reaches across the table and takes my hand.

"That's what we're doing, Mel," she says. "Fixing one thing at a time. We were sweaty and disgusting – we've cleaned ourselves up. We were hungry – we're eating. We need a distraction – we're concentrating on having an epic second breakfast and admiring the way Sam looks in your dressing gown."

I glance at Sam, and he strikes a half-hearted pose. "That part's working," I say, smiling.

"And the shower, and the food." She hands me the orange juice. "And the vitamins, if you let them."

"OK." I nod, taking a sip. "Point made. One thing at a time."

"When can you see him?"

Sam looks up from his phone and shrugs at Georgie. "When he's out of surgery. I'm waiting for his dad to call."

I lean back against my bed and close my eyes. I should be sleeping, but Sam has stolen my bed, and Georgie has taken over my TV.

"What should we watch?" She scrolls through my streaming menus. "Vampire hunters? Some sci-fi thing? Something kick-ass and loud?"

I groan, and Georgie shoves my knee with her elbow. "Come on. We have a duty to keep Sam awake. He needs to be ready when Fai's dad summons him."

I don't hide my yawn. "Sam is welcome to stay awake. I want to close my eyes and not wake up until everything is back the way it should be."

"Fine." She sighs. "Sam? Come down here and sit with me. Mel needs to sleep. She's getting cranky."

I stick my tongue out, and she laughs. "See?"

Sam sits up and pats the duvet. "All yours," he says, and shuffles onto the floor, my dressing gown trailing behind him.

I fall onto my bed, pulling my pillow under my cheek and wrapping the duvet round my shoulders. My friends argue about vampires and spaceships and I sleep through whatever it is they choose to watch. My dreams are jumbled and confusing. Angels, feathers, endless long, dark hallways. I don't know what I'm looking for.

I wake to Sam shaking my shoulder, his face grey.

Georgie sits on the floor, staring at her phone, and for a moment I think something has happened to Fai. That it's bad news from the hospital. I glance at Sam, but the way he's looking at me makes my stomach sink.

"What?" My voice is a croak. Nothing makes sense. I'm still tangled in my dreams.

"Oh." Georgie presses a hand to her mouth. "Oh, god. Mel?" She holds her phone out to me. "You need to see this."

There's ice in my chest as Sam reaches out and passes me the phone. I shuffle upright and the room spins. I make myself focus on the screen.

It's a live feed, from Patrick. A figure on a rooftop, looking down at the camera. The colours shift and flare as the lens picks out the dark silhouette from the white sky, and then I see the wings.

The figure steps to the edge of the roof – bare-chested, male, dressed only in jeans. Wings lift from his back and he looks up, away from his audience, his face too dark to see. He balances on the precipice for a moment, then steps back, bending double and resting his hands on his knees.

His feathers catch the light and I see rainbows, dancing as he moves.

My stomach twists. Grey wings, rainbow shimmer.

Jez. It's Jez. On the roof of his building.

He's showing his wings.

It's impossible. He's kept them hidden, his entire life. He's been taught to be ashamed. He doesn't believe they're beautiful. He doesn't want anyone to see.

But here he is. He lifts his head and I can see his face. I have to make myself breathe.

I hurt him last night. I embarrassed him. I made him angry.

And now he's showing himself to the world. It doesn't make sense.

He's a secret angel. He's ashamed.

My breath freezes in my throat. With a jolt, I realise what he's doing.

He's not showing off his wings. He's not standing tall and proud on the roof.

He's hurting and angry and messed up.

I think about our conversation, on the same rooftop. Questions about my family, comments about his mother. The way he tugged his T-shirt down and pulled away from me. The way he asked me to leave.

He's not showing the world who he is.

He's going to hurt himself.

He's going to jump.

Chapter 37

For the second time today, I'm up and awake in moments, pulling on shoes and grabbing my coat and phone on the way out of the door. Georgie yells something after me, but there's no way I'm stopping. I sprint down the stairs and out onto the pavement, pushing through groups of people in their Sunday best and running as fast as I can.

I need to get to Jez. I need to stop him.

I don't want to call him. I don't know how he'll react, and I don't want to find out.

I need to be there.

I run, ignoring everything. The people in my way, the traffic, my hammering heart, even the phone ringing in my pocket until I realise it might be Jez. I tug it free, losing my focus on the pavement in front of me, and trip, skinning the heel of one hand. I'm on my feet again in seconds, pushing away the pain, weaving around the queue at a bus stop and sprinting as soon as I can.

I glance at the phone screen before looking up at where I'm going, keeping my feet pounding onto the concrete.

It's Georgie.

I ignore her. I don't want to know what she's seen. I don't want to know what's going on on Patrick's livestream.

If I don't answer, if I don't find out, maybe I still have time to save Jez.

"Patrick!"

I stumble as I reach the crowd in front of Jez's building, steadying myself against Patrick's arm.

"Mel?" He stares at me, eyes wide. "I thought you'd be ..." He waves a hand at the scene in front of us. "... in there."

I shake my head, trying to catch my breath. My lungs are burning.

"What's going on?"

I don't want to look. I don't want to see where Jez is. I fix my eyes on Patrick's face, ignoring the noise and gossip around us.

He shrugs. "He's ... not jumping." He glances over my shoulder. "But he's not coming down, either. They're trying to talk to him. They keep calling him, and he keeps hanging up." He squints at me. "Did you know he had wings? Was that a *thing* for you two? All that angel-sexual stuff?"

I stare at Patrick. I can't believe he's thinking about this.

I can't think of anything to say. I turn on my heel and push through the crowd towards the building. Every part of me is shaking.

"Hold it!" A policeman steps in front of me, hand held up. "No one comes through here. Turn around, please."

I realise there's a strip of police tape keeping the onlookers back.

"I'm ..." I begin, and I wonder what to say.

I'm nothing. I'm no one.

But I need to get to Jez.

"I'm his girlfriend." I point up at the roof, and catch sight of Jez for the first time.

Grey wings and rainbows against bright clouds. A figure standing tall at the edge of the roof, eyes closed. His fists are tight at his sides.

My heart slams against my ribcage. I feel dizzy. I feel sick.

The policeman raises an eyebrow.

"I think I'm the reason he's up there."

I don't know what happens next. I'm looking up at Jez as he stares out at the rooftops. At the view of London I know he can see. The police are talking – arguing – but I'm not listening.

And then someone is lifting the police tape, taking my elbow, guiding me onto the lawn.

A policewoman with a kind face asks my name, and I whisper an automatic reply.

"Hello, Mel," she says, gently. "I'm Kate. Has something happened between you?" She glances up at Jez and back to me.

I nod.

"And you think that's why he's on the roof?"

My throat is tight. I have to make myself breathe. I nod again.

"Do you think he'd listen to you? Do you think you can talk to him?"

My stomach cramps. I taste bile, and press my hand over my mouth.

I don't want to be here.

Kate is leading me across the grass. There's a bench, and she helps me sit down.

"Tell me what happened," she says, sitting next to me. I look up at the roof – at Jez, silhouetted against the sky. "Don't worry about him. He's OK for now. Tell me what he'll do if you try to speak to him."

"I ..." It hurts to speak. My throat feels tight and gritty. "I don't know."

Kate nods. "Did you break up? Did he hurt you?"

I shrug. I have no idea how to explain. "I'm not an angel," I say, and there are tears in my eyes.

"Did he ..." Kate takes a breath. "Did he want you to be? Did he think you were?"

I can't believe she understands. I can't believe she gets it. I'm nodding and brushing away tears and fighting sobs at the same time.

She puts a hand on my shoulder. "I'm sorry," she says. "It happens more often than you'd think."

"He ..." I shake my head. I need to explain. "He was hiding his wings. I didn't know."

"About him?"

I nod. "His mother ... she made him hide them. He had this harness ..." I realise I'm waving my hands, trying to draw his bindings in the air. "Marks on his skin. He wasn't supposed to show anyone."

"And he thought you were the same?"

"Yeah."

"I'm so sorry, Mel," she says. "And I'm sorry this is happening." She glances up again. "Do you think you can help us?"

My breath catches in my throat. "You want me to talk to him?"

She nods. "I think a friendly voice might make him think twice. See if you can distract him. Get him away from the edge."

I curl my fingers into fists, fighting the red-hot fear in my chest. "I haven't called him," I say, my throat tight. "If he sees my number ..." I give Kate a pleading look. "I don't know what he'll do."

She holds up a chunky black phone. "I'll call him from here – he'll know it's us. Let's see whether he'll listen."

"Sure," I say. But inside I'm screaming.

Chapter 38

"You understand what we need from you?"

Kate's colleague hasn't introduced himself, and he's definitely not kind. He's cold, professional, and efficient.

I make myself concentrate. "Talk to him. Distract him. Get him to step back from the edge."

My hands are shaking as he nods at Kate, and she hits the dial button on her phone.

"Say whatever it takes," her colleague says. "Do you understand? Whatever he wants to hear."

I nod.

My stomach is a boulder. My knees feel like jelly.

Jez is at the edge of the roof, and I'm supposed to make out that everything is OK.

"Just ... don't provoke him. He's threatened to jump if we try anything he doesn't like, but we're going to take a risk with you. We think he'll stay and talk."

I stare at this man, who knows nothing about Jez and me.

"Based on what?" I'm shouting at a policeman, yelling into his face, and I don't care. He's willing to risk Jez's life because he thinks I can help.

He gives me a sad smile. "Not the first case like this we've seen, I'm afraid."

I close my eyes and take a breath.

This is happening. I'm here, and Jez is messed up, and everyone thinks I can make things better.

Kate is talking, so Jez must have picked up, but I can't hear anything over the sound of my pulse thumping in my ears. I don't know what I'm going to say to him.

What do you say to someone standing on the edge of a roof? What do you say when you're the person who put them there?

Everyone is counting on me. They all think I can help.

I think about Jez. About the look on his face when I told him I didn't have wings. That I wasn't the angel he thought I was.

Horror and confusion and hurt. The anger in his voice.

What would you know about wings?

I make myself keep breathing.

Kate gives me a quick smile and hands me the phone. "Jez?"

I look up, watching his response. My heart is kicking my ribcage, and my hands are shaking.

He's at the edge of the roof, holding his phone to his ear. His wings are tucked behind him, and as he looks down at the lawn they lift, rainbows shattering across his feathers.

He's beautiful. Breathtaking, like a renaissance painting. I half expect him to be holding a sword and slaying demons.

My eyes meet his. His attention is on me, and my breath catches. He looks like Kane, in my mother's portrait.

I wonder whether he's planned this – whether he's trying to look like Kane. He's wearing jeans and boots, his chest is bare, his wings spread. I can imagine this moment, painted in shades of bronze and gold.

Except where Kane's eyes held confidence and pride in their sapphire-blue depths, his expression burns with anger.

"You," he says, his voice flat.

I shrug. "Me."

"Don't." His voice is a growl. "Don't try to stop me."

"Jez," I say, taking a step towards the building. "What is this? What are you going to do?"

He laughs. "You come here and ask what I'm doing? *You*? Really?" He sounds desperate. He sounds unhinged.

I shake my head. "I don't understand."

"Do you know what it took, for me to show you … what I am? Do you know how much *trust* I placed in you?"

I take a breath. Steady my voice. "I'm not an angel. I can't show you wings I don't have."

"I trusted you."

"And I never told you I had wings. I never lied. I didn't do …" I wave a hand in frustration. "… whatever it is you think I did."

His shoulders slump, and he glances at the sky. He looks as if he's praying.

"You didn't tell me who you are, *Melodie*." There's pain in his voice, and confusion.

Anger sparks in my chest, and I'm shouting before I realise what I'm doing. "It's not something I like to remember! It's definitely not something I go around talking about. That moment – that *photo* – doesn't define me. I thought you'd understand that, Jez-the-angel."

Kate touches my shoulder, and I jump. I'd forgotten she was there. "Gentle," she says, so only I can hear.

We stand, staring. Jez on the roof, me on the ground. Phones to our ears, fists clenched, each a mirror of the other.

Slowly, deliberately, he takes a step, until he's balancing right on the edge. I realise I can hear gasps and shouts from the crowd behind me, cameras and phones clicking.

Everything slows. I can't feel the ground under my feet.

An angel, standing in front of me, showing his wings to the world, moments from his last breath. I can see Jez, and I can see Kane. I can hear cameras. Sounds of traffic from the road. The roar of an SUV in the crowd.

"Please," I say, my voice broken. "Don't jump."

He looks out at his audience, then back at me, and shrugs. "Why not?"

I take a breath, uncurling my fist, remembering what I'm doing here.

Say whatever it takes. Do you understand? Whatever he wants to hear.

There are tears, pricking my eyes. A lightning pain in my chest.

Whatever it takes.

"Because I'm not worth it, Jez," I say, as loudly as I can. "It's not worth throwing your life away over me."

I feel as if I'm falling. I feel as if I'm drowning. My chest is tight and I'm fighting for breath.

And I realise Jez is laughing.

"You think this is about you?" He raises his wings, his feathers fluttering. "You think you're the reason I'm up here, Melodie Abbott?"

I make myself breathe. My lungs are on fire. I'm thinking back, to everything he's said. Everything he's done.

I don't understand.

"Then why ...?"

His face twists into a sneer, and he steps away from the edge.

"Do you know what my mother did to me?" He runs a finger over the marks on his chest. "Do you know what she thinks about these?" He flexes his wings.

I nod. "I'm sorry, Jez. And she's wrong." He laughs again. "You really are beautiful."

"No," he says, and he sounds absolutely certain. "No. I'm a freak, I'm deformed, I'm a disappointment. I have to hide all this, so people will never find out." He spreads his arms and looks towards the crowd. "And yet, here I am! Showing myself to the world."

"I'm proud of you," I say, quietly. "This is brave, showing your wings. This is ... amazing."

He shakes his head. "This isn't brave. This is desperate and stupid." He shrugs. "I know what I'm doing. I know it's idiotic and destructive, but I want her to know. I want her to see."

I blink, his words sinking in. "You're doing this to spite your mother?"

"She told me to marry a human. Did you know that?" I shake my head. "If I can't do that, I need to find an angel who hides her wings. Someone my mother won't suspect."

I can feel heat rising on my skin. All the pieces falling into place.

Jez going home. Our awkward, creepy conversation on the roof. His comments about my tears at the Angel Club.

The ground is falling away. I step back to find my balance.

"And you thought that was me?" My voice is cracked. Broken.

"The clues were all there, Mel," he says, exasperation in his voice. "Songs about wings upsetting you, that angel infatuation, the angel-sexual comment." He shrugs again. "Of course I thought it was you."

I stare up at him, trying to think of something to say.

"I'm not marrying anyone, Jez! At least, not now. What were you thinking?"

He shrugs. "That you understood? That you and I were the same? That I wouldn't have to hide any more?"

I tighten my fist and let out a scream of frustration. "You could have asked!"

"*You could have told me!*" His shout is ragged. Full of pain.

I shake my head. This doesn't make any sense. He's blaming his mother, he's blaming me – but he's the one on the roof, showing his wings and threatening to throw himself off.

"Jez," I say, holding out my hand to him. "Don't jump."

His shoulders slump. He bows his head and tucks his wings behind him.

When he looks at me again, he's running a hand over his face. With a start, I realise he's brushing away tears.

"Mel," he says, his voice like gravel. "Mel."

And he holds out his hand.

I'm running towards the building, ignoring Kate as she calls my name. I know where the gate is. I know how to get to the roof.

This is my chance. This is how I get Jez out of danger.

My heart is hammering, the phone still pressed to my ear. Someone shouts and I glance behind me.

I can see the crowd, watching us. TV camera crews. A hundred mobile phones held up, pointing at Jez. Ambulances and police cars in the road.

I blink, and see a bank of cameras. Bright lights and shouting. Kane, flying backwards towards me. Broken wings.

It's happening again.

"Mel," he says. "I'm sorry."
And then he's falling.

Chapter 39

Jez jumps.

My heart slams in my chest. I'm fighting for breath.

I barely have time to scream.

He's falling, and there's nothing I can do to stop what's coming.

At the last moment, Jez raises his wings. My stomach twists as he turns his fall into a glide, his feathers shivering around him.

For a moment I can breathe again. I can imagine the fall is over.

He's beautiful. Storm-grey wings spread, shimmering with rainbows. For a few seconds he looks like an angel in a painting or a stained-glass window. He looks as if he's flying.

And then he hits the ground hard.

He's thrown by the impact, tumbling across the grass.

I hear cameras, and screaming. Flashes and bright lights and shouting.

Grass, phones, Jez, pain. The world twists. Pavement, cameras, blood, Kane.

I'm on my knees on the lawn, reaching out to the broken, shining wings.

I don't know where I am. Which angel is dying.

I don't want to look. I don't want to see what happened.

My head feels as if it's been hit with a hammer. My hand stings where I fell on the pavement. My throat is on fire, and my face is hot with tears.

I reach down to touch the grass, like paintbrushes under my fingers. Green grass, blue jeans, pale skin. The texture is comforting, grounding. I take a slow breath, and there's a raw pain in my chest.

I'm still here. Jez jumped, and I'm still here.

I tried to stop him, but he didn't listen.

I'm breathing. It hurts, but I'm breathing.

Someone in a green paramedic uniform drops to their knees next to me, calling my name. Then Kate is holding my hand, gently taking the phone from my fingers and cutting off the call.

Someone is shouting, and I can hear Georgie's voice.

"She's my friend! Let me past. Hey! She's my friend!"

And then she's there, on the grass, throwing her arms round my shoulders. Her fiery hair falls over my face as she leans against me.

I want to say something. I want to let her know it's OK – I'm OK – but my voice doesn't work. I can't tell her.

I feel as if I'm somewhere else, watching Georgie as she strokes my hair. Whispers my name.

I want her to stay. I want her to keep talking to me, but she's pulled away.

"Mel?" Someone is shining a light in my eyes. "Mel – can you hear me?"

I try to answer, try to say yes, but all I can do is blink. The light hurts and my chest hurts and I can't make myself move.

"Good," someone says, stroking my hand. "That's good, Mel. You're OK. We've got you."

Then everything I see, everything I hear flows together like dark water. The paramedic, Kate, Georgie, the buildings and the crowd – and I'm tumbling into the black.

The images come and go. Flashes of colour and sound in the dark.

An angel, falling. Feathers, glinting in the light.

Cameras, shouting. The sound of an engine and the screaming of a crowd.

Gold and grey and shimmering rainbows.

Stay with me, someone says, their hand in mine, and I grip their fingers before the light falls away.

When I wake up, Georgie is next to me.

"Hey." She smiles, and I realise she's holding my hand.

"Where—" I say, squinting in the bright light.

"Ambulance," she says. "Don't worry – we haven't gone anywhere. They're just checking you over. Making sure you're OK." She glances over her shoulder, out of the open doors. "They'll let you go once you start talking."

I shake my head, trying to follow what she's saying. It's like thinking through fog, and I'm trying to remember why I'm here.

"I can go?"

"As long as you're making sense." She grins.

I shut my eyes for a moment, trying to make my thoughts line up.

"What happened?" My voice sounds wrong. Drowsy. Confused.

Her expression darkens, and she squeezes my fingers.

"Jez," she whispers. "On the roof?"

And the memory slams into me like a body blow. Like being shot.

Like falling and hitting the ground.

Jez fell. He *jumped*.

He was talking to me. He was explaining, and he jumped.

I thought I was helping. I thought I was saving him.

The angel with the storm-grey eyes and beautiful rainbow wings, who wanted something I couldn't give.

There are tears spilling over my face. My whole body is shaking.

Georgie grips my hand.

Jez did this. Jez made this happen.

"Mel," Georgie says, gently. "It wasn't your fault. You can't blame yourself for this."

I shrug.

"This was Jez, not you. You did your best, and he ..." She waves a hand at the back of the ambulance. "He chose this."

"And?" Anger is swelling in my chest. I want to know what happened. I sit up and stare at Georgie, my fingers locked round hers. "Did he get what he wanted? Suicide on a hundred phone cameras?"

My lungs are impossibly tight. I can't take a breath. My throat is burning.

I'm shaking. I'm fighting rage and hurt and fear. I'm fighting flashbacks – blood and screaming and shattered golden wings.

I don't know what she's going to say.

She shakes her head. "He's hurt. Really hurt. His wings ... I don't know. They looked pretty beaten up. But he's alive."

He's alive.

I feel as if I've put down a heavy bag. I'm bending over, gasping for air.

Jez is alive.

It all happened again – cameras, crowds, an angel, falling – and I couldn't stop it. I couldn't save him.

But this time the angel survived. This time no one had to watch his life slip away, or cradle his head as he died.

I think about the way Jez looked at me. How it felt to have his full attention on me. How it felt to be tested and challenged and brought into his private world.

How it felt to look into his eyes.

And how it was all a lie.

Georgie wraps her arms round my shoulders and holds me as the tears come.

Chapter 40

When we get back to the flat, Sam is waiting. He's sitting on the floor outside our front door, his head in his hands.

"Shit," Georgie mutters under her breath, and I reach a hand out to the wall to steady myself.

I can't lose Fai. *We* can't lose Fai.

"Sam?" I kneel down next to him and put a hand on his shoulder. Without speaking he wraps his arms round me and pulls me close. He buries his head in my shoulder, and I hug him back.

He doesn't let go.

I hear Georgie unlocking the front door, then she sits down beside Sam and puts her arms round both of us.

It's a long time before anyone moves. It feels safe, kneeling here on the floor. It feels as if someone's hit the pause button on everything that's happened.

"Come on," says Georgie, pulling away. "We need tea. Or coffee. Or something stronger." She stands up and holds the door open. "Comfy chairs. Duvets. Dressing gowns. Cake."

I untangle myself from Sam and tug on his hands. He nods and we both stand, slowly.

Every muscle in my body hurts. My head is a ball of pain. My hands are cold and aching. The paramedic said this might happen. PTSD, fight-or-flight, emotional shock – when you calm down you feel as if you've been running and fighting for hours.

I feel as if it was me, not Jez, who fell from the roof. I feel bruised and broken and defeated.

I follow Sam into the flat and close the door behind us. Georgie is filling the kettle and pulling mugs from the cupboard. Sam slumps into a chair, and I sit down across the kitchen table from him. He looks up, and I can see he's been crying.

It's a relief, for a moment, to be concentrating on someone else's drama.

"Tell me," I hold a hand out to him. "Tell me what happened."

He closes his eyes and takes a breath.

"Fai's OK," he says, and I feel air rushing into my lungs, a bubble of relief growing in my chest. Tears sting my eyes, and I realise I'm smiling.

"That's great, Sam," I say, taking his hands in mine. "That's fantastic."

Georgie joins us at the table. "You gave us a scare, there, Sam," she says. "I thought for sure it was bad news."

He shakes his head. "We don't know yet. It still might be." He sounds exhausted.

"Dancing?" I tighten my grip on his fingers. "Can he dance?"

"It's too early to say. They've put the pins in his arm and a cast on his ankle. We won't know for months."

Georgie gasps. "What about his degree? What about his future?"

Sam shrugs. "We don't know. We need to …" He sighs. "He needs to talk to the university. To his tutors. Try to figure something out. Maybe defer and come back next year, if he can. If he's fit enough."

"I'm so sorry." It's all I can think of to say. I can see Fai on the stage, dancing as if that's what he was born to do. His body flowing as if he was made of water. And I can see him in hospital, bruised and bandaged and still.

Sam gives me a sad smile. "Thanks," he whispers, squeezing my hands.

Georgie jumps up as the kettle boils. "Right. Tea, coffee, hot chocolate. What's everyone having?"

We choose our drinks and she makes herself busy.

Sam is staring at the table. He lets go of my fingers and rubs a hand over his face.

My stomach sinks. I know my friend, and I know there's something he hasn't said.

"Sam?" I try to catch his attention. "What aren't you telling me?"

He shrugs again.

"Sam," I say, gently.

He rubs his eyes and looks at me. "It's not important."

"Something's bothering you. Of course it's important."

Georgie puts three mugs down in front of us and drops into her chair.

"We're here for you, Sam," she says. "Not going anywhere."

He nods, and looks at both of us. It's a moment before he says anything.

"I'm going to sound like an idiot."

Georgie wraps her hands round her coffee mug. "Let us be the judge of that. You haven't exactly had a lot of sleep."

I can't help commenting. "Neither have you," I say. "Neither have I. We're not exactly reliable judges at this point."

"Might as well tell us, then." Georgie grins. "We're all too tired to take anything personally."

"It's not that ..." Sam shakes his head. "It's just ... while I was there, someone else came to see Fai. One of the dancers."

Georgie's eyes snap to mine. I take a sharp breath.

"What?" Sam glances between us, his eyes wide. "What do you know?"

"Kyle?" Georgie asks, carefully.

Sam's jaw tightens.

"We ..." I wave a hand, trying to find the right words. "We had a run-in with Kyle. At the hospital."

"Last night?" Sam sounds breathless. Angry.

I nod. "This morning. He recognised Georgie from the recital."

She mimes holding a camera. "Backstage photos. He's the director, so it was his permission I needed to photograph the dancers."

Sam's fingers curl into fists. "What was he doing there?"

"He came to see Fai." I close my eyes, trying to remember what he said. "I think Fai texted him."

Sam slumps back in his chair. "Well," he says, spreading his hands. "At least I'm not an idiot."

Georgie leans her elbows on the table. "We sent him away," she says, sounding proud, and I can't help smiling at the memory. The look on Kyle's face when I told him he couldn't see Fai.

"You did what?" Sam raises an eyebrow at my smile. "Why do I think this is going to make me feel better?"

"It should. Your loyal friend here ..." She points at me, "... accosted him in the corridor. As soon as she realised who he was. She told him not to disturb you two, and when he didn't get the message she used him as a punch bag."

Sam gapes at us both. "Mel ..." he says. "Did you ... did you *hit* Kyle?"

I shrug. "More of a firm shove." He gives me a sideways look. "What? I was angry. And hungry. And I hadn't had enough sleep."

"And he deserved it." Georgie shakes her head. "Ran away with his tail between his legs."

Sam drops his head back and stares at the ceiling. "Wow," he says. "Wow, Mel. I don't know what I would have done if he'd turned up in Fai's room when

I'd been waiting all night to see him." He gives me a quick smile. "Thank you."

"So what happened today?" I ask. "Were you there when he visited?"

"I went to get a coffee for Fai's dad. He hasn't been home yet." Sam shakes his head. "I wanted to help. And Kyle was there when I got back. He left quickly, though. And it was just before the end of visiting hours."

"Did Fai ask him to come? Did he want Kyle to be there?"

Sam shrugs. "I don't know. It was weird. And I only saw him in passing. I didn't know anyone else had Fai's room number."

"You didn't ask Fai?"

Sam shakes his head. "He's really groggy. Strong painkillers. I didn't want to upset him. I thought it was nothing." He closes his eyes. "It was only when I got here, waiting for you, that I started to think about it."

I give Georgie a look. "We should show him."

She glares at me. "But ... you said ..."

"I know. But I think he deserves to see."

Chapter 41

"Are you sure about this?" Georgie pulls her chair up to her desk and opens her laptop.

I glance at Sam. He's staring at the screen, his jaw tight. I nudge his elbow and he nods.

"Show me. Whatever it is, show me."

Georgie pulls up the folder of rejected images. She pauses before she clicks and turns to Sam.

"It's not what it looks like. I need you to know that. A couple of seconds, that's all. I just happened to catch it on camera."

He nods again, and she opens the photo.

Fai and Kyle, forehead to forehead, Kyle's hand on the back of Fai's neck. It's a beautiful image. Intimate, joyful, powerful, using black and white to focus on the two men and their shared emotion.

Sam gasps, and runs a hand over his face.

"Are you telling me …" He stops to take another breath. "Are you telling me there's nothing going on? That this is a completely innocent picture?"

Georgie spreads her hands. "All I can tell you is what I saw. Fai came offstage, smile too big for his face, high on adrenaline. Kyle was delighted with his performance. It was over in seconds. I just got lucky with my timing."

"Lucky." Sam's voice is hollow. Flat. He stares at the screen.

No one speaks. No one moves.

"Sam," I whisper, my hand on his arm. "It's Fai. He wouldn't ..."

He shrugs my hand away. "Don't," he says. "Just ... don't."

"We didn't send it to the papers." Georgie looks up at Sam. "We didn't want that to be the public image from the performance."

He scowls. "I suppose I should be thanking you for that."

"Come on, Sam." I don't mean to sound angry, but I'm exhausted. Everything hurts, and I need a distraction – not more pain. "You know how one image can change ... everything."

He nods.

"You know how a single photo can make you public property." I can feel tears in my eyes. A pebble in my throat. "One photo, one lucky shot, and now everyone knows who I am. Everyone knows my name. Everyone has an opinion about me." I take a breath. My hands are shaking. "Whatever I do, I'll always be the girl in the photo. I'll always be stuck in that moment with a dying angel." I give him a pleading look. "You were there. You saw it happen. You saw the news feeds and the coverage. You saw the comments online – you know how people talked about me, as if I'm not a real person." I shrug. "We didn't want that for Fai. And we didn't want it for you."

He takes a long breath.

"So you knew about this image, and you didn't tell me?"

Georgie turns towards him. "Sam. I've told you. It was nothing. It just ... it looks more intimate than it was."

"We didn't want to upset you. Either of you." I sound as if I'm begging.

Sam stares at me, his jaw clenched.

"You did this to protect me."

I roll my eyes. "I know what it's like, to have your image broadcast to the world. To have strangers assume they know who you are because of one photo. This ..." I point at the screen. "This looks like something it isn't. I don't want anyone else to go through what happened to me." I shake my head. "I never want to go through it again, and I wouldn't wish it on my friends."

"So this ..." Sam points at the screen. "This is why you stopped Kyle at the hospital." I nod, and he runs a hand over his hair.

"I didn't want him barging in on you and Fai."

He shrugs. "Thanks." He doesn't sound grateful.

"Sorry, Sam." Georgie sounds tired. "We screwed this one up. Mel is right – we didn't want to hurt you and Fai, so we kept the photo to ourselves." She shrugs. "We should have told you. We should have given Fai a chance to explain."

"Sorry." I nod. "Bad call." I want to say more. I want to apologise properly, but exhaustion is clawing at me. I can't find the words.

Sam takes a breath, his hands curled into fists at his sides.

Georgie's phone chimes. She pulls it from her pocket and opens a message.

"Uh ... Mel?" She reaches for the remote control and switches on her TV, flipping through the channels until she finds the news. She turns and grips my hand in hers. Behind me, Sam gasps.

We're watching Jez, on the rooftop. Shouting into his phone, looking down at someone on the grass.

Looking down at me.

I watch myself reach out a hand. I see myself turn and run, and I know what happens next.

I don't want to watch, but I can't look away. I'd managed to forget, for an hour. I'd managed to focus on Sam.

And now I'm thrown back. Jez is on the roof. I'm running for the gate. I can feel my heart racing, my breath catching.

I feel heavy. I feel dizzy. The edges of my vision are turning black. Everything is moving in slow motion.

I'm in two places at once. I'm safe, in Georgie's room, and I'm back on the lawn, the phone pressed to my ear.

On the screen, Jez jumps. My stomach twists. The camera closes in as he falls.

In those final seconds, as he spreads his wings, he doesn't look like the man I met at the Angel Club. The journalist who laughed at my tears.

He looks like a classical angel. Like something from the art lecture – a sculpture or a painting.

Something holy. Something beautiful.

The footage cuts off before he hits the ground. The newsreader is talking, but I can't follow what she's saying. Georgie's grip tightens on my fingers.

There's an image on the TV. A grainy, distant image of me on the grass, talking into the phone. Blue-black hair, no makeup, jeans and trainers.

The screen splits. Two images of me. One from today, trying to save Jez.

And one from the night of the Angel Exhibition. The photo everyone knows. Me, in my mother's dress, screaming for help. Kane, resting against my knees. My arms held out, my hands bloodied, golden wings broken around us.

I can't breathe.

The room turns and Sam grabs my arm as my legs crumple. He holds me up, and helps me sit down on Georgie's bed.

My chest is tight. My throat burns. I feel as if I'm drowning.

It's happening again. Another angel, falling. Another photo. My image on TV, the worst moments of my life served up for everyone to see – and there's nothing I can do to stop it.

"Mel?"

I shake my head and close my eyes. I feel sick.

"Mel." Georgie sits down beside me. "Mel. Breathe."

She's switched off the TV. I can hear my heart, drumming against my ribs. Every muscle in my body is screaming with pain.

"I'm sorry," she says. "The message. Patrick said to turn on the news. I didn't know there'd be video ... I didn't think."

Her arm is round my shoulders. Sam is kneeling next to me on the floor, his hand pressed against my back.

"We've got you," Georgie whispers. "You're OK. We've got you."

I lean into her embrace. I can feel tears on my cheeks. I'm shivering, teeth chattering, my hands shaking in my lap.

It takes a long time for the shivering to stop. I sit between Georgie and Sam, their touch connecting me – pulling me back to the room, the bed, the floor under my feet.

"Well," Sam says when I open my eyes. "This has been a spectacularly shit weekend."

Georgie barks a laugh. Sam rests his head on my knee. I brush away tears, my shoulders shaking.

I don't know whether I'm laughing or crying.

Chapter 42

"Get some sleep, Mel."

Georgie leans against the door frame, watching as I pull clothes from my wardrobe and stuff them into a bag. Sam sits on the floor, his back against the wall, arms resting on his knees.

"We'll grab a takeaway. Wake you when it's here." She waves at the bag. "Sort all this out in the morning."

I shake my head.

"I can't be here. I can't be where Jez showed me his wings. Where he said awful things to me."

"OK then," she says. "Stay for Sam. Stay for Fai."

I glance at Sam, and he shrugs.

"I'm sorry," I say.

He nods. "It's OK – I get it. Go home. Let your mother take care of you. Eat some of your dad's home cooking. Make your brother's day."

I can't help smiling. "You know me too well."

Georgie taps Sam's knee with her foot. "Hey! Whose side are you on?"

"Mel's," he says, his voice serious. "She needs to get out of this flat."

Georgie folds her arms.

"What?" Sam spreads his hands. "I know what it's like to want to get away. I know how much a place – a room – can remind you of someone. Mel needs a break from that." He looks back at me. "Plus her mother would never forgive me if I tried to keep her here."

"Thanks, Sam," I say. "You know you can stay, if Georgie agrees. Have my bed. I don't want to send you back to an empty flat."

"I'll let Georgie decide. Once we've had that takeaway." He grins, and Georgie laughs.

"Sure," she says. "Keep me company, while my flatmate swans off to her family. Just – no hogging the bathroom, put the toilet seat down, do your washing up, and don't eat all the food."

Sam gives her a look of mock outrage and I can't help laughing.

"He'll be a model flatmate, I promise. Well – except for the food thing. You might want to go shopping when you fetch the takeaway."

The taxi drops me home at dinner time.

"Hey, sis." My brother opens the door. He's trying to play it cool, but I can see the smile he's hiding. "Good to see you."

"You, too," I say, pulling him into a hug. He hugs me back, and I notice he's stooping to rest his chin on my shoulder. "Did you get taller again?"

He lets go, grinning. "Maybe you're shrinking, Mel. Take your bag?"

"Sure." I hand him my duffel bag and pull my rucksack onto my shoulder.

I don't make it past the hall before my father emerges from the kitchen, untying his apron and wrapping me in a bear hug.

"Pumpkin," he says. "Welcome home."

When he lets me go, my mother and grandfather are waiting, and we end up in a big family hug. I feel warm and safe, wrapped in their arms.

"There's food," says my father, pulling away. "Take a seat. Bags can wait. Dinner is ready."

We sit and eat a feast of home-grown vegetables and home-made nut roast. I've never been a strict vegetarian like my father, but his food always makes me smile. I realise it tastes like home. The dining room is warm and cosy – there's a fire crackling in the grate and the dark red curtains are drawn against the dark outside.

They know why I'm here. They've seen the TV coverage, and I told them what happened when I called to say I was coming home – but no one mentions the angel on the roof. No one asks about Jez, or talks about Kane. My mother tells us about her latest project, my father raves about the harvest from the garden, and my brother grudgingly admits that he's won a prize for his artwork at school. My grandfather waits until the two of us are clearing the table to ask about Fai, and I tell him everything I know.

"Shameful," he says, shaking his head. "The way people lash out at things they don't understand. I'm sorry Faisal and Sam are going through that."

I nod. "It's so unfair. Fai may have to give up dancing, and Sam will have a scar. He'll find it harder to get picked for auditions." I put down the plates I'm carrying and rest my hands on the table. "All they did was hold hands and wear sequined wings. They weren't hurting anyone. Just round the corner from the Angel Club, too. You'd think ..." I shrug. "You'd think they'd be safe."

"They should be safe." My grandfather's voice is edged with steel. "They shouldn't have to worry. Not here. Not today."

"I don't understand. I don't see why they made those men so angry."

"They didn't." He shakes his head. "The hate those men feel? It starts with themselves. They haven't lived up to the macho expectations they were raised with, and they're looking for someone to blame. Why not angels? Why not two boys holding hands?" He puts down the pile of placemats and spreads his hands. "Anyone who doesn't look like them. That's who they blame. People with wings. People with different coloured skin. People who love who they want to love, and people who live confidently – who don't care what angry old white men think."

"People who don't follow their rules?"

He gives me a sad smile. "Exactly."

I think about the men, beating up my friends. Turning their anger outwards and using other people's pain to feel good about themselves.

And I think about Jez, standing on the roof. Everything he'd been taught to hide, everything he'd been taught to feel ashamed of, and how his anger turned inwards. He hated himself. He hated who he was. And he turned on me when I wasn't what he wanted me to be.

I know Sam didn't like him. I know Georgie wanted him to leave me alone, but I thought I could see more. I thought I could see the person behind the arrogant front.

I thought he was letting me in.

But he only liked me when he thought I was an angel. When he thought I was exactly like him. When he found out I was different – that I'm just a girl, without wings – he lashed out. He called me *basic* and *unremarkable*. He called himself a freak. He defended himself by hurting me.

And I wonder what makes him different from the men who beat up Sam and Fai, or the man who killed Kane. He didn't use his fists and his boots, or drive a car through a crowd, but everything he said was calculated to wound me. To punish me. To *blame* me.

To make himself feel superior. To make it all my fault.

I'm leaning over, gripping the edge of the table, screwing my eyes shut against the tears. My grandfather pulls two chairs out and sits with me while the pain unfolds in my chest. I'm home. I'm safe, and it's all I can do to drag breath after jagged breath into my burning lungs, choking out sobs and trying to soak up the tears with my sleeves.

He's there, quiet, next to me. No platitudes. No empty words. I know my grandfather understands, and he's giving me the space to grieve.

I need this. I need to cry and scream and shout and *feel*. I need all the hurt to bubble up and boil its way out of my body. I need to find myself again.

When the crying is done, I lean my head against his shoulder and he gently strokes my hair.

"Look after yourself," he says, his voice soft. "Walk away. Your angel? He has to face his own demons, and you can't help him with that." I start to protest, but he holds up a hand to stop me. "He's too willing to hurt you, Mel. You don't have to let him. Wish him well, and move on. Wish him happiness – just not at your table."

I take a breath. I hate that he's right.

I can wish Jez well. I can hope he finds a way to be happy.

But I need to protect myself. I need to leave him behind.

Chapter 43

When I wake, I feel light. Clean.

I feel new.

My eyes are puffy and sore, and my throat feels like sandpaper, but I feel … what? Euphoric. Joyful.

I feel at peace.

I feel free.

It takes me a moment to remember what happened. Fai, Sam, Jez. Bruises and scars and broken wings. Kicks and punches and hurtful words. Last night's messy crying.

It all feels distant, as if it happened in another life. I'm home. I've left all that behind.

Winter sunlight filters through my curtains. The room is cold, and I curl up under the blankets and bedspread, thankful that I'm in my own space.

When I drag myself out from under the covers, I sit on the edge of my bed, and I can feel my mood darkening.

I'm staring at my wall – Kane, in a hundred photos, magazine cuttings, sketches. I'm looking at my shrine to a murdered angel.

Golden wings, sapphire eyes. Red carpets and dazzling partners. Pride and confidence and smouldering good looks.

Blood on my hands. Broken wings. Cameras and shouting.

Jez on the roof. An angel falling.

I pull on slippers and a warm sweatshirt and hurry downstairs to breakfast.

How's home?

There's a sequence of messages from Georgie waiting when I get back to my room. My father has always had a strict 'no phones at the table' policy for meals, and it's lovely to talk to my family while we share porridge and toast and tea. My brother has a Food Technology assessment this morning, so we send him off to school with everything we know about pastry and pie-making ringing in his ears. It's loud and chaotic, and we're all shouting over each other and laughing as we remember all the things he needs to know.

Are you free?

I sit down on my bed and catch up with what she's sent me.

Can you get to the hospital later? Fai's dad is going home (finally!) and we can get three people in at visiting time.

3pm.

338

Come with us?

Mel? You OK?

I can't help smiling. My flatmate is so used to me having my phone in my hand that she's worried when it takes me half an hour to get back to her.

Fine, I type. *Thanks for asking. Home is good.*

No phones at breakfast, though.

She responds with a laughing emoji.

Poor Mel! It's like living in the Stone Age!

I shake my head and start typing.

If the Stone Age had fancy marmalade and posh tea …

Well, she types back. *Now you're making me jealous.*

I send her a grin and wait for her reply.

So – can you come this afternoon? I know you need to keep up with coursework, but if you can get to the hospital it would be great to see you.

And I have something to show you …

I send an side-eye emoji. *Mysterious!*

She sends a grinning face back.

So we'll see you there?

I need to contact the Art Department and let them know I'm at home. I need to sort out deadlines and what they're expecting from me this week. It's a two-bus journey from here to the hospital, and I'll need to allow an hour to get there.

I check my watch. Plenty of time.

Sure, I type. *See you there. 3pm.*

Meet you at the main entrance, she sends. *He's been moved to a proper ward. We'll track him down together.*

"So – wait, slow down. He's where?"

Georgie waves at me as I walk through the door, her phone pressed to her ear. I give her a grin and leave her to finish her conversation.

"How do I get there?" She turns, looking for signs, one arm held out in a shrug. "Sam – I don't see what you're talking about."

There's a small gift shop in the hospital entrance hall, and I find myself staring at the shelves of colourful overnight bags and wash kits, greetings cards and stuffed toys and bunches of shiny balloons.

"*Which* way?" Georgie's voice echoes along the corridor.

There's a teddy bear with pink fur wearing a shiny leotard and a rainbow tutu, its arms in Fifth position, paws next to its ears, toes pointed. I can't resist buying it for Fai. By the time Georgie ends the call, Ballet Bear is tucked under my arm.

"You didn't," she says, tucking her phone into her pocket. I give her an innocent look, then hold the bear up for her to inspect.

"OK." She nods her approval. "That's cute."

"I couldn't find a decent Get Well Soon card, and then I saw this ..." I bob the bear from side to side, and Georgie smiles.

"Much better." And then she grins. "Hold on," she says, searching the back pocket of her camera bag.

When she hands me a packet of tissues and a bunch of safety pins, I know what she's thinking.

We find Fai, following Sam's instructions and checking for maps and signs on the way. We only go up the wrong stairs once, and when Sam calls to see where we are we're already on the right ward.

Sam gets up from his chair and gives me a crushing hug.

"You OK?" I ask, and he nods, standing back so I can take his seat next to the bed.

"Hey, Fai." I sit down and take his hand. His face is still puffy and bruised. There's a plaster cast on his elbow and a plastic support boot on his right foot. He's still on a drip, and it takes him a moment to focus on me.

"Hey, Mel." His voice is slurred, but he manages a smile. My stomach sinks. I can't help thinking of my mother, exhausted by surgery and painkillers when we finally got to see her after the Angel Exhibition.

After Kane.

I push the thought away. "How are you doing?"

"Been better," he says, still smiling. "My gorgeous boyfriend is inconveniently busted up, too."

"That he is." I glance at Sam, but the look on his face is full of pain. I turn back to Fai.

"We brought you something, Georgie and me. Someone to keep you company."

He stares at me, waiting, while Georgie produces Ballet Bear from behind her back and tucks it gently into the crook of his uninjured elbow.

Sam laughs. Fai's smile spreads.

The bear still wears its tutu, but its right foot and right arm are bandaged with strips of tissue, neatly secured with safety pins. There's another tissue tied round its head, pinned behind its ear. Its injuries match Fai's, but it is still a dancer – toes pointed, costume neat, a look of concentration on its face.

"He's perfect." Fai grips my fingers. "I love him. Thank you." He wraps his arm more closely round the bear. "We can get well together."

"You'd better." I pull a strict face, and Fai looks down.

"I'll try," he says, his smile fading.

"Promise?" I give his hand a squeeze.

He nods. "Promise. We'll do our best."

Georgie reaches into her bag. "If you need some inspiration, I kept my promise."

Fai raises a bruised eyebrow as she pulls out a glossy magazine. "The recital?"

She nods. "Photos, article – full coverage." She grins. "You're famous, Fai!"

Sam brushes tears from his eyes as he pulls a chair to the far side of the bed. Georgie opens the magazine to the right page and holds it out for the boys to read. I let go of Fai's hand and angle my chair so I can see.

It's a double-page spread. Colour, action, contrast. Photos, and a write-up. Credits for Georgie and Patrick.

It's stunning.

"He wrote you up as the star of the show." Georgie points to the text.

"And the photos …" I tilt my head to get a better view. "They look amazing!"

She gives me a satisfied smile. "They do look good plastered across a national magazine. I have to agree."

The editor has chosen her images of the dancers on stage – all bright colours and dramatic lighting. One side of the spread is a collage of pictures and text. The other is a full-page photo of Fai, mid-leap, his arms thrown back as he dances into the spotlights. The sleeves of his costume are fringed with scarlet feathers. As he stretches his arms, the feathers glow, fragile against the dark background.

In that instant, caught by the camera, they look like wings.

"How did you …" Fai asks, taking the magazine with his good hand and resting it on his blanket. "Everyone reads this! This is huge."

Georgie shrugs. "One of the lecturers has a contact in editorial. They got you in."

"And you." Sam waves a hand at the credits. "This is all thanks to you and Patrick."

"You know me," she says. "Married to my camera. Fai and the others did the rest."

I can't help thinking about Fai's injuries as I look at the photos. I don't want this to be the record of his final performance. Angelism, racism, homophobia – that shouldn't be where his ambition ends.

Fai's expression darkens. He stares at one of the photos. "Is that ...?"

Sam inspects the image. "I think so. In the background."

Fai gives a frustrated sigh. "He can't leave me alone. Even in print."

"Kyle?" Georgie's voice is quiet. Sam nods. "Shit. Sorry. I hadn't noticed." She leans over to inspect the photo. "Yep. That's him."

I glance between my friends. "What did I miss? I thought we were worried about ..." I wave a hand. I can't bring myself to say his name. I know how upset Sam was about the backstage image.

Fai shakes his head. He speaks slowly, his words uncertain. "I've been telling him to back off for months, but he wouldn't listen. He's got this ..." He searches for the word. "... fascination with me. I thought it was the dancing. He's the director. I thought he wanted me for my dance skills."

"No?"

He looks at me and shakes his head again. "No."

"So there wasn't anything going on with Kyle?" I can feel a weight, lifting from my shoulders.

"Not on my side." He points at the photo. "All in his head."

"Did something happen?" Georgie folds her arms across her chest. Fai nods.

"Here? After we sent him away?" I can't help sounding indignant. I thought we'd got rid of Kyle.

He gives me a tired smile. "Sam told me about that. Thank you."

"Any time. Just tell me who needs a gentle roughing up, and I'll make it happen."

Sam laughs. Fai shifts his shoulders against his pillows, and I catch the wince of pain on his face.

"So?" Georgie taps her fingers on the guard rail of the bed. "Don't leave us hanging!"

Fai looks thoughtful, as if the memory is cloudy. "He came to see me. Sam had gone somewhere ..."

"Coffee machine."

"Right. Sam was fetching coffee, and Kyle walked in. I was out of it." He shrugs. "Drugged up. I wasn't sure it had happened until Sam mentioned it later."

"And?"

"My dad left us together."

"Toilet break," mutters Sam, scowling. "He shouldn't have left you."

Fai takes Sam's hand in his. "I know that now. Then, I was ... out of it. And Dad hadn't slept. I can't blame him."

Sam nods, and grips Fai's fingers.

"So Kyle came in, and he tried to kiss me."

"He *what*?" Georgie looks ready to punch someone.

I sit back in my chair. I can feel anger knotting in my stomach. "That's ... that's awful, Fai."

"Like a proper, proper kiss?"

He nods at Georgie. "Unfortunately."

I feel sick. I can't believe anyone would do that. I think about meeting Kyle in the corridor. The look on his face as he staggered away from me. He deserved more than a quick shove.

I rest my elbows on Fai's bed. "I hope you broke his nose."

"I think I told him to piss off. Something like that. And then Dad came back and Kyle left. Quickly."

"Yes!" Georgie punches the air. "Well done, drugged Fai!" She shakes her head. "That's disgusting. Kyle is disgusting. I'm sorry that happened."

"That's horrible, Fai." I wave a hand, trying to think of something else to say. "Horrible. I'm so sorry."

Fai nods. "He hasn't come back, so ..." He shrugs.

I look at Sam, and he meets my gaze. He looks uncomfortable.

"So are you guys OK?" I don't want to ask the wrong question, but I don't want to see my friends getting hurt.

He looks away. His voice is a whisper. "I might have accused the love of my life of messing around with Kyle."

"After that?" I don't know whether to laugh or throw the magazine at him. "Sam! He's ..." I wave a hand. "He's all drugged up! Completely defenceless!"

Sam shakes his head. "I know."

Fai laughs, still slurring his words. "He saw Kyle leaving. He told me about the photo. I know why he was upset."

"Yes, but—"

Fai cuts me off. "I'm not losing this gorgeous man because of an idiot like Kyle." He looks at Sam. "All is forgiven."

There are tears in Sam's eyes as he plants a gentle kiss on Fai's head.

"We're good," he says.

I give them a quick smile, my chest tightening. They've made up, in spite of Kyle. In spite of Sam's accusation. They've got through this – through judgements and mistakes and misunderstandings – and I'm happy for them. I'm relieved that they still have each other.

But it hurts to know that I can't have this. That there's no making up for me and Jez. No way to bring back the way he made me feel.

There's a pain in my chest. A rock in my throat.

Without wings, I'm no one to him. I'm nothing. There is no way to bridge this gap.

I know I shouldn't want to fix us. I know he'll only hurt me again. My mind is made up, but my heart still wants the angel with the storm-grey eyes.

Looking at Sam and Fai, I feel as if someone's punched me in the stomach.

"Mel?" Georgie raises an eyebrow.

I nod. "I'm OK."

There's a puzzled look on Fai's face. "Have you seen Jez?" He says, picking up on Georgie's question. "He's here somewhere. In hospital. After ..." He frowns, and looks at me, his thoughts lining up. "Oh."

Georgie takes a hissing breath. "Mel, don't even think about—"

"No, I haven't." I shake my head, interrupting my friend. "And I'm not going to." I sound much more confident than I feel, as if I'm making the decision as I speak. I hadn't thought about where he would be now. What would happen next. "I can forgive his hang-ups. I can forgive his shitty home life. I can't forgive—"

"The manipulation? The crappy attitude? The way he treated you?"

I give Georgie a nod. "He had his chance. He had plenty of chances. He doesn't want me – Jez never wanted me." The pain is like a bruise blooming in my chest. My throat is tightening. I curl my fingers into fists to stop them shaking, and make myself breathe. "He needed me to be ... something else. There's no going back."

Sam shrugs. "I'm not going to cry over him. Good riddance."

"Fine," I say, fighting to stay calm. "You're probably right. But I've cried, and I'm probably going to cry some more."

I know my grandfather is right. I know I need to let Jez go, but the pain in my chest tells me we're still knotted round each other. That this is more messy than I thought it would be. That this is going to be like Kane. I think I'm over it, and then something small will throw me back and I'm there, all over again, watching an angel fall.

"It really hurts, Sam. He couldn't see me. He only saw another shamed angel, and when I wasn't what he wanted, he left." I can see him on the roof. Hear his voice through the phone. My lungs have frozen, my eyes are shut tight. I can't feel the chair underneath me. I can't take a breath, and my voice is a gritty whisper. "He wouldn't let me save him."

I couldn't save Kane, and I couldn't save Jez. I watched as a man filled with hate murdered the most famous angel in the world, and I watched as the angel I adored threw himself from a roof. I tried. I ran to both of them. I did everything I could.

Now Kane is dead and Jez is broken. I still see both of them when I close my eyes.

I can't do this. I can't keep wishing for a different ending. I can't keep waiting for Kane to stand up, or Jez to step back from the edge of the roof. This isn't like Sam and Fai – there are no second chances. It doesn't matter how many times I watch it happen – Kane, the SUV, the cameras; Jez, the roof, the crowd – it's not going to change.

Kane is dead. Jez is shattered.

Leaving them behind is up to me. I'm the one who needs to move on.

When I open my eyes, my friends are staring at me.

"Mel," Georgie says, stepping round the bed to put a hand on my arm. "Breathe."

But I'm already standing up, making myself concentrate on feeling the floor under my feet. Using the chair for balance.

"I have to go," I say, to nobody in particular. "I have to leave. There's something I need to do."

Chapter 44

I'm standing in my room, staring at my shrine to Kane. At expensive boats, cars, and planes. Movie premieres and red-carpet parties. Naked torsos, dinner jackets, crisp white shirts and golden wings. Piercing sapphire eyes.

Interviews, fashion shoots, billboards. Photos, cuttings and sketches, carefully fixed in place, lovingly arranged to reveal the world's most famous angel. Timeless black and white and vivid, popping colour – everything blurs together into a single wall, a single person, a single face looking back at me. Over and over again.

My heart kicks in my ribcage. I wrap my arms across my chest, gripping my elbows, trying to hold myself together.

I can see Jez, wings spread as he stood on the edge of the roof. I can see Kane, bloodied, his golden feathers falling.

I take a breath and focus on the images in front of me. I'm safe here, surrounded by paper memories. There are no clattering cameras, no revving engines, no crowd lifting their phones to see the drama. No blood and pain and screaming.

This is how I've put Kane back together – how I put myself back together. Holding on to the shrine. Celebrating his life, his joy, his beauty. A place of golden wings and gorgeous smiles. A place where I could pretend I wasn't the girl in the photo, and he could live on.

Where I could dream of a night by his side. A moment in his orbit.

Where I could be his angel.

I'm done with this. I'm done with angels and dreaming and impossible endings. I'm done with violence and hate and shame.

I don't need wings. I don't need angels.

Two relationships that weren't real. Two angels who left me behind.

I don't need Jez, and I don't need Kane.

And I'm tearing at the wall, ripping and pulling at the images. Magazine pages and glossy photos and sketches fly apart in my hands, ragged white edges slashing like lightning across the paper as I tug them free from the wall. The pieces flutter around me like leaves – like feathers, falling.

Part of me is screaming, my chest breaking open as fragments of an angel scatter from my fingers. Here and there I see a golden wing, the edge of a tailored jacket, part of his face, still smiling. My throat is raw, my hands bruised as I punch at the wall.

And part of me is singing. Flying. Setting myself free as I tear the images apart. Kicking at the pieces as they settle round my feet. Dragging the shrine from my wall, shredding the wallpaper and uncovering the blank canvas beneath.

I'm putting an end to this obsession – to the story I thought I was telling. Kane's life ended in violence, in front of the National Gallery, but mine didn't. All this time I've been living in that moment, trying to escape the truth.

Trying to find another angel.

Kane is gone, and I'm still here. I wake up every day, I create the art I love, and I have a whole life ahead of me to live. I can decide who I want to be, while Kane is fading from the world. He exists only in these photos, these interviews, these slices of a life.

It's not fair. He deserved better. He deserved love, not hate. Warmth, not violence. Smiles, not tears. I have grieved for him and for everything he lost.

But I'm still here. I can't wait in his shadow forever.

I reach up and tear another photo from the wall.

There's one image left. I didn't realise I'd been saving it, and something stops me from pulling it down.

It's a famous image of Kane, wings wrapped round his shoulders, his dark blue jacket artfully slashed at the back to show off his golden feathers, a flash of scarlet lining showing under the collar.

It's the image from the Angel Club. The icon at the side of the stage.

I reach up, brushing my fingers over his wings, tracing the line of his jaw.

He's beautiful. Laughing, smiling, his eyes full of joy. Full of life.

A hundred photos, a thousand magazine cuttings, and this is the one I save.

I can see why the Angel Club chose this as their reminder of Kane. His first billboard might be the image everyone recognises, but compared with this it is cold, impersonal. Stark. We're supposed to look at his wings, not his face. We're supposed to be shocked.

This image is warm, joyful, full of life and colour. He looks as if he is sharing an unguarded moment with the person behind the camera. It's intimate, in a way the billboard could never be. It feels real, not staged. It feels as if he's smiling for me.

"Keep it."

My mother's voice makes me jump. I hadn't realised she was standing in the doorway. As I catch my breath, I realise my hands are shaking.

"I can't," I say, glancing at the destruction on the floor around me. "I have to ..." I wave a hand, looking for a way to explain.

She nods. "I know. I understand. But keep that one. You never know when you might need inspiration."

"I need ..." I shrug. The feelings in my chest are too real, too raw. I can't find the right words. I reach out and touch the wall, rough and cream-coloured where the wallpaper has torn away.

"You don't have to keep it on the wall. Just ... keep it." She steps into the room, fallen paper rustling against her feet. "Don't throw everything away. I know you want to remember him."

I nod. She's right. One photo – that's all I need. I'll regret it if I save nothing.

I reach up and gently peel the cutting from the wall – carefully, so as not to damage the paper. I take the photo down, handling it is if it is made of gold. Kane smiles at me, completely comfortable in his own skin, proudly wrapped in his shimmering wings. I pull open the drawer where I keep my sketchbooks, and slide the photo underneath. Out of sight, but not entirely out of mind.

My mother takes my hands. "I'm proud of you," she says.

I shake my head, staring at the destruction on the floor. Years of work, years of dedication, reduced to piles of shredded paper in a few moments.

"I had to," I whisper, round the pebble in my throat.

"I know." She looks round the room, at the ragged strips of wallpaper still clinging to the wall, glimpses of pale green ivy pattern fading into the cream liner paper. She grips my fingers. "We should redecorate. Give you a fresh start. New wallpaper, new curtains, new bedspread. What do you say?"

I should be excited. I should be happy, but this is all too big, too raw.

"Sure," I say. "New room, new me." I force myself to smile. "Thank you."

She smiles back. "That's great. Put together some ideas – sketches, colour schemes – and we'll go shopping at the weekend." She tilts her head. "If you're staying that long?"

This time my smile is genuine. "I'll be here."

She drops my hands and gives me a quick hug, then steps back and looks at the drifts of paper on the floor. "Let's get this tidied up. I'll fetch a bin bag." And she leaves me alone in the bare, miraculous, transformed room, with no one but myself for company.

Kane is gone. Jez is gone. This space is mine again.

It feels amazing.

Chapter 45

I dream of flying.

I stand at the edge of the roof, the London skyline laid out around me. Trees, churches, rooftops. Skyscrapers in the distance, like glinting glass beads on a necklace.

I plant my feet in the gravel, roll my shoulders, and feel my wings unfurl. Light as bird bones, they rise from my back, muscles from my arms to my waist tensing to stabilise the feathers. They rustle like leaves, whispering, and I feel the anticipation. The breathless moment before the jump.

These wings need to fly.

I take a breath, balancing myself over the drop, and then I take a step.

I know I should fall. I know I should be afraid – but instead, I fly. My wings pull against the air, every feather straining against my fragile bones to lift me higher.

There is joy in my chest. I'm smiling as I reach up, climbing towards the sky.

London is beautiful, spread beneath my feet like a painting. From here it's all green parks and red roofs and glass, golden in the sunlight.

I can't see my wings. I can't tell what they look like, but I know they are full of colour. Bright, vivid feathers, bold and unashamed. No shimmering rainbows, no glistening gold, just joyous splashes of all the colours in my paint box.

I should be tired. I should be aching from the effort of keeping myself in the air, but the longer I'm up here, the more at home I feel. I swoop and dive, throwing my wings out to catch my fall and climbing again, over and over.

The feeling is exhilarating. Addictive.

I don't think I can ever come down.

When I wake, it's to joy and despair. I don't want the exhilaration to end. I know how it felt to have my own wings, to fly – impossibly – by myself, to be my own kind of angel.

I don't want to give that up.

Part 3

Finding Mel

Chapter 46

June 2025, Age 22

"Changing your mind, Mel?" Sam throws his hands in the air. "The exhibition is in – what? Three weeks?"

I nod, pressing another golden feather onto the wire armature and holding it in place while the glue sets.

"I thought you were using the model of Fai for your sculpture piece. The dancer."

I nod again. "I was. And now I'm not."

It's unbearably hot in the studio. The glue is taking forever to harden, and my arms and hands are streaked with gold paint. I'll have to spray another coat onto the wings before I add them to the plaster cast. I'm hungry and I'm tired, and Sam's right. I have changed my mind. I am making more work for myself.

My friend sighs, and drops himself into the chair. "OK. Tell me about this one."

I wave a hand at the golden feathers, spread out on the table top. The wire wings. The plaster cast of my head and shoulders, hands clasped across my chest as if in prayer. The photo of Kane, saved from my bedroom wall.

"It's an angel thing," I say, and Sam smiles.

"Of course it is."

"But it's not an angel."

Sam nods slowly. "Right," he says, raising his eyebrows.

It's so hard to explain what I'm trying to make. I know it will make sense when I've finished – I know he'll be able to see what I'm trying to say – but it's difficult to put into words.

"It's me, but with wings." I shake my head. "No. That's not it."

Sam gives me a puzzled look. "It's you," he says, pointing at the plaster model, "and there are wings."

"Yes, but ..." I shrug. "It's me, but not me. And the wings are Kane's, from the Angel Club photo." I've shaped the metal structures to match the shape of his pose, lifted and wrapped lightly round his shoulders. "It's ..." I pause, searching for the words.

"A metaphor?"

"Yes!"

Sam grins. "So – something to do with Kane being a part of you, and what happened to him being part of your story?"

"Yes!" I say, punching the air. "Exactly. He's part of my story, I'm part of his. We can't separate ourselves. I've been trying to find a way to show this connection."

Sam nods. "The connection you hate."

I close my eyes and take a breath. He's right. I hate our photo – me, Kane, blood and feathers. I hate that that's how everyone sees me. But it's true. I can't deny what happened. I can't pretend I wasn't there. That I wasn't screaming for help as the cameras flashed and Kane died.

I shrug again. "All part of the story."

"You look sad," he says, his eyes on the plaster cast of my face. "Like an angel on a gravestone."

I give him a half-smile. "Appropriate, don't you think?"

He smiles back.

"It's good, Mel," he says. "Really good."

I wish I could believe him. He's understood what I'm trying to do, and he likes it, but I know there's something missing.

This is my final exhibition. My final, graduating grade. I want to express myself – I want to show what I can do, and I want to be authentically myself. I want to show who I really am to everyone who thinks of me as the girl in the photo.

I want to reclaim my story.

"Angels, Mel? Is that really what you want?"

Georgie places the lasagna on the table and drops the oven gloves next to her plate as she sits down. We've been sharing a house this year – me, Georgie, Sam, and Fai – and it's become a habit to cook for each other on Thursday nights. The full works, with wine and dessert. It's Georgie's turn today, and the lasagna smells delicious.

"I thought you were using the dancer." Fai glances at me as he holds out his plate.

"I was," I say, with a note of apology in my voice. "And I do love that sculpture. But I need to make something more personal."

Georgie laughs. "I'd say a model of my photo of Fai's famous dance recital is pretty personal." She grins at Faisal, and he grins back.

"Not personal enough," he says. "We've been rejected."

She winks at him. "There are angels involved, Fai. It was inevitable."

I roll my eyes. "It's not about you! I'm not rejecting either of you! I just ... I need to do this."

"Mel needs to fly." Sam shrugs, and nudges his shoulder against mine. "If she wants to bless herself with golden wings, I don't think we can stop her."

I can't help smiling. Sam gets it, even if the others don't.

He's right. I want to give myself wings.

"How's your portfolio, Georgie?"

The lasagna dish is empty, along with our wine glasses. No one is ready for dessert, and no one wants to move.

She shrugs at me. "You know. Getting there."

"Another late night tonight?"

"Probably. Sorry, everyone. I'll try not to type too loudly."

Sam makes a face. "I can't believe they make you write. I thought that was for the words journalists. Aren't you supposed to be able to communicate everything with your photos?"

Georgie sighs. "Yes, and no. I have to create stories with my images, but they want me to show my working."

Fai laughs. "Like maths, in school. It's not enough to have the right answer – you have to show them how you got there."

"Bingo." She nods. "I have to be able to explain and analyse my own photos, and tell them why I'm good at my subject. Oh – and what's wrong with each image, and how I could improve it next time."

Fai groans. I roll my eyes.

"All that, and an exhibition?"

"Words and pictures." She smiles. "At least I get to show off my favourite photos, as well as analysing them to death. You're all coming, right? Come and say nice things about my work, just when the examiners walk past?"

I give her a serious look. "You come to mine, and say nice things, and I'll come to yours and do the same. Deal?"

"Deal," she says, grinning.

Sam lounges back in his chair and puts on a fake posh accent. "I know you'll all come and watch me redefine theatre. And I know you're all going to sing my praises in the bar after the performance. I will, with a little calorific persuasion, do the same for you two."

Georgie laughs. "Are you asking for dessert, Sam?"

"Of course he is." Fai shakes his head.

Sam nods, and takes a bow over the table.

"And Fai?" I don't want my friend to feel left out. He's come back this year to take a Choreography module, alongside some intensive physiotherapy. No one knows whether he'll be able to go back to dancing, but if not he'll be an amazing choreographer. "I promise I'll come back next year, or the year after. Whenever you need cheerleaders for your finals."

"Thank you, Mel." He smiles. "I'll hold you to that." He looks around the table. "All of you. And this year, I'll be your biggest fan." He presses his fingers into the shape of a heart. "Promise."

I'm lying in the dark, listening to the sound of typing from Georgie's room down the hall.

I can't sleep.

Something Sam said is echoing in my head, and I can't stop wondering where I'm going wrong with my sculpture.

Mel needs to fly. If she wants to bless herself with golden wings, I don't think we can stop her.

He's right. Giving myself wings is exactly what I want to do. I want to show that I can fly. That I can be a success on my own terms.

I don't have to be the girl in the photo, frozen forever with a dying angel. I don't have to be the girl without wings – the girl who couldn't save Jez.

And I don't have to be Alice Abbott's daughter. Painter, angel-lover, always working in her shadow.

I want to find my own way to fly.

Angelica's words come back to me.

Of course you have wings. We all have wings. We all have something to be proud of. Sometimes it just takes someone special to see them.

I can't help wondering – who am I doing this for? Who am I trying to convince, by adding Kane's wings to my shoulders?

What does it mean, that the wings I've chosen belong to a murdered angel?

I can't tell Kane I'm over him. I can't tell Jez he doesn't understand me. If I'm trying to break free, why am I stealing Kane's golden feathers? Why am I letting them define me?

My art – my expression – that's my wings. That's what I want people to see. Not Kane, not Jez, not my brush strokes mimicking my mother's talent.

I take a breath. My heart jumps in my chest.

If I want other people to see my wings – to really see the things I'm proud of – maybe Angelica was wrong. Maybe it's not about finding someone special. Maybe it's not about letting other people decide who I am.

Maybe I have to see them first.

Chapter 47

This time in my dream, I'm painting the sky.

My wings are strong and steady as I fly into a pale blue evening, brushes in my hand. I pick a vibrant flame-orange, and sweep the colour across the space in front of me, summoning the sunset.

The paint glows, sinking into my canvas, blending with the ice-blue air.

I follow it with a golden yellow, a fiery pink, a dusky, pale rose.

The clouds I pick out in electric purple, outlined with dazzling silver-white highlights.

There's drama here, and beauty. I am honoured to have this moment, to show the world who I can be.

And as the day fades, and the colours bleed into a fragile twilight, I can feel them. The hurrying man who stops in the street and glances at my work. The busy nurse, taking five minutes to watch the day end before heading back to her patients. The restless child, awake too late and peeking through the curtains of their darkened room.

And I know they understand. I know they've seen my art. I know I've made a difference.

When my feet touch the ground I look down at my hands, and find them stained and transformed with all the colours of the sky.

Chapter 48

I know what I have to do.

I eat breakfast, thinking through my plan while Georgie drinks coffee and tries to keep her eyes open. Her hair is scraped back into a severe pony tail, and her face looks grey.

"Late night? Or very late night?"

She blinks at me and holds a finger to her lips. "Shhh. No talking. Only caffeine."

"Tell me you got some sleep."

She shakes her head and shushes me again.

"Georgie! You're not a night-shift person! You're the most morning person I've ever met, unless there's a party involved. Or a hospital … What happened? You never leave assignments to the last minute."

She shrugs. "I know," she says, sounding drunk as she holds up her coffee cup. "Hence the caffeine."

"At least tell me you finished. Tell me you don't have to pull another all-nighter."

A smile spreads slowly across her face. "All done," she says, proudly. "Well. Apart from the formatting and the checking and the editing and the word count and the printing. Apart from that, it's all done."

"That's fantastic!" I offer her a high-five across the table, and she throws her hand onto mine. "You know," I say, watching her reaction. "You could go to bed. Ditch the caffeine, catch up on sleep."

"No," she says, sitting up straight. "No day sleeping. Coffee, carbs, meeting with my tutor."

"Are you serious?"

She nods. "Deadly. Caffeine is my friend."

"Good luck with that," I say, shaking my head. "Make sure you take chocolate and snacks."

"Sleep Replacement Therapy." She grins. "I know the drill. I *invented* the drill."

"If you find yourself needing a nap, you know where my studio is. Sign yourself in and keep me company. There's something I need to do."

She raises an eyebrow. "Mysterious. Do I sense a breakthrough in the artistic chaos?"

"Maybe," I say, thinking about my dream. About Angelica's words. About wings. "I hope so."

"Then good luck with that," she says.

The wings have dried overnight, feathers glittering in the sunlight that streams into my workspace. Kane' wings, lifted and curved to fit the shoulders of my plaster cast.

To fit me.

I run my fingertips over the edges of the painted feathers, remembering the gentle warmth of Jez's wings. The soft, downy velvet where the fragile bones met the skin of his back. The imprint of the bindings. Scars, storms, and rainbows.

These wings are lifeless. Hard, rigid, cold. Held in place with twisted metal and hardened glue. No gentle rustling of feathers, no tiny movements. A parody, like Angelica's sequins – created with love, but never enough. Nothing like a living, breathing angel.

I lift the wire frame from the table. It's awkward, but not heavy. Paint, glue, and feathers, shaped in imitation of something magical. Someone I can't forget.

Careful not to bend the wire or scuff the paint, I settle the wings onto my shoulders. There's no harness, like Georgie's, but they sit against my skin, wrapping around my shoulders and falling to my waist like a golden gown.

I can feel each feather where the wings press into my arms. The subtle weight as they rest against my shoulders.

I remember my dreams of flying. Brightly coloured paint-box feathers, dancing in the air. Hollow bones and strong muscles.

Nothing like this embrace of wire and glue.

I glance at my reflection in one of the glass frames on my studio wall, and my breath catches. Kane's wings curve across my back, stunning golden feathers offering protection and shelter.

My wings. My face in place of his.

I see Kane, in my dream. Flying with him into the sky above London.

"You see?" He says, looking into my eyes. "It's beautiful. It's all beautiful."

And I see cameras, flashing. I hear the roar of an engine that shouldn't be here.

Flashbulb moments. Golden feathers falling. Blood on my hands.

I'm shaking, trying to breathe, my heart pounding an alarm in my chest.

I twist the wings from my back and let them fall, trying to forget my reflection. Blinking away the image of myself, tangled with my memories of Kane.

This is not who I want to be.

I need to step back. I need to forget the angels I loved – the play of light on their feathers, the storm-grey eyes, the sapphire gaze.

I need to define my own pride.

I need to create my own wings.

By the time Georgie arrives, I've pulled every paintbrush from my shelves, every crushed acrylic paint tube from my worktop, and every coloured pencil from my boxes and tins. Watercolour pans, drawing pens, oil pastels and half-empty bottles of ink are piled on the table, traces of their contents smudged across my hands.

I'm surrounded by colour.

"Bad time?" she says, slipping her camera bag from her shoulder.

"Amazing time," I say, grinning. I feel electrified. Fired up. Ready to create.

Ready to make something special.

"So ..." she points at the mess in front of me. "This is a good sign?"

"This is ..." I wave a hand, looking for the right words to describe how I'm feeling. "Yes. This is good."

She covers a yawn with both hands. "That's brilliant, Mel. Do you want company, or should I leave you to ... whatever it is you're doing?"

"Company's great." I don't lift my eyes from the table. The image in my head is coming into focus, and the objects in front of me are shifting into patterns and blocks of colour. I move my hands over the piles, pulling out a paint tube here, a pencil there, and placing them together. Turning them until the shapes flow into each other, the colours singing as they blend and oppose.

"I'll be over here." Georgie's voice cuts through my trance. She moves a stack of art books from my battered arm chair and sinks onto the cracked leather. "Shout if you need help," she says, through another yawn.

I don't know how long I spend, picking up art supplies and arranging them on the table. Georgie is asleep when I step back and take a look at what I've made.

On the table sits a pair of wings, but instead of feathers, every piece is a fragment of my studio – an expression of the art I want to create.

At the top, the oil pastels and short pencils nestle together, suggesting the softest feathers. Twisting down, appearing from under the smaller layers, are the half-empty tubes of paint. Shaped by my fingers, and the acrylic inside, they look sculpted and textured, shiny metal edges criss-crossing the brightly coloured labels. Next come my brushes, soft paint from the tubes smudged along their shafts and bristles. Finally, the pencils and pens feather the lower edges of the wings, spilling a rainbow of ink and pigment in their nibs and sharpened points.

This is what I wanted. This is personal, and vivid, and bright. Just the right colour in exactly the right place.

We all have wings. We all have something to be proud of.

Angelica was right. And these wings are mine.

Georgie stirs and shifts in the chair when I start pulling chicken wire and hot glue from the boxes on my shelves and setting up a space to complete the sculpture. I need another wire armature, fitted to the layers of the new wings. I need the hot glue gun, and a steady hand.

I need to keep working, and watch the wings grow.

As I work, I realise I don't need the plaster cast. I don't need a sad copy of myself – a graveyard angel to wear my wings. I can hang them alone, or mount them on a white-painted board. The pigments, the shapes, the objects – they speak for themselves. They are joy and colour and potential. They are the art I will create, waiting to be born.

I'm grateful for Georgie's steady breathing as I recreate the wings on the wire frame. It's fiddly, challenging work, starting from the bottom edge and working up through pencils, pens, brushes, paint and pastels, layering each piece like a feather over the object below and balancing the colours across the sculpture. The wire curves, arching the wings outwards and suggesting the shape of an angel underneath. It's like putting together a puzzle, but wrapping it round a barrel as I lock each piece into place. I'm constantly having to change the design to match the contours of the frame.

I want the curves to be graceful and life-like, and I want the colours to pop and shout. Dark blue next to violent orange, moss green next to electric pink, yellow with purple, black with white, red with gold.

When I'm done, I add watercolour pans and ink bottles, filling gaps or throwing in colour where the layers are too dull. I spread acrylic paint over the brushes and neaten the edges of the wings.

Up close, the effect is chaotic, like an explosion in a studio. But step back, and the pieces come together. Lightweight feathers at the shoulders, long, graceful plumes at the tails. And in between, all the colours of the rainbow in a joyful jumble. Feathers in all the colours of my paint box. All the tools that help me to fly.

"Wow."

Georgie's voice makes me jump, and I realise the bright sunlight has faded, filling the room with shadows. I stretch my arms and roll my shoulders. I have no idea what time it is.

"Is this the finished sculpture?" She sits up in the chair and shakes the hair out of her eyes, then squints at the window. "Did I sleep all day?"

"Just the afternoon." I glance up. "Maybe the evening, too."

She groans, and pushes herself out of the chair. "I'm glad one of us has been productive. Can I see?"

I stand back and switch on the lights as Georgie steps up to the table.

"Seriously, wow." She points at the wings. "Did you do all this today?"

I nod, noticing the paint on my fingers. Strings of glue over the backs of my hands. The ache in my wrists and the stinging blisters on both thumbs.

"I did," I say, and the surprise in my voice is real. "I really did. I still have to varnish them, once the glue is dry. And mount them. But ..." I wave a hand. "This is it. This is my sculpture piece."

I'm shaking, and I don't know whether it's joy or exhaustion. I feel as if I could keep working all night. I feel as if I could lie down on the floor and sleep for a month.

Georgie throws an arm round my shoulders. "They're stunning, Mel. Artist wings."

I can't help grinning.

Chapter 49

I take a slow breath, ignoring my shaking hands, and give my outfit a final check. Brand-new skin-tight indigo jeans, white shirt, navy jacket, smart black boots with low heels, and one of those cheap conference badges in a plastic wallet with my name on. Georgie styled my hair in a messy up-do, and I lost count of the number of clips and bobby pins she pushed against my scalp. The charity-shop diamanté clip sits to one side of my head, curls of blue-black hair tumbling around it. The whole style is stiffened and held in place with industrial-strength hairspray. I feel as if I'm wearing a helmet.

I don't feel like me. I feel as if I'm pretending to be an artist. I'd be much more at home in paint-covered jeans and a T-shirt, but we've been told to dress up. Looking around, I can see that the other students have all made an effort. At least they all look as nervous as I feel.

The gallery space is a long white box, washed with bright, cold light. We've each been given a section of wall space to display our final pieces, with lights on overhead metal rails positioned to highlight our work. It's taken a week to move all the art into place from our studios, to supervise the hanging and placement of each painting and spotlight, and make sure everything is labelled. In contrast to the noise and chaos of the last few days, the room feels hushed and quiet. The stepladders and dust sheets are gone, along with the shouting, hammering, and swearing.

This is it. This is our final exhibition as students.

It feels like my mother's exhibition at the National Gallery – nerves, anticipation, smart clothes and hairspray – but this time I'm not waiting outside while the guest of honour meets the artists. I'm on the inside, waiting for the audience. This time, the art is mine.

I check my phone. Four minutes until opening time, and there's a message from Sam.

We're in the queue, he says. *See you soon!* And there's a photo of Fai, Sam, and Georgie, grinning and holding up their invitations.

Ready for you, I reply, my fingers shaking. *See you soon!*

I remember standing in the crowd outside the Angel Exhibition, clutching my ticket and programme, feeling overwhelmed by the occasion. I remember feeling like a fraud – a sixteen-year-old schoolgirl among all those people in suits and gorgeous dresses. I catch my breath, remembering the church-like gallery space, the surprising paintings of ordinary angels, and Kane, kissing my hand.

I close my eyes, and concentrate on today. This gallery, these white walls, this stark lighting. My work on display.

When I open my eyes, it's the sculpture that catches my attention. The shapes and colours of my studio, woven and curved into brightly coloured life-sized wings. I finished them with a glossy resin varnish, and mounted them on a white-painted board. Under the spotlights the cascading rainbow colours glow and sing. Against the bright white background, they look like a stained-glass window – eye-catching and beautiful, commemorating something important.

My studio, my ambitions, my passion.

I'm proud of the work I'm displaying today. I'm happy with what I've achieved, but I still feel like a fraud. I feel as if I've been stuffed into this outfit, pinned into this hairstyle, and dropped into a room of real artists. I feel as if I have to justify my presence, to explain why I get to be here.

I have my wings. I have my acrylic painting of Sam. I have prints, sketches, watercolours, and studies for finished pieces. The display on my wall is an explosion of colour in the white room, and I know it represents everything I'm proud of.

I glance around the gallery, at the nervous faces of the other students. Maybe we're all feeling like imposters. Maybe this self-doubt never goes away. I think of my mother, talking with Kane in front of his portrait. Chatting easily with journalists and guests. I wonder whether she is ever truly at home showcasing her work, or whether she's just learnt to hide her nerves.

I squeeze my hands into fists and then force my fingers to relax. I take another slow breath. I'm sweating into my shirt, and I'm glad I wore the jacket. I feel as if there's an electrical charge flowing across my shoulders as the doors open and the first ticket-holders step into the room.

"Mel!"

Georgie skips to my display and gives me three exaggerated air kisses before crushing me with a hug. I can't help grinning. In her black jacket and green shirt, she could be my mismatched twin.

"Look at you," she says, pulling away and glancing behind me at my work. "A proper artist!"

Before I can react, Sam gives me a quick, tight hug. "Gallery life suits you," he says, smiling. "I knew it would. Your stuff looks amazing in here."

I shrug. "The lighting helps. And the whole big-event-with-tickets thing."

"Mel, no." Sam gives me a stern look. "Your work is brilliant, you're brilliant. You deserve to be here. Enjoy it."

I nod, surprised to be blinking away tears. "Thank you."

"He's right." Fai waves a hand at my wall space. "This is gorgeous." He grins. "I especially like the wonderfully handsome subject of your ..." He leans in and squints at the label. "Portrait, Acrylic on canvas. That one," he says, pointing at Sam's painting.

"Well," I say, grinning at Sam. "I could always introduce you. I mean – he is my muse, so we'd have to share him, but ..."

Fai laughs, and plants a kiss on Sam's cheek.

Sam raises an eyebrow. "I'm your muse? I don't remember telling you to ditch two perfectly beautiful sculptures and then stick everything in your studio to a metal frame in a fit of artistic genius."

"Oh, you definitely helped inspire the wings. You, Angelica, Kane …" I stop before I mention Jez. I don't want him intruding on my exhibition.

Sam presses both hands to his heart and smiles. "Such glorious company! I am honoured."

"Wait …" Georgie steps closer to the wings. "Isn't that what Angelica said, backstage?"

"The title?" I watch as she stoops to read the gallery label.

"'We All Have Wings'. Assembled sculpture with found objects. Melodie Abbott, 2025." She looks at me. "*We all have wings.* That's what she said to you, after the Angel Club show."

I nod, remembering Angelica's husky voice, the smell of her perfume in the crowded dressing room. "We all have wings. We all have something to be proud of."

Georgie steps back from the wall and nudges my shoulder with hers. "Demonstrably true," she says, smiling.

"Pumpkin." My father wraps me in a warm hug, and I hear my mother cough behind him. "Sorry," he whispers, standing up straight. "This is your exhibition. Apparently I'm supposed to call you 'Melodie', because that's what it says on your artwork. And your badge." He winks. "Your mother's rule, but I guess she knows how these things are done."

We share a smile. "Well," I say, as seriously as I can, "if that's the rule, then you'd better stick to it."

He makes a show of clearing his throat and lifting his chin. "Melodie," he says, and it sounds strange. He always calls me 'Pumpkin'. "This ..." He waves a hand at the wall behind me. "This is stunning. Congratulations."

"Thank you," I say, for the hundredth time tonight. "I'm glad you like it." I'm trying to sound grown up and professional, but inside I'm glowing.

"Melodie." My mother wraps one arm round my shoulders, the other braced against her walking stick. "I'm so proud of you."

She slips her arm through mine, and we both stand, looking at my artwork.

"Sam's portrait," she says. "It's very mature work. You've captured so much more than his looks with your exaggerated colour scheme." She tilts her head. "The catchlights in his eyes ... excellent."

That makes me smile. I remember coming back to the portrait over and over, trying to perfect the eyes, and the balance of colours.

"I learnt from the best, Mrs Abbott," I say, and she laughs.

"And the sculpture. It's beautiful. I can see what you've done, claiming elements of your work as metaphorical wings. But you've also pulled something positive from everything that happened. You've made something ugly and violent into something ... opposite. Powerful."

I'm aware of her arm through mine. The way I'm taking her weight, and the walking stick keeping her balanced. The scars on her leg that will never heal, and the memories that trip me up, over and over.

"I wanted to reclaim my story," I say. "I want people to see me, and who I am. Not the girl in the photo, or the girl on the screen."

She nods. "It's clever. Redefining how you want to be seen. Brave, too. You could ignore the past and try to reinvent yourself, but instead you're facing it. Making it your own."

I give her a sad smile. "It's hard to reinvent yourself when everyone knows who you are. It's only a matter of time before people I meet figure it out, so I might as well have an answer for them. I might as well turn the hurt into beauty."

"Spoken like a true artist." She smiles as she releases my arm. "If it hurts, make it into something amazing. Fill it with light. Don't let the darkness win."

"She's right." My grandfather stands next to me, arms folded. "What happened with Kane, what happened with your angel – you've taken it and created something new. Something better." He gives me a bright smile, and lowers his voice. "I really love the wings, Melodie. They suit you."

I can't help returning the smile. I want to tell him about my dreams – about flying and freedom and painting the sky, but I know I don't need to say anything. I know he understands.

And then my brother is there, leaning one elbow on my shoulder, asking questions about all my work. Where the materials came from for the wings, how I chose the colours for Sam's portrait, what I think of charcoal as a sketching medium – and it's great to get into technical details and forget the emotions behind the work. He knows what happened with Kane, and he knows how much it changed our lives. He knows about Jez, and how much it hurt me to see him give up. He knows where the inspiration comes from, and he wants to know how, not why. He wants to understand my artistic decisions, not the pain behind them.

It's exactly what I need, and before long we're waving our hands and debating better ways to glue pencils onto chicken wire, and the best lighting for portrait painting. I'm pointing at one of my watercolour paintings and describing the brushstrokes when I realise that I don't feel like an imposter. I don't feel as if I shouldn't be here.

I'm Melodie Abbott. I'm an artist – my own artist, not my mother's shadow.

I'm not the girl in the photo.

I'm the woman with paintbrush wings.

Chapter 50

"Tea break!" Georgie's voice echoes through the house as I pick up the last of my toiletries from the bathroom. "Also, Patrick's here."

I'm packing up the last of my belongings and Sam and Fai are clearing their room. We're moving out tomorrow, and I can't believe how quickly everything is coming to an end. Our courses, our final shows, Thursday night dinners, sharing a house with my best friends.

"Coming!"

I slide the box into my room and head downstairs, Fai and Sam behind me.

"So you're coming tonight?" Patrick pushes the Angel Club flyer across the kitchen table.

"Already in the diary." Georgie smiles, and raises her mug. "Wouldn't miss it."

We're all dressed in our shabbiest clothes, ready to pack boxes and deep-clean the house. Patrick looks out of place in his clean jeans and polo shirt.

I'm not sure what he's doing here. He could have sent a text.

But then he wouldn't have seen Georgie.

Sam drapes an arm around Fai's shoulder. "We'll be there," he says, and Patrick raises an eyebrow.

"After everything—" he says, and stops when he sees the look on Sam's face.

I catch my breath, and Sam glances at me. I can see the anger and hurt in his eyes.

"We're not letting the idiots win." Fai responds before I can think of something to say. He sounds angry. He sounds determined. "We're not going to let them stop us."

"OK." Patrick nods, and makes an approving face. "So can we expect the usual costume parade? Wings, drama, deadly heels?"

Georgie winks at him, taking his attention away from the boys. "I guess you'll have to wait and see."

"Hmmm," he says, smiling at her over the top of his mug.

I can't believe how insensitive he's being. I'm speaking up before I realise what I'm doing.

"Did you really come all the way over here to invite us out tonight?"

Patrick gives me a quick glance. "It wouldn't be the same without you," he says, and turns back to Georgie. "And what's next for our silver angel?"

I roll my eyes, and she covers a laugh. At least he's not bothering Fai and Sam.

"After the summer? Norwich," she says. "Photography Masters. You?"

"No way!" He grins. "I'm starting at the East Anglian Daily Times next week. Staff reporter. I'll be just down the road from you."

She shakes her head and clinks her mug against his. "A proper job – a proper newspaper! To East Anglia, I guess. And print journalism. Good luck." She's definitely trying to dissuade Patrick's attentions, but I'm not sure he notices.

"What about you, Mel?" Patrick asks.

"No idea," I say, grinning, and Georgie whoops.

"Freedom!" She shouts, punching the air.

Patrick pulls a confused face. "I heard you got a First. How come you don't have something to go on to?"

"I did get a First, and I've been offered a place on a sculpture course, but I don't know whether that's what I want to do." I shrug. "I figured I'd take a year, work with my mother, borrow her studio, see what commissions I can pick up. Figure out what I want. Try to be creative on my own terms."

"You just can't bear to leave us." Fai grins at me across the table.

"It's true," I say, smiling back at my friend. "I'm staying in London so I can watch Sam on stage every night, and keep you company while the love of your life is off auditioning for the next part."

"Sounds good to me." Fai clinks his mug against mine and drinks. "Come and keep me company, and keep Sam out of trouble."

"Hey!" Sam nudges him. "Maybe she's offering to keep you out of trouble!"

Patrick winks at me. "Maybe she is the trouble."

Sam gives me a grateful smile. I roll my eyes as Georgie tries to hide a smirk.

"You know there are trains, right?" Georgie says later as we pack up the kitchen cupboards, and the boys deep-clean the bathroom. "You can come and visit me in Norwich."

I give her a smile. "I know. And I will. And you should come and see Sam in whatever he gets a part in. If it's anything like his final show, he'll be brilliant."

"I know he will. I wouldn't miss it."

"I can't believe …" I stop, putting down the bag of pasta I'm holding. "I can't believe this is it. Our last night in the house."

Georgie grins. "And if I have anything to do with it, we won't be spending much of it here. We need to celebrate, big-time."

"It's just …" I take a breath. "You're going miles away. Sam and Fai will be just round the corner with Fai's dad, but you'll be …"

"I know." She says, and her grin fades.

"I'll miss you."

She nods. "I'll miss you, too. All of you."

I glance at the Angel Club flyer. "You and Patrick …" I begin, and I'm not sure what to ask. "Is there something going on? Did he come over today to finally declare his adoration?"

She stares at me for a moment, then laughs. "God, no. I mean, he might have come here to hit on me, but ..." She laughs again, shaking her head. "That's why I called the tea break. I didn't want to give him the chance."

"So he might have been inviting you to the Angel Club. Just the two of you for a romantic evening of drinks and wings?"

"You can talk," she points at me over the boxes. "Pink cocktails, creepy hidden angels ..."

"Fine, yes. OK." I raise my hands in surrender, but I can't help teasing her back. "Just – poor Patrick! After all this time the guy has no hope?"

"Mel," she says, fixing me with a stare. "You know my rule. Does he run on batteries?"

I pretend to think about it, biting down on a smile. "I really, really hope not."

And we're both laughing. Big, belly-aching laughs as we gasp for breath. I lean against the table and Georgie folds her arms across her stomach, grimacing.

"Poor Patrick!" It's all I can say, over and over.

"Batteries!" Georgie wipes tears from her face.

"Are you guys OK?" Sam stands in the doorway, Fai behind him, watching the two of us as we try to make serious faces. I feel bad, but I don't think we're really laughing at Patrick. There's an empty space in my chest, and for a moment the laughter filled it. I'm pretty sure laughing is better than crying.

I shake my head, taking a slow breath. "We're going to be wrecks tomorrow."

"Oh, god. Tired, emotional, hungry, hungover. It's going to be carnage." Georgie takes my hands over the top of the boxes and gives my fingers a squeeze. "It's only this house we're saying goodbye to. Don't forget that."

I brush away tears, and give her a smile. I've taken my artwork and most of my clothes home early, so I only have a bag and a couple of boxes still to pack. But already the house looks empty and cold, clinical, all our personal touches removed. It feels as if the four of us are already gone.

"Angel Club tonight," she says, tugging on my hands and smiling at Sam and Fai. "Let's not be sad. Let's have a brilliant time."

The last Angel Club night of the summer term is packed. There's a party atmosphere in the queue, under the gaze of the Guardian Angels, and we're lucky to get in.

Patrick and the other journalists have claimed their usual table, and we all pull up chairs from anywhere we can find them.

Georgie is wearing her silver catsuit and wings. We've replaced some of the feathers, and they're looking tattered around the edges, but in the dark of the club she still looks like a real angel. Her face is highlighted with silver glitter, and we've piled her red hair up on her head, held in place with bobby pins and her sparkling tiara. I'm wearing my cartoon wings over a little black dress, but I've spent the last week sewing golden feathers on top, and extending them so they reach my waist. Georgie helped me to melt the glue and rescue the feathers from my sculpture, and now I have my own pair of wings to match hers. Fai and Sam found matching midnight-blue shirts with a pattern of tiny golden wings. The boys look fantastic under the lights in the club, but when we walk home they can cover the wings with their jackets. I hate that they have to think like that, but I understand their fears. Sam's scars are fading, almost invisible in the shadows, but Fai still doesn't know whether he'll ever dance again.

"Wing upgrade?" Patrick raises his glass to me. We're all drinking bubbly tonight, celebrating the end of term, and the end of our courses.

I raise my glass back. "I might have found myself some actual feathers. Something to rival Georgie's glamorous efforts."

"Very Kane," he says, nodding. "Very appropriate."

I open my mouth to protest, but he's right. I'm honouring Kane, here at the Angel Club. I didn't use the feathered wings to define my art, but instead I'm bringing them to a place where everyone understands. Where everyone knows who Kane was, and I can be one person in a crowd – not the famous girl in the photo. I'm paying tribute to him, not me. Tonight is about angels, and celebration.

The lights dim, the music builds, and the cheering and clapping feels louder than ever. Georgie and I are on our feet before the curtains draw back, and we're dancing as a singer with a guitar takes the stage to the opening beats of 'Fly Away' by Lenny Kravitz.

The audience whoops and cheers, singing along, stamping feet, drumming on tables.

It's going to be a great night.

The energy in the club is climbing, the excitement mounting with every song, every new act. It feels as if everyone is here for a final party – an ultimate send-off from all the work we've put into our courses. A goodbye, and the start of something new.

We sing along with songs about how it feels to fly, men given wings, birds of prey and circling skies. Every performer gives their salute to Kane, kissing their fingertips and touching his photo as they file offstage.

There's a bubble in my chest, lifting me. I feel light. I feel connected – to the singers on the stage, to my friends around me, to every person in the club. Every angel, every angel-lover, everyone who knew Kane and loved him. Everyone who longs for wings.

The beat of the music becomes the heartbeat of the club, my pulse lining up with the pounding of the speakers. It's dark and hot and we're all here, now, together. It doesn't matter whether we have real wings, stunning fakes, or wings we can hide when we leave. We're all dancing together, loving angels, and remembering Kane.

I don't want this to end. I don't want any of this to end. But too soon the singers crowd onto the stage with Angelica, and the first notes of 'Angels' echo through the club.

I catch Georgie's elbow and pull her to a space behind our table, beckoning to Sam and Fai. By the end of the first line we're standing together, arms round each other. Georgie, me, Sam and Fai, swaying to the music and singing as loudly as we can.

After everything that's happened – after Kane and Jez, after Sam's scars and Fai's injuries, after Kyle and Georgie's photos – I've found my wings. Singing together – singing for Kane, for Fai and Sam, for Georgie's new start, for everything we're leaving behind – it feels amazing. It feels free.

I'm building my own life. Finding something of my own to be proud of. Claiming my painted, colour-filled wings. Leaving university, saying goodbye to Georgie – it's terrifying. It's an end, and a beginning.

It feels like stepping off a roof into nothing but air.

A rush of excitement fills my chest. I don't know what's coming next – what happens after that first step – but I know I want to find out.

It feels dangerous. It feels exhilarating.

It feels like flying.

A Note From the Author

Thank you so much for reading *Angels*! It is amazing and terrifying to think that there are people out there reading these words and meeting my characters, so I hope you've enjoyed the time you've spent with Mel, Georgie, Sam, Fai, and the Angel Club.

If you enjoyed the book, can I ask a small favour? Would you mind leaving a short review? Reviews on Amazon and Goodreads can bring the book to an entirely new audience, and let other readers know they might enjoy it.

A review doesn't have to be long. A star rating and a couple of sentences would mean a lot, and make a HUGE difference to this author. (Thank you!)

Of course, if you're on TikTok or YouTube or Instagram, a review on your feed would be amazing. I'm more than happy to share good reviews and promote reviewers. Drop me a note (I'm RachelChurcherWriting on TikTok and Instagram), let me know where to find your post, and I'll make sure my followers see it.

And tell your friends! Word of mouth is the most effective way to market a book, so few moments of your time would be massively appreciated – and help support me to write more books in the future!

Thank you, thank you, thank you.

Acknowledgements

Where to begin?

This book took me a year to write – about the same as the first five books of the Battle Ground Series, and (without going into details and breaking confidences) it's personal.

Once again, the story has been patiently shaped and improved by my amazing proofreaders: Alan Platt, Holly Platt Wells, Reba Sigler (AKA the Typo Ninja), Joe Silber, and Reynard Spiess. A huge thank you to you all for your time and feedback.

Another huge thank you is due to my beta readers, for detailed feedback on what should have been a finished novel. Julia Blake, Jasmine Bruce, and Bea Purser-Hallard – take a bow!

Thanks to Joe Silber and Franki for their LGBTQ+ sensitivity reads and incredibly helpful comments. I hope I've got everything right, and any mistakes are absolutely my fault, not theirs.

And thank you to all my proofreaders, beta readers, sensitivity readers and others for your comments on the various (and varied) cover designs. I honestly didn't think I'd find something that worked for this story, so I hope we made it in the end.

Thank you as always to Alan Platt, for continuing to bravely build a life with a writer, for your magnificent support, and for bringing your business brain and roadie skills to the running of Taller Books.

Thank you to all the Writers of Bury and Beyond, the authors who have contributed books to the Local Author Shelf in Bury St Edmunds, and everyone who's showed up to the many book fairs, festivals, online events and conventions where we have signed books and given talks since 2019. Special mention to my frequent partners in crime: Instagram Queen Julia Blake, Festival Co-conspirator Jackie Carreira and Nerd-Lit Eyebomber Extraordinaire MT McGuire. We've got this!

I can't end without thanking everyone who got me started on writing novels, a whole six incredible years ago. Alex Bate, Janina Ander, Helen Lynn, everyone at NaNoWriMo, and everyone at YALC – this is what you started.

This book is for the friends who keep us going when everything else falls apart. Thank you.

About the Author

Rachel Churcher fell in love with space flight at the age of five, after watching the launch of the first orbital Space Shuttle mission. She fell in love with science fiction shortly after that, and in her teens she discovered dystopian fiction. She went on to earn a Masters Degree in Science Fiction Studies, and spent many years working as a magazine writer and editor.

Her UK-based friendship-centred dystopian Battle Ground Series has won two international book awards, a Five-Star Seal from Readers' Favorite, and five-star reviews from readers aged 11 to 80. She's always happy to meet writers and readers, and talk about SF, YA fiction, politics (in the widest sense), dinosaurs, writing, and the merits of various fictional starships.

Follow her online at RachelChurcherWriting on Instagram and GoodReads, and find her books at TallerBooks.com

By the Same Author

The Battle Ground Series

What would you do if your government turned against you – and what if you had the chance to fight back?

The Battle Ground Series is set in a dystopian near-future UK, after Brexit and Scottish independence.

The award-winning series is available from Amazon, Waterstones, Barnes and Noble and all good bookshops.

MAKING TROUBLE
RACHEL CHURCHER

9 781916 386860